LURE OF THE HUNT

FANTASY, FUTURISTIC, AND PARANORMAL ROMANCE WRITERS

AKIRA ANGEL   JAYLEE AUSTIN

KORIE BETH BROWN   CLAIRE DAVON

FENLEY GRANT   B.L. LUCAS   LEAH VEGA

NATASHA WILCO

CONTENTS

FOREWORD BY FANTASY, FUTURISTIC, AND PARANORMAL ROMANCE WRITERS

Welcome to Our Worlds,

Immerse yourself in *LURE OF THE HUNT,* a Sci-Fi Romance anthology by Fantasy, Futuristic, and Paranormal Romance Writers. Journey through distant galaxies where star-crossed lovers and interstellar warriors navigate love and adventure. Each standalone story blends high-tech wonders with deep emotions, offering tailored heat levels for the perfect mix of passion and escapade.

Heat Levels Within the Anthology

🔥 Sweet - No sex on or off the page

🔥 🔥 Sensual - Off-page sex mentioned in story

🔥 🔥 🔥 Steamy - At least one "Closed door" sex scene

🔥 🔥 🔥 🔥 Smokin' - At least one "Open door" sex scene

🔥 🔥 🔥 🔥 🔥 Scorcher - Explicit erotic romance with HEA/HFN*

Fantasy, Futuristic, and Paranormal Special Interest Chapter of RWA is an international association of writers dedicated to the genres of fantasy, futuristic, and paranormal romance. Our members range from pre-published new writers to best-selling authors with multiple series. This year, we are thrilled to share with you our inaugural anthologies in both sci-fi and fantasy. Our intention is to continue this tradition and publish more collections of imaginative and captivating stories in the future. We hope you enjoy and treasure these tales, and we look forward to your continued support.

2024 Anthology Committee
Fantasy, Futuristic, and Paranormal special interest RWA
www.FFPRWA.com

THE MISSION: SEARCH FOR SURVIVORS

FENLEY GRANT

Triggers: infertility, attempted assassination, and off-page murder.

Heat Rating: Steamy

CHAPTER
ONE

June 13, 2141
Aviemore Ruins, former country of Scotland
EuroAnglica Province

Killing the man isn't an option.
The mantra ran through my head multiple times per day.

Even though my mission's purpose was to locate postwar, post-pandemic, reproductive survivors, I debated…often…whether the world would be better off without Darren Davis's inclusion. He and his band of less-than-merry military-trained personnel had been a thistle in my side for the past three weeks.

The man in question, visible from the doorway and standing outside in his uptight, forthright manner, side-eyed me as if he'd heard my thoughts.

He's not clairvoyant, is he? I gripped the container I held so tightly that I risked collapsing it and crushing the contents.

Fingers snapped in front of my face in a repeated rhythm. "Jane? You with us, Doc?" Roan, my colleague and assistant, stepped into view.

I jerked, nodded quickly, and passed Roan the labeled crate of Aviemore's biological samples. "Can you put this on the truck before I have to hear them complain about our brief amount of time remaining before we leave this location?"

He grinned in his boyish fashion, his fresh, freckled face perched with his chin resting atop the box. "No problem. You plan on reminding them again that the government says they work for you and not the other way around?"

"Not sure they're getting the message." At least Captain Davis wasn't—I knew he believed he should be in charge instead of me. A breeze blew through the shattered window of the former town's library, our current base of operations, sending a tendril of my hair flying. At the brisk swirl of air, my skin rose in goose bumps, and I tucked the wayward curl behind my ear once more.

Through the spiky remnants of the glass-framed opening, I watched three members of my research team scurry to load our equipment into our supply van. The sun momentarily peeked from behind the gathering dark clouds to shine on my crew as if to sanction our work. I'd like to believe the blessed Mother and her feminine energy thought our efforts holy.

Hefting his crate higher, Roan laughed and called out over his shoulder, "Maybe threatening their jobs would help. Hard to find work as a soldier now that the world wars are over, eh?"

True enough. The last of the battles ended less than a decade ago. Soldiers were forced to find new career paths.

We as a species had decimated the population to the point humanity faced the danger of becoming extinct if we didn't act immediately. All life was now precious. Due to the wars, the diseases, the pollutants, and the genetic manipulations of over half the population—including my ancestors—the world contained fewer and fewer people capable of reproducing.

I counted as one of those infertile humans. A pit hollowed

out in my gut, a place as empty as my womb. *Quit wallowing. Focus on your work.*

My job was to find and keep safe those fortunate few who could still reproduce—the Repopulators.

During our mission's first week, where we'd toured the outer islands of what once was the country of Scotland, we'd managed to locate fertile folk on the remote island of Raasay, but, sadly, the people of Raasay didn't want our help in rebuilding their isle's number of inhabitants. When the protesting mob of locals came after us to "get off their land," the security team had to extract us from the island.

The government then reclassified Raasay as a rogue colony, one outside the EuroAnglica Province's oversight, to be contacted at a later date when the people might feel a little less hostile toward the new world repopulation centers being built throughout the province.

We'd experienced less luck in finding living residents on the mainland. Most towns were like Aviemore—deserted, bombed-out shells of their former selves. They'd been reduced to decaying scars on the land devoid of any living animals, flora, or people.

I labeled another box of samples and surveyed the area, pressing a palm against my lower back to stretch the cramped muscles of my spine. Skeletons of digital machines once dispensing books to those hungry for knowledge sat forlornly on shelves, their insides stripped for parts and their databases gone with the electricity that once powered them. A familiar ache settled in my bones at the losses.

The loss of this town came from the wars.

The wars were carried out by soldiers. People like Davis and his ilk.

I glanced over at the leader of the squad assigned to assure my safety and that of my scientific crew as he entered the

5

doorway. Darren Davis should be someone I'd find attractive—athletic build, striking blue eyes, chiseled features, and close-cropped light brown hair that tried to curl despite its short length.

Damn it, I did find him appealing.

However, "pretty is as pretty does" as my mother would have said…if she and my father hadn't been killed in the past war by people like the captain.

Why the government sent this team of mercenaries with us as protection still made no sense.

Seemed to me, so far, the biggest threats to my people and our assignment all held positions on Davis's team. They were the ones uttering the snide comments. Giving the rude glares. Showing the outright hostility toward us and our mission.

Captain Davis must have felt the heat of my stare because he turned his head toward me. "Scarlet, we're out of here in ten."

Scarlet? Using my not-from-nature hair color as a dig? Like I had a choice in my genetically altered appearance.

He jerked his head toward the waiting van. "You and your crew need to finish up. No survivors, so no need to stay." His tone was clipped, curt, and cold.

A familiar burn heated my veins at his callous disregard for the frailty of life. This mission would help secure the future of humanity through the work of the world repopulation centers. Discovering and protecting fertile humans. Locating willing surrogates for those unable to carry their own children. Establishing banks for viable sperm and eggs.

The man in front of me felt the human race should let nature take its course. We'd already done that and look where we were. Science deserved a turn to save humanity instead of creating weapons to destroy them.

I leaned forward on the table. "My name is Dr. Carter. If we were friends, I'd say call me Jane. But we're clearly not on familiar terms, and no one has permission to call me a derogatory name." Scarlet, indeed. *For this operation, I outrank you.*

I stretched to pull another crate closer and stumbled over a gnarled piece of wood poking out from the base of the table, tipping the box. Thankfully, the container had yet to be filled with samples. Of all the people to witness this... My skin temperature rose as if I'd been roasted over a fire. Making a simple error in front of a man who already considered me weak and incapable of leading this mission couldn't be worse.

"Nice to see a human side to you." His tone held a playful lilt.

You're not playing. You're making fun. I glanced up enough to send him a scathing stare. "You don't think my genetically altered kind are human."

He slowly shook his head, the semi-smile still in place. "Never said that."

"You didn't need to." *I see the truth in your smirk, you jerk.*

"I know you're human, and your hair color isn't a curse word."

It is to me. "We're done, Captain Davis, when I say we're done. We owe it to the people of Aviemore to determine what either drove them away or killed them, so we don't make the same mistakes in the future."

A frown pulled at his lips, his shoulders locked into his familiar military stance, and he glanced toward the windows' jagged glass pointing upward from the sills like predatory tusks. "Unless you want to gather samples in the rain, dear doctor, you'd better load up in ten. A torrential downpour is predicted." Pivoting on his booted heel, he headed outdoors. The sounds of him ordering his people to get ready to move filtered in with the wind.

I tucked my errant hair behind my ear again and loaded more samples into the third crate. When the clouds opened up in this part of the world, the resulting rain could last for days. Despite the late spring date, we'd be cold and miserable, and the overcast skies would leave us without the solar power needed for us to get very far. We'd be behind on our mission's schedule, which I couldn't abide.

Another wind draft blew through the place, carrying with it the promise of wet weather. By the sacred Mother, I hated it when he was right. Rain would arrive at any moment. *Move faster.*

Whenever Davis irked me, like now, I pondered the possible ways to permanently remove him and the rest of his security team. I didn't want them here with us, and they distracted from the science.

Some of the other exploratory teams across the world had experienced attacks from the extinction purists who felt our time on Earth was coming to an end, and we should embrace the final days as our punishment for our crimes on humanity. Since we hadn't run into any survivors since Raasay, I felt fairly secure. My team took enough measures to protect themselves, so I had few worries there.

As for me, my safety didn't overly cause concern. The mission did. We had to find what remained of humanity and get them to the protection of the domes under construction in the new world repopulation centers. These centers would shelter them from poor air quality, pollution, nuclear fallout, and disease, and would provide medical care to ensure their and their future generations' survival.

Roan reentered the main doorway. "These the last two containers? I hear from the doom squad we're in for some nasty gales."

I jerked my head toward the already loaded and labeled box. "Heard the same. You take that one, and I'll add the final samples to this container. Meet you at the supply van."

From the windows and the doorway, I could see the gathering

8

gray in the cloudy sky. The storm would arrive quicker than anticipated. *Curse Davis for being right.* Moisture grew heavy in the air, and a chill rippled over my skin like the frigid waters of the North Sea.

Roan nodded, took the crate, and raced for the truck idling in the distance.

Good thing we'd loaded our personal gear at dawn or Davis and company would've taken off without us having our things. You'd think they feared death-by-precipitation the way they were pushing us to get going. I swiftly loaded the rest of the items, sealed up the box, slapped on the label, and raced for the van.

Thunder rumbled and cracked in time with a jagged lightning strike. *Damn it.*

The first chilly drip landed on my nose as soon as I left the building. More followed, pelting me in a sharp barrage of raindrop bombs as I ran for the open loading door. Roan grabbed the box from me and slid it in place, then motioned for me to get in the truck parked in front of the cargo vehicle.

Not yet. I watched one of Davis's men shut and lock the freight area, making sure our samples and equipment were secure, before snagging Roan's arm and dragging him toward the truck's door. "Get in. I'm not sitting in the middle this time."

He grimaced but entered the vehicle first.

Another crack boomed, and a swift jolt to the shoulder smacked my body into the vehicle's unyielding metal exterior.

Air left my lungs, my legs slid out from under me, and I landed with a thump on the hard earth.

Captain Davis's handsome face came into view. He gripped my cheek in the palm of his hand and turned me to stare at him, but his features fogged. The deep blue of his eyes seemed to bleed like watercolors on the page. "Dr. Carter. Jane. Stay down."

Stay down? Wasn't I already on the ground? "Wh-wha…?" I

listed, falling to my left, and dropped to lay on the dampening dirt.

"Shit, you're bleeding. Harris. Taylor. Secure the area." The captain bent down and hovered over me like a shield. "Stay with me, Jane. I've got you—" His voice drifted off.

Drifting sounded like an excellent idea.

My muzzy brain decided I should do the same.

CHAPTER
TWO

My body swayed back and forth, back and forth, like someone rocking me in an old-time cradle. The rhythm felt familiar.

Oh. I'm in a vehicle.

Opening my eyes to slits to peer into the murky light, I tried to rise, levering up on my elbows. Pain radiated from a nexus just below my left shoulder, waves of agony threatening to submerge me.

A scream rose from the depths of my soul, fighting to break free, and I pressed my lips together to contain the sound.

"Shh. Shh. You're okay. You're resting on a stretcher in the rear of one of the vans." Someone's warm hands guided me back to a reclining position, then gently brushed my hair away from my face. "Dr. Carter, it's Captain Davis. Do you remember what happened to you?"

I blinked a few times to bring him into focus. *Captain Davis? Why is he here, and what did he mean by the tender touch? Wait. He asked me a question. What happened. Yes.* "Lightning crack. Did I get struck?" *No. That's not right.* I'd be feeling something completely different if I'd been hit by lightning. No burning internal organs. No seared skin. Just…throbbing pain and heat radiating from the left shoulder area.

"You were hit by a bullet. Fortunately, the sniper missed any vital organs. Through and through shot. The medic field-dressed your wound." His tone was as grim as the set of his jaw.

Someone shot me? The idea hit so hard I might as well have been struck by lightning. "Bullets are illegal for all non-security personnel," I blurted out.

His intent look let me know how big of an idiot he thought I was. Based on his frequent stares at me throughout our trip, he thought my normal level of idiocy already significant. "When in the history of the world did declaring something against the law stop someone from doing so?"

"I, um…" I pressed my lips shut. He was correct, of course, but it wouldn't do to let him know I agreed. The man too often forgot who was in charge of this mission. "Who, ah, fired a gun at me?"

He lowered his head. "Unfortunately, one of mine. Smith."

Shock rippled through my limbs, jerking my shoulder, making me inhale so hard it hurt my lungs. "Amy Smith? The quiet brunette?" I could picture the small woman going about her work, silent, methodical. "Why? What did I ever do to her?"

He glanced up, piercing me with his baby blues, a blue more natural than the perverted, gene-manipulated shade of mine. "You didn't do anything. You exist. A genetically engineered human on a crusade to find breeders. Her words, not mine." His face reflected an emotionless mask, but I knew better.

Captain Darren Davis hated our directive to find fertile individuals. He disagreed with the entire premise. He'd remarked on numerous occasions that government intervention in naturally occurring biological functions never improved the situation.

He just didn't disagree with me much as Amy did.

Yet.

My mouth dried. Was I surrounded by enemies waiting for the perfect moment to pick me and mine off one by one?

If Davis came for me, I'd never see him coming. The man moved like a silent predator. My gut twisted. "So, where is Amy now? Contained?"

"Dead."

The single word lay between us like a minefield. My emotions halted, ready to detonate at his one-word declaration.

"H-how is she…dead?"

"She shot you. I shot her. She missed your heart. I didn't miss hers." He stated the facts as unfeelingly as he'd previously discussed the weather.

Bile churned and threatened to rise. "You killed one of your own. She was fertile. All of you and your team are." My whispered words echoed in the van, horror infusing every syllable. "Why—"

His irises appeared to take on a steely hue. "Amy Smith disobeyed orders. Personal feelings have no place during an operation. She didn't have to agree to come on the assignment, yet she did. I trained her, so she knew better." His voice held a bitter aftertaste.

I licked my dry lips and could swear I tasted the acridness of his tone. "The rest of your crew agreed to the job. So did you. How do I know my team is safe with yours?"

"Anyone who had any ideas about harming any other member of this squad now knows the consequences for violating my trust. As for me, when I make a decision, I stick by my word." A note of sincerity sang through every bit of his speech, but I'd keep my guard up.

Once upon a time, Amy Smith seemed harmless.

"Wonder why she waited until now to act?"

"Guess we'll never know." His firm, flinty tenor stated he didn't care to discuss her further.

"Guess not." *How can you be so cavalier about taking the*

life of one of your own? I swallowed hard. "Where is everyone else?" *Am I alone in here with you?*

"My soldiers are evenly distributed among your crew."

That notion didn't fill me with confidence.

"Your people and mine are roughly paired up, four duos per vehicle, except for this one. Your O'Hara and my Taylor are up front."

Roan was near. The thought instantly soothed me, my muscles relaxing slightly. While the man couldn't offer any sort of physical protection, I thought of him as the baby brother I never had—someone to protect. Davis's Taylor was the unit's medic. "Guess I have Stephanie Taylor to thank for dressing my wound."

"She did what she could do in the time allotted. We'll make camp once the solar batteries die out and the vehicles are forced to stop and recharge. She'll reassess you once we arrive."

The morning meal's meager contents curdled my stomach at the mere suggestion of her poking at my injury. "How far are we toward our target? How long have I been out?"

"We're probably going to be just shy of making Elgin. Had to steer clear of the coast. Too much bomb damage to the terrain that's never been repaired or purified from after the past war. You've been out for the better part of six hours. Taylor felt you'd fare better if anesthetized for bumpy travel along the rough road."

I did the mental math. Elgin stood about two hundred kilometers from Aviemore. Even with the minimal mileage these solar-powered vehicles managed, we should have been at our destination three hours ago at the latest. "Why is it taking us so long to get to Elgin? Unless…"

He huffed a breath. "Your assistant insisted we stop in Inverness, per the original plan. Said that's what you'd want. Your people took samples. My crew checked out the remains of the town. Empty, like every other city we've encountered."

Warmth flooded me. Dear Roan. He kept us on plan. We wouldn't have to backtrack. I wouldn't have to file an exception report. Well, I wouldn't have to file one in addition to the two for my injury and for the death of Amy Smith.

Amy. I closed my eyes and squeezed them tight against her loss.

Davis placed a hand on my harm. "You okay, Doc? Are you in pain? You got awful quiet there."

I nodded and opened my eyes. "Sorry, just thinking about Amy. Did she have family?"

"You think I should've let her live to shoot you another day?" His lips flattened along with the timbre of his voice.

Choose your words carefully. "I appreciate you saving my life. I wish that didn't come with ending hers. She was young. She had a future." *She could have had her own family.*

"You don't have a future? You're not young?"

He thinks I'm questioning his judgment call. "I'm twenty-nine. Life spans of my kind don't match that of yours."

"Even for a GE, you still have plenty of time left. You seem fit. You've got at least fifty years."

"You're being generous. I've got thirty-five to forty, tops, even for a fit GE."

GE. Derogatory term for those of us who were genetically enhanced, or, as most Repopulators called us, the genetically engineered. But he wasn't wrong. What my ancestors and those who were like-minded did in the name of vanity ruined us as human beings. "Which is why as a GE my remaining life span has to count. Thanks to my forebears and other people who continually tinkered with our genes, I'm the first generation who can't reproduce. What I can do is help save and protect those left in this world who are able."

"I'm one of those. I don't need you to save me. I'm fine on my own, thanks." The snark in his tone let me know his sarcasm mode still worked, but his hard gaze stayed focused on me as if I wore a target on my chest.

I returned the stare and looked at him. Really and truly examined him. Handsome. Strong. Tall. Most people would find him irresistible...until he opened his cynical mouth. "Are you fine on your own? Postwar soldiering jobs are few, which is why you're here. Where is your home base? Why are you alone? Why haven't you found a partner, Captain?" *Why am I asking you all of these questions?*

He narrowed his gaze. "Edinburgh is my base, not that you need to know. And don't even think about trying to pair me up with someone. I can manage that by myself too."

"Oh." Maybe I'd misread the whole situation. He'd never shown me or any other person on the crew anything but professionalism...and in my case, acerbity. Was he asexual? Did he not want the closeness a coupling would bring? "Do you prefer men or women?" *Why did I ask that particular question?* I slapped a hand over my mouth as if I could shove the words back in and swallow them down dry.

"Women, and I don't need a matchmaker. Last I heard, Dr. Carter, 'professional cupid' wasn't in your mission specs." His lips twitched as if he fought a snicker.

"No, I...no. It's just hard for someone like me to understand why a man of thirty, a fertile man in his prime, wasn't looking to build a life with someone. Have children. Create a family." I couldn't keep the wistfulness out of my voice.

He leaned closer, the move squeaking the frame of his folding chair, the portable type we kept in the back of the vans for field use. He never took his eyes off me, resting his forearms on his thighs and lacing his fingers together. I couldn't read his emotions by the closed-off expression on his face. "When I find the right woman, I'll think about that kind of life." His stare lengthened as if he waited for me to respond.

How was I supposed to reply? Good luck?

16

He shook his head, breaking eye contact. "Until then, I have a job to do. So do you."

The vehicle faltered, then began to slow. Damn the batteries. Guess our conversation was at an end. I was no closer to understanding the man than I'd been before. Probably for the best. After this mission, we'd most likely never see each other. I'd be back in London, overseeing the new labs being built as part of the domed area of the city set to house the surviving population. He'd be off doing only the holy Mother knew what former military people did.

Another lurch later, and we ground to a halt. If the sun shone, we should've banked more power than this. "Wonder where we are?"

He got up. "I'll go find out. It's still raining like the great flood's returning, so we'll need to scout out shelter—especially for you. Taylor will need a dry environment to fix you up."

Blood abandoned my limbs at the reminder.

He headed for the rear doors but paused with his hand on the latch, staring at me from over his shoulder. "You place a lot of stock on children being a required part of what it means to be a family. Not everyone should have children. Not all of us want them. A married couple in love can be whole enough." Silence lengthened while he locked me in his mesmerizing gaze.

"You would be satisfied with that? If not for personal reasons, then for the betterment of the world. How can you not want to continue your bloodline?"

"Finding the person you're supposed to be with and procreating are two different things. Love can be enough. Think about that, Doc." His powerful scrutiny seemed to burn a hole through my soul.

He turned, then twisted the handle.

Love can be enough.

We must live in different worlds because in mine, love could never be enough.

Darren Davis stood in the open doorway of the van, the deluge pounding the ground in a deafening beat. He tilted his head like a raptor on a hunt, listening for his target.

A boom sounded over the driving rain.

"Curse it." He leaped from the van, pulled his gun, and slammed the door.

I wanted to believe thunder made the sound.

The throb near my shoulder said otherwise.

CHAPTER
THREE

The sniper remained at large, but the side panel damage to one of the vehicles and the blown tires on two others told us we either had an unhappy local firing at us…or a traitor in our midst who somehow managed to get out of the van and take the shots. After Amy Smith's attempt on my life, a part of me wondered if the threat was internal. Either way, after a futile search for the gun-wielding attacker, we had to fix the tires, recharge the vehicles, and proceed on to our targeted location for the day.

The camp we'd set up southwest of Forres defined roughing it. Rocky, uneven ground. Pouring rain. Not a lick of green growing things in sight. Nothing but soggy brown soil as far as I could see from my vantage point. Normally, I'd expect every member of the team to sleep in the tents—the equipment and collected samples must remain dry, not us.

However, Stephanie Taylor needed to clean out and mend my injury in a drier, more sanitary environment, so I stayed in the van. She'd completed the full sterilize-and-fix-the-gunshot-wound procedure on my shoulder area and loaded me up with the good stuff, so I currently felt no pain.

For once, I thought I deserved the drugs. During the procedure, the anesthetic did little to minimize the agony of repairing a bullet wound.

"So…you and the captain, huh?" she asked while winding up the sterile dressings.

I jerked my head to better see her facial expression, thankful for the meds because the movement didn't hurt. Mischievous came to mind—the tilt of her lips and the sparkle in her eyes read playful. "The captain and I what?"

"You know…the thing you two have." She used the rolled wrap to gesture between us.

Roan snickered from behind me. I couldn't see his face, but I could picture the look. Eyes crinkled up, cheeks as red as his hair, mouth curled in an impish smile. "Stephanie, you might as well be talking to Jane in a dead language. She doesn't speak romance."

Stephanie laughed softly and put the repackaged piece back in her kit.

I craned my neck to see my assistant, but the medication disoriented me, and I couldn't quite get him in view to give him my dragon-lady look, as he called it. "We're here for a higher purpose. Love and romance are not on the table…or anywhere else," I added before he could twist what I said into something suggestive.

Because he would.

"Tell that to Harris and Ward. I'm surprised you can't hear them from here."

Stephanie's words penetrated the fog of my brain. "Wait. Paul and Bonnie?"

Roan tsked. "Jane, for all your powers of observation in the field or a lab, you are sometimes clueless about interpersonal relationships. I don't claim to be an expert, but even I've noticed the banter between them, the knowing glances, and the tent rocking at night if those two aren't on sentry duty."

She nodded. Or at least I thought she did. My vision blurred a bit. "Dr. Carter, I've got to agree with O'Hara here. Harris and Ward started sharing quarters on week one of this trip. If you didn't pick up on those two, it's no wonder you didn't notice Captain Davis's interest." Her voice rose and fell as she spoke as if she drew close, then moved away from me during the conversation. Why was she conversing this way?

"He dislikes me." A distorted version of my own voice came out. What kind of medication did she give me? I should've asked more questions.

Roan's face came into view. Well, a hazy version of him. He must have stood up and bent to look at me. "Captain Davis hates our mission...doesn't hate you." His words skipped and paused periodically. Damn it. The drugs.

"Caught him watching when you're not looking. Didn't need to use stealth...didn't pick up on his attraction. Killed one of our own to save you. If that doesn't speak to his feelings...don't know what does." Stephanie's piecemeal words registering with my brain surprisingly lacked any venom. Odd. I thought she and Amy were friends.

"Didn't ask for her to die." My words slurred together as if I spoke the dead language Roan talked about.

"What'd she say?" Her question didn't appear to be directed at me.

"...feels terrible...Amy's death." Roan spoke in a soft, sad tone.

"Amy Smith didn't follow orders," Stephanie replied with an edgy sharpness. "...captain was clear. Personal opinions about the mission were unwelcome. We've...under his leadership... know his reactions...challenges to his command. Plus, Smith... kill...first woman...shown sentiments for." Her words stuttered in my brain. I doubted she said them this way.

"No...feelings." I tried to speak, but only garbled sounds emerged from my throat.

A small, cool, gentle hand pressed against my cheek, my forehead. "About time. Drugs...kicking in...sleep until morning."

No, wait. I need to know more.

———

The familiar sight and swaying sensation of the van greeted me when I woke...along with the fine-looking face of Darren Davis.

Creases on his brow smoothed as he took me in. "How are you feeling, Doc?"

Glancing away, afraid to read anything into his presence at my side, I focused on the wound and butterfly-touched my tightly wrapped shoulder. *Ow, ow, ow.* Pain spiked as if someone skewered me, and my eyelids fluttered. "Uncomfortable, but I'll survive."

"We're currently on track and proceeding to the next scheduled town, if you can call it that, but we can make camp there and give you a day to recuperate before we start the search."

I snapped my head toward him, which jerked my body, and I sucked in a breath through my teeth. The drugs had worn off. "We stay on plan."

He nodded with what almost looked like approval. "Sun's out, so the solars are recharging en route. Should reach our destination soon." He cocked his head. "Sure you're up for this? Based on our searches to date, chances are good we won't find anyone."

"People could be in the mountains. Those landforms have proven helpful in other locations in blocking some of the poor air quality. Makes survivability more likely. Look at Raasay."

He laughed. The sound suited him. "My ancestors are from Raasay. We're just pigheaded people."

I paused. "You never mentioned you were from the island. Not even when we were on the island."

With a shrug he said, "Many generations ago, my family left there for jobs in Edinburgh. Not many career opportunities on a small isle. We've been on the mainland ever since. Have you always been in London?"

"Always. Big-city people. My great-grandparents were keen on being viewed as trendsetters. Unnaturally vivid scarlet hair. Luminous blue eyes. The perfect genetically enhanced height and weight and form. Hard to show off and be seen in the suburbs." Disgust dripped from my tone. Damn my family for their genetic decisions. They ruined me.

"You know, you're the first enhanced person I've ever met who hates the way she looks. For the record, you and your family have mild modifications. I've seen elf ears, green skin, horns, permanently purple hair, elongated fingers, you name it."

"Yes, I guess in comparison, the Carters are less flamboyant." I stared at the ceiling of the van, not wanting to see the expression on his face that would tell me what he really thought about what my ancestors did to our genes.

"I once heard you tell one of your people that you're a freak. You're anything but. In fact, I'd call you attractive, Jane." His voice, soft and velvety, made me turn toward him. Sincerity showed on his stoic soldier face. In the past, I would've bristled at the flattery, sure that he never intended his meaning to be complimentary. After what Stephanie and Roan stated, however, I took a moment to consider he might mean what he'd said.

"You, um, you're not so bad yourself." *Well, that sounded genuinely awkward.* Roan was right. I had no expertise in this area. Besides, I hadn't thought through what my feelings were toward him if he did, in fact, find me worth his notice. He'd been flinty and acerbic toward me from the start.

Maybe he was as clueless about how to initiate contact as I was.

23

"I'm not so bad? Did Dr. Jane Carter just give me a compliment?" A small smile curled his lips.

A warm, gooey sensation spread through me at his grin, and I laughed. "Maybe. Don't let it go to your head."

"Not to worry." He chuckled, deep and husky, and the vibration touched me in virgin parts of my soul.

The van wrenched to a halt, sending my makeshift bed to swaying.

Darren immediately caged himself over me, our faces so close I could see the concerned creases at the corners of his arresting eyes and inhale his pleasant woodsy scent. "Let me see why we stopped so fast." In seconds, he rose with his gun out and managed to get the vehicle's back door open to a mere slit of visibility.

My ears echoed with my heart's rapid rhythm. *Thump-thump. Thump-thump.* Was someone else going rogue? Weren't we supposed to be close to our destination making this a normal, if abrupt, stop?

He peeked his head out of the door, weapon held in both hands. "Situation report."

"Local with a gun," Stephanie replied. "Harris and Ward on approach."

My heart rate rabbited. *Another damn gun?*

"Stay with the van. Protect the team. I'm heading on scene." Darren Davis dropped down to the ground and slammed the cargo door shut hard enough to shake the vehicle.

Hell no. These trigger-happy soldiers might kill the resident citizen. I pushed myself up, gasping against the sharp pain of the movement, and swung my legs off the bed. After a wobbly few seconds of standing, I followed Davis's path, opening the back door and easing myself to the ground.

"Sir, we mean you no harm," I could hear the captain say.

"Then why the guns? Why the military vehicles? You're clearly soldiers. Haven't you people done enough to this land?"

24

The unknown local had a strong Scottish accent, which sounded strange to my ears. These days, most people spoke in a blended, common version of English. In fact, the world repopulation council's global government had discussed making English the world's standard tongue. By his tone, this man seemed intent on keeping to his own ways.

We had to be at our target site or close. As I rounded the side of the van, I could see an attractive man in his early thirties, with light brown hair and a stocky build, standing with the Cairngorm Mountains as his scenic backdrop. A verdant green tinted the ground and the surrounding hills, and the man held the unmistakable steel barrel of a rifle sighted at us.

The mutinous set of his jaw and the way he held the gun let me know he wasn't bluffing—he'd use it.

Davis and his team had the same stance.

I ran, the pain ignored in my effort to stop a bloodbath.

Interjecting myself between the two factions, I approached the man and held out my hand. "Hello, sir. I'm Jane Carter. Pardon my team's response, but as you can see"—I tilted my head toward my visibly bandaged shoulder—"I've been recently shot, so they're a bit concerned for my safety. We're not here on a military mission but one based on helping people."

He took in my hair and my eyes, and his lips firmed further. The man ignored my attempt at a handshake and gripped his gun tighter. "How can the likes of you help me?"

The likes of you. Though not surprised by his response, the sentiment still stung.

"We're assessing the environments of the surviving pockets of humanity and offering them safe spaces to live."

"In the damn domes you're building? Even in this remote area, we've heard about those."

"Among other options, yes."

"We don't need you and your kind. You've no place here."

"Da? Mum sent me to ask what you're about."

I froze and turned in the direction of that sing-song sound.

A sense of wonder unfurled and bloomed inside me, raising the fine hairs on the back of my neck, a sensation that dominoed down my arms in a rippled, raised-skin effect.

This miracle, the unmistakable, small, high-pitched voice of a little girl, made me sway.

A child. We'd found a fertile family.

The probability of our mission's success changed trajectory, exploding from a mere 10 percent chance of finding a fruitful pocket of humanity to full-mission goal…if I could persuade them to come live in one of the domes under construction.

One look at the local in front of me torpedoed my elation. Success wasn't guaranteed. I'd have to use my nonexistent people skills.

My work here had just begun.

CHAPTER
FOUR

T he mutinous man in front of me, the assumption the little girl's father, flexed his fingers, gripping the rifle more firmly.

"Jocasta, get back. Go to your mother," he called out, not taking his eyes off us or releasing his hold on his weapon.

"What's going on, Da?"

I pivoted toward the speaker. A sweet face, a perfect face, peered over the rise. The small child wore her auburn hair in two long braids, and her eyes and bow mouth grew round at the sight of us.

Tears sprang and began to course down my cheeks at the angelic vision of her.

"Go, I say," her father yelled.

The little girl whirled around and disappeared from view. I could hear her repeatedly calling "Mum" in her high-pitched, squeaky tone.

"You'll not be getting your hands on her. I see the coveted way you look at my daughter."

I swiveled my gaze to view the angry, wary look on his face.

"We have no interest in separating you and yours, sir. Our mission is to find families and keep them safe."

"By poking guns in their faces?"

Without looking at my crew, I motioned my right hand in a *put it down* manner. "Lower your weapons, please."

I didn't hear any movement to indicate they'd done so. While I often admired the natural command skills the captain demonstrated with his people and the devotion they showed him, now wasn't one of those moments. "Captain Davis…Darren… please ask your team to stand down." The words ground out between my clenched teeth.

"Disengage," he growled out in his gruff tone after a few tense seconds.

"Sir," I said to the local man. "I'd appreciate if you did the same. You have my word our group will not harm you and your family. Your well-being is our mission." I dashed away the tears streaming down my cheeks.

"Evan, what's going on?" This voice, distinctly female, came on approach from the direction the child had taken.

"Lianna, return home. I have the situation in hand."

"I'll be the judge of that." An auburn head appeared, the hair worn loose and the same color as the little girl's, and soon the woman's face and body came into view as she hustled our way. Short and pretty, in an unadorned way, she'd clothed her slender figure in denim overalls and a plain dark T-shirt. The gloves on her hands made it appear as if she'd been working in the soil, and she had a baby perched on her hip. She halted at the top of the hillock.

My mouth dried. *A baby.* I waved. "Hello, ma'am. My team and I have been sent to help the pockets of surviving people. I've just been talking with…your husband?"

She continued toward us. "He is that, and I doubt he's been talking."

A red flush crept up from his shirt collar to tint his face. "Lianna, I've got this. Go back and tend to the children."

Children. Plural. *They have more than two?* A full-body tremble rippled through me.

"I'll do as I please, as you well know. Besides, Jocasta has the other two in hand. Brian's with me."

He cast a quick glance over his shoulder and closed his eyes, his features creasing as if in pain. "You brought the baby into this situation? Have you lost your sense?"

"Have you? Let's hear these people out before we start brandishing firearms." She'd reached his side and extended her free hand to me. "Lianna Bain."

I clasped her dirty, gloved hand. "Jane Carter."

"Tell me why you're here. Wait. Are you all right?" She paused and cocked her head, side-eyeing her husband for a second. "Did Evan make you cry? Do you need a handkerchief?"

"I'm fine. Perfect, in fact." Tears continued to trickle at the sight of this woman holding a precious, rare child, and I swiped the wetness away. "I'll tell you what we can do for you."

"Oh, we're fine as we are. Just regular folk. Join us for a meal, and we'll talk. I'd started pulling some vegetables to cook, so we'll have plenty."

"Lianna," Evan said with a warning note to his voice.

"Evan, we were raised to be hospitable. I'll not go back on our values."

"We have food to share," I added in case they were worried about trying to feed so many people.

"It's a picnic, then. We don't have table space for…how many in your party?"

"Twenty-three. And a picnic sounds lovely."

"Follow me." Lianna turned and headed back the way she'd come. "Bring your man and the rest of your crew."

My man?

I glanced behind me. Darren Davis had silently taken point less than a foot from me, mirroring the stance of Evan Bain.

———

We sat upon blankets and tarps, enjoying a fine spread of their fresh produce and our contribution of sterilized beef. They seemed as wary of eating the meat as I was of eating the carrots, spinach, and strawberries. I hadn't checked the pollution levels in the area—it seemed rude to do so before the shared meal—so I had no idea what lingered in the soil or the air that could contaminate the food supply.

Her husband, Evan, sat beside her while the baby, Brian, munched happily on the pureed carrots Lianna served him from a spoon.

"How old is he?" I couldn't help the note of longing in my question.

"Nine months. He'll have an additional sibling in another seven."

"You're pregnant." Reverence breathed through my statement. This woman had to be protected at all costs.

The laughter of her daughters, Jocasta, Brigid, and Rose, rang through the area as they ran and played, having quickly devoured their food. Lianna birthed four children, ages seven through nine months, and she was expecting a fifth. This family defied the norms, even for Repopulators.

"You've no children of your own?" She gestured between me and Darren.

"Oh, we're not—"

"Not able to have children." Darren finished the sentence for me.

My eyes welled. I glanced at the blanket and traced the quilted pattern with my finger. "He is, but I'm not. My genes are defective." The one thing I ever wanted—a family encompassing children—was the one thing multiple-generations-worth of genetic manipulations ensured I'd never have. My parents were lucky to have me, their only child. The Carter line would die out with my death.

I raised my chin to meet Lianna's gaze, a tear tracking down my face. I'd blame my emotions on hormones but those had been genetically altered too. So, why couldn't I stop crying today?

Her features softened. "I'm sorry for you. Clearly, you were meant to have babes of your own."

My smile wobbled. "The deeds of my forebears prevented that. The best I can do is ensure the safety of those like you who can."

Evan used his carrot like a pointer. "As you can see, we do just fine on our own. Don't need anyone's help." He gestured to the surrounding area. "We left Elgin shortly after the last war destroyed our apartment and settled here, where we've found fertile soil and plenty of game to meet our needs. Built a home. Created a family. We've even put a name to our settlement— South Elgin, in honor of our birthplace."

Darren leaned back and took in the area. "Nice area to establish a community. Are there others nearby you can socialize and trade with?"

Evan nodded. "Recently ran into another man while out on a scouting expedition. Maybe six weeks ago?" He looked at his wife.

"Sounds right." She wiped some carrot mush from Brian's face.

Jealousy's sharp, green spike stabbed at witnessing their obvious connection, their clear love and ease with each other. I'd never allowed myself to ever consider such a gift for myself. Science became my spouse. Seeing Lianna and Evan's relationship, however, made me ache for things I could never have.

Evan chucked his son's chin before refocusing on us. "Ran

into the other man about a half hour east of here. Scared each other near to death, since we both had weapons at the ready. Took a few minutes to figure out we were both foraging to feed our loved ones."

Lianna smiled. "Our families got together a couple of weeks ago. Felt good to meet a new neighbor and know others are close enough to reach out to if needed. They have two boys about the ages of Jocasta and Rose. Nice people. We're planning on another outing next week. I'm happy we're now able to visit with others. We lost our families to the pandemic, then the war took our home. No place to raise children. Took baby Jocasta with us, and the rest of the children were born here."

Born without medical treatment. I quelled a shudder. So much could have gone wrong.

"So, with all of this plenty," Evan said, "what can you do for us that we can't do for ourselves, Jane?"

"Ensure a safe food supply, one free of pollutants, and guarantee you'll have medical care available to you. Clean air. Clean water. Make certain no one can harm you."

"By building a dome around us like animals in a cage?" Evan's tone made clear he wouldn't go for such a plan.

Darren turned to me and raised a brow. "I'm sure we can work out other options. My people are looking for places to settle, to build a life. Soldiering is no longer a profession, but my crew is trained to keep others secure. Some might be interested in staying here. Plus, we have equipment like air scrubbers to help improve the environment, don't we, Jane?"

I nodded, the emotions lingering at the surface too much to allow more than that agreement. After taking a few moments to collect myself, I responded, "We do. We could discuss the possibilities for ways to assist." *As in build a dome around you like the bubble wrap of old.*

Lianna leveled a strong stare my way. "I'd like to talk about those options. I watched my parents and my sisters die from disease. Watched Evan's parents and sisters succumb to the most recent virus too. I couldn't bear to lose my husband or children that way. Come with me to the house. We'll have some thistle tea and talk. Evan and Darren can discuss things they don't wish to say with us women around."

Evan snorted but didn't disagree.

Neither did Darren, come to consider it.

She stood, hefting the baby and settling him on her hip, then waved me forward. "Let's go, Jane."

I followed in her wake, then caught up with her.

She patted my shoulder. "I think you and I share common concerns. Together, we might come up with workable solutions, maybe even become friends."

"Yes. I think so too." My soul warmed as if Lianna were the sun and shone her rays upon me.

This first contact felt like a pivotal moment in time—my lifetime—one that would forever shape my future. I made a silent vow.

I would keep Lianna Bain and her family safe…persuade them to embrace dome life…if it was the last thing I did.

CHAPTER
FIVE

I left the Bain's homestead with a new hope shimmering in my heart. Humanity wasn't doomed. If this family could survive and thrive in this environment, then we as a race could overcome all the disaster we'd brought upon ourselves. We still had work to do, but a light beamed on the possibilities for the survival of our species.

Lianna and I would talk in greater depth tomorrow, but tonight she'd said she needed family time with her husband and children.

Family.

Children.

Husband.

Though I couldn't have children, maybe I could have one of those. I knew which man I'd choose, but my thoughts about Captain Darren Davis confused me. He'd behaved so differently on this leg of the mission. More relaxed. More open. More like someone I'd wish to know more intimately. I liked this version of the man and found myself wanting to believe Roan and Stephanie's thoughts about his romantic feelings for me.

"Jane, wait up." The thud of his bootsteps pounded behind me until he sidled up to my side.

His unique, spicy scent triggered an endorphin hit—one that could be addictive if I weren't careful. I cut my gaze to him. "Good start, don't you think?"

He raised a brow.

A flush raced through me. Damn it. Did he think I meant a beginning for us? "The initial contact seems hopeful."

The brow remained up.

Guess you could take that two ways too. My skin warmed from the inside, and I'm sure I wore a blush. I never blushed... except around him. What a mess I was making of things. Better clarify. "You know, to the mission."

He glanced ahead toward our troops' vehicles and nodded once. "Yeah, to the mission. You and Lianna seemed to hit it off." His tone of voice changed from one of resignation in the first sentence to one of the cold, callous captain I'd known for the previous part of our journey. Was he disappointed I didn't mean the start of an *us*?

No, I'd read more into this than he intended. I should get back to business too. "You and Evan got on as well. I think we should debrief and compare conversations while they're fresh for the report."

"Sounds logical. Where would you like to talk?" The brisk note to his words were so cold they made me yearn for a sweater.

Stay on task. Answer his question.

We'd need some privacy, and ahead of us I could see the rest of our team members who'd straggled back from the picnic either in the process of setting up a tent or already in one. I flashed to Stephanie and Roan's conversation about Paul and Bonnie. Best not to look too closely at the tents to see if any were moving in a rhythm not caused by a breeze.

"We could meet in the van? Or a tent? I'd rather keep this discussion private for the report. Lianna and I spoke of some matters she'd probably wish to remain known to only a select few." The old-world phrase of "girl talk" popped to mind. My conversation with her qualified. We'd started with the practical —overviews of what the government hoped to do to help the survivors of our world's destruction. The talk evolved into a more personal chat about our families, our backgrounds, and our men, even though Darren wasn't technically mine. Her referring to him as such made me consider *what if he could be*?

When I'd told her the truth of Darren's and my relationship, she'd offered suggestions of how to manage the situation if he was who I wanted. Lianna's no-nonsense, joyous approach to life left her with little filter. She spoke her mind. Often. One or two or twelve of her comments about the intimacies of married life made me blush at the time.

The reminder triggered a heat rush to paint my skin all over again.

"Embarrassed, Jane?"

His question pulled me out of my head but did nothing for the arousal triggered from my wanton thoughts. "Ah, no. Just reflecting on bits of what Lianna shared."

He smiled for the first time in a while. "Based on your reaction, I look forward to the debrief. I'd think you'd like to avoid the van. You've spent a lot of time there lately. As for the tent, I considered a joke about your tent or mine, but I don't see you being able to pitch a tent with the full use of only one arm or ask someone to help you do so. Asking for help is against your religion. I also don't think you'd appreciate the innuendo, so I'll offer to set up a tent far away from the madding crowd for us to share knowledge."

"Why do you think I'd not welcome the innuendo?" *Did I say that out loud?*

He halted midstride and turned to me. "Do you?" The way he asked the question telegraphed so much optimism.

My pulse picked up and sweat slicked my palms. Maybe

with this man, I could take the risk. Admit my interest. Entertain the possibility that he and I could have the closeness the Bains shared.

What could I do but answer honestly?

"I do." My words came out in a whisper.

A happy grin expanded across his face. "Stay here. I'll raise us a tent." He sprinted toward the cargo van and grabbed one, along with some blankets and bedding.

I'd never seen someone set up camp so quickly. Darren moved like a vid-screen image on fast-forward.

He raced back to me, grabbed my hand, and all but hauled me into the canvas abode. The blankets he'd seized lay across the floor, padding the area like colorful rugs, and the bedding had been wedged against the far wall, the two sets still in their rolled-up form. Pillows lay in a stack beside them. "You need something soft to sit on?"

"No, I'm—"

"Fine? You're always 'fine,' even when you're not. Know what?" He snatched two of the pillows, placing them on the ground in parallel lines. "Have a seat. You always do for others but never for yourself. Let someone else take care of you for once." He didn't use the tone of a coworker or a captain or a callous man on a mission he didn't believe in. His words soothed and seduced and left me spellbound.

I lowered myself to sit on the cushion.

He claimed the one opposite me and took my hand. His warmth seeped into my trembling fingers, and the contact eased my ratcheted-up nerves. "I'm not a man who speaks often, especially in a social setting, but when I do, I intend for what I say to count. We share this trait, I believe."

Since I seemed incapable of producing sound, I nodded.

He tightened his hold on my hand, and the intensity of his stare held me hostage.

"Today is the first inkling I've had that you might consider seeing me as more than a teammate. Am I wrong?"

"No." My voice sounded like a croaking frog. I cleared my throat. "You're correct. I... Today changed things between us. For me." I looked at our hands. "Sorry. I'm making a mess of this. Emotions aren't an equation I can solve. I've made this awkward."

"Not awkward. For me, today created a chance of an 'us.'" Our fingers still entwined, he brushed the rough pad of his thumb across the back of my hand.

"I like the sound of 'us.'" I smiled, my lips wobbly with wonder. Possibilities flowered of something fresh and fragile and completely off-mission...and worth the risk.

He leaned closer. "What if we waited on the report and the Bains and the whole mission and we put ourselves first and explored what we might have here."

His scent enticed me to narrow the gap between us further. "I'm not sure I know how."

"Me either. We'll work on it together. Joint taskforce, if you will." Humor lit his eyes.

"Collaboration is key, I think." I zeroed in on his mouth. His lips tempted, enticingly near, and I wanted them on mine. Flirting wasn't my forte. What to do? *Be bold. Try one of Lianna's suggestions regarding seduction.* I licked my lower lip.

As my new friend promised, his gaze tracked the tip of my tongue. He didn't make a move, though. Shifting my attention to the hope embodied in our clasped hands and our intertwined fingers, I racked my brain to think of how to proceed.

"Jane?"

I jerked my head up. "Yes?"

"Would it be too forward of me to kiss you?"

Forward? Certainly. Risky? Without a doubt. Welcome? Hell yes. Every nerve ending in my body woke up as if they'd been roused from a coma.

Instead of answering him, I closed the distance between us. His breath feathered over my face. I inhaled his heady scent, and the lock surrounding my shriveled, caged heart snapped open. I took the leap and pressed my lips to his.

"I'll take that as consent," he murmured against my mouth.

I consented to many things that night.

Guess the government was right when they sent him on that mission with me.

I did need him for security.

He'd secured my heart.

EPILOGUE

*S**even years later*
South Elgin World Repopulation Center (SEWRC)

I climbed into bed, the joy of the day and the stress of the massive move finally taking its toll on my muscles and my mind.

Darren welcomed me into his arms, and I relaxed for the first time since I'd awakened early this morning. He cuddled me close and brushed a tender kiss on my lips. "Everyone settled in?"

I rested my head on his chest, bare like the rest of him, where the reassuring beat of his heart sang my favorite song. "Yes, every last one of them. The Bains, the Martins, the Kerrys, the Wards, the MacDonalds—every family who agreed to live under the new dome. All are in their new quarters. You should've seen the kids. So excited to explore their fancy new rooms." I traced one of his old war wound's raised ridge of scarred skin with my fingertip. "I hope they continue to love their new home, their new surroundings."

"Kids have short attention spans. They're adaptable. Don't you remember being a child?"

"Yes, but I lived in the city. These are country children. They'll yearn for their former open spaces soon enough."

"You've built greenhouses, and they have the courtyard in the middle of the complex for them to play in, not to mention the animal habitats in the facility's northeast corner. But, my darling Jane, not everyone living here will like it. Can't please everyone."

Why not? I wanted, no, needed these people to be happy and build their lives here. One unhappy new resident stood out. "Especially can't please Evan Bain."

"His love for his wife is a powerful motivator, and she wants to be here. Hell, she helped design this place with you. So, Evan will stay." He laughed, soft and low, and the pleasant sound reverberated through my cheek against his warm chest. "What we men won't do for our wives." He picked up my hand, brought it to his lips, and kissed my wedding band.

I laced my fingers with his and tilted my head up to stare at his striking, sculpted features. "Thank you for agreeing to relocate with me to London."

"Facing another move, especially to that town, wasn't my first choice. I'd have preferred to remain in the pre-dome South Elgin, but home isn't a place. You're my home. I go where you go."

I breathed him in, the slightly spicy scent wafting. "How did I get so lucky? You've sacrificed so much for me."

"You're my family. I can't imagine my life without you."

Here's my opening. "Speaking of family...I have a favor."

"Shoot."

I winced, and my shoulder spasmed at the memory reminder. The bullet wound from years ago never felt fully healed.

"Sorry, poor word choice, Janie. What do you need?"

41

"I want to bank your sperm." The request burst from my mouth like the discharge from a pistol.

He paused, his body immobile. "Say again?"

"You're amazing. Perfect. Everything a man should be. The world needs your bloodline to live on."

"We're not having this conversation." His jaw went as taut as the muscles in his body.

"Why are you so set against this? I want your children." My pleading tone shifted to a demanding one in seconds.

"We do not need to have kids to make us whole. The only woman I'll procreate with is you. Why can't you understand that you and I are the only family I'll ever want or need?"

"Because I'm not enough."

A gleam sparked in his eyes. "You are everything. Somehow, someway, I will make you understand I mean what I say."

I nibbled my lower lip and glanced down at his chest.

He tilted up my chin with his free hand. "Let me take this time to show you how much I love you. Miracles happen in this world. When science catches up with us, I'll consider the options. Until then, we can keep trying to have a child." He skimmed his hand down my side and began to gather up my nightgown, pleating it like ruching. "Trying is fun, too, don't you think?"

My body answered for me. *Yes.* Desire quickened and tightened in anticipation at the crux of my thighs, and adrenaline mainlined through my system.

Damn the man. Darren knew the map of my contours well enough to know how to tease and tempt and lure me away from a topic he didn't want to talk about.

Fine with me...for now. He stripped off my gown and rolled me atop him. The man was firm and fiery and mine. For the next few hours, we let passion override all else.

As we lay in the afterglow, my head once again on his chest,

I thought about our situation…and devised a fresh plan, a new mission. One I'd see to personally.

Science would find a way. Darren Davis would live on through his children. The universe needed this man's gifts.

Smiling into the dark at my decision, a blissful peace surrounded my soul, and I could sleep.

Darren's genetic legacy would live on.

The man who now dominated my dreams and made me whole had once irritated me to the point I'd wondered if the world truly needed him. The world did.

More importantly, I did…and he made me believe the world just might need me too.

Good thing I didn't remove him from the mission all those years ago.

ABOUT FENLEY GRANT

Fenley Grant is an award-winning author of urban fantasy, time travel, and paranormal romance. She moved from cold northern climes--she's shoveled her last driveway--to live in the sunny Dallas/Fort Worth area with her family and her greyhounds.

facebook.com/FenleyGrant.Author
x.com/FenleyGrant
instagram.com/fenley_grant

AUKERA

LEAH VEGA

Heat Rating: Smokin'

ONE
ALESANDRA

I never thought I'd be a criminal. I'm not ashamed of it. What drives me to it floods my core and fuels me. If they ever identify me, they'll hunt me down and kill me. But I keep on in the name of my brother.

"Hurry!" I rasp, waving Laeeda and her mate toward the hidden entrance to the underground city.

My gaze darts around the forest, sweeping across filtered slivers of light between the trees for any signs of movement. Being the escort in this operation was *not* the plan. I'm supposed to be a silent partner. But when the driver of the transport gets caught u-minutes—a nomenclature for universal minutes— before reaching the checkpoint, improvisation must prevail.

From behind me, the snapping sound of a twig pops in my eardrum. I nod to the entrance guard as he reaches for the interior panel to close the camouflaged limestone door. In the narrowing passageway he nods back, his visage disappearing along with any evidence of the door.

Another twig snaps. I swing around, my gaze sweeping the forest again, scouting for anything lurking around, while I wipe my sweaty palms down my trousers. I see nothing, but I'm not stupid. Those search drones can be anywhere and look like anything.

I reengage my holo-repeater to disappear into my surroundings and lift my hand up for inspection. Then it hits me. *Drones fly, they don't snap twigs.*

I plaster my back against the rock wall near the entrance and swivel my head, my gaze sliding back and forth. My erratic breathing is heavy, raspy.

Can drones detect breathing?

I suck in a breath, not daring to release it just in case. Maybe they hadn't sent drones. Maybe they had sent interplanetary marshals, and they're snapping twigs to disorient me.

Movement on my left draws my attention. A glint of the sun shines off the metal body of a bird drone the size of my hand, zigzagging between the branches of dark orange pine trees. Somerika's lands are mostly rain forests with leafy deep purple-and-blue trees, but just north of Zeru, the capital city of Somerika, there's a singular swath of land that grows long-needle pine.

Any other u-day, it wouldn't matter to me. Today, my life depends on it. Drones are easier to spot through pine trees than large-leafed ones.

The drone comes to a stop, hovering a dozen feet before the entrance, and runs a laser scan over the rock wall. I've never known it to be true that the Imszoranians know where the entrance is located, but the drone stopped to scan the very spot where I had just stood while hustling the latest pair of asylum seekers inside. As the laser begins to reach the side of my body, I stiffen, my thoughts focused on burying the breath I can't release.

A tornado of my life's memories spins up in my mind, circling around the single thought that this may be my last moment alive. My hammering heart quickens, and my throat flexes as I fight every instinct in my body begging for a breath.

The light glides across my body, then the drone's sensor clicks off. I'm just about to release my breath when the little drone whizzes as if it's powering up to beam a death ray at my head.

I squeeze my eyes shut. *This is it. The end.*

Caught between accepting my fate and running like mad, my mind stalls until the drone lets out a mechanical bird chirp and turns toward the trail leading to my transport.

I ease out the long-held breath, my eyes fixed on the fog filtering out from between my lips and swirling in the chilly air.

The corner of my eye catches movement again, and I stretch my vision to the farthest reaches of the shadows.

A male voice emerges from nowhere, his tone as prickly as the pines. "I know you're there."

My bones lock in place as my gaze flits all around me. I don't dare let out another breath, hoping my last one has not given me away. A chill shoots down my spine.

Lips quivering, I hold tight on my breath, the lump in my throat building up pressure. My ability to function devolves as though I'm powering down like a machine, causing me to lose sight and sound. No rustling of branches or birds chirping or bugs buzzing reach my ears. No movement, not even the movement of pine needles in the slight breeze, catches my eyes. It's as if my surroundings have become paralyzed with me.

A masculine fragrance carried on the breeze reaches my nose, and I follow the scent to the origin where a male figure takes shape on the trail as his holo-repeater disengages.

The Imszoranian's eyes scan the rock wall in a search pattern. I wonder if he hasn't thought to use his thermal reader to find me or if he's just toying with me. Either way, I don't move a muscle. He takes careful strides up to the end of the trail and drags his gaze around him as he turns in a circle.

I use this opportunity to exhale, cursing the breath as it dissipates into the air, and ease in another breath. His head snaps my way, and he angles it, studying the space around me.

51

The irony of the situation, being less than an arm's length away from safety, is not lost on me. Azpian City, the hidden refuge for batasurna mates, rests behind that concealed door. If I had the nerve to kill this male and seek asylum for myself, I would. But murder goes against everything I stand for. Even if he *is* Imszoranian. With nimble fingers, I reach behind me to slowly unzip the side of my pack and fish out whatever I can get my hand on to use for self-defense.

He takes a step toward my position. Unless he can see through a holo-repeater, it's not possible for him to track me, but somehow I sense him piercing through me, puncturing my soul in a thousand places.

I'm so lost in thought I don't track him until he's right in front of me, his gaze somehow catching mine despite my invisibility.

"Got you," he says with a satisfied grin.

TWO
BAKAR

A soft female voice emerges from thin air, the fog of her breath billowing out from an invisible mouth. "How did you spot me?"

I pause at the question—not because the answer is not clear, but because it's *very* clear. "I'm drascking good at my job. That's how."

The figure of a female materializes before me, and as her face takes shape, I compare it to the face burned in my memory. For good measure, I angle my arm up and let my wristband scan her retina for an identity match.

"If you're so good at it then why did I hear you?"

Ah, she challenges my intellect. All right, then. "What makes you think it wasn't intentional? It made you pause long enough for me to reach you, didn't it?"

She purses her lips into a thin, white line.

"You think I didn't see you before you engaged your holo-repeater?" I ask. "I just needed you to stay still. I prefer not to energy-harness females. Not while on duty anyway."

"Gross."

"By the way, that's illegal tech you're using. If you weren't facing maximum punishment already, I'd add it to your list of crimes. But since you led me to the entrance of Azpian City, I'll let it slide. Turn around. Don't make me harness you."

"Harness a blast from *this*."

The bottom edge of my vision catches a glimpse of her hand, followed by the pressure of an object pushing on my abdomen. I snort. "Do you plan to comb me to death with your hair tool?"

The once soft voice I first encountered deepens, her tone drenched in disdain. "Anything can be a weapon, big dummy."

I arch a brow. "Name-calling is juvenile."

"So is arrogance!"

Her lip snares as our gazes lock, and I'm drawn in. The dark rims of her eyes exude a cunningness, while the expression in the softer brown interior dulls the effects of her sharp insults. Unruly black hair falls around her diamond-shaped face and down to her waist. The faint flowery fragrance of her skin reaches my nose and strikes me in a way that's almost nostalgic.

I break the mental hold just in time for my eyes to catch her free arm slinging a metal container at my groin. My vision goes dark. I double over, fighting the invisible hand that seems to have dived into my lower abdomen and taken hold of my guts to wrench them out with one merciless yank. I fall forward, expecting to fall into her, but my hand lands on the rock wall. I finally suck in a hard breath and massage my balls, focusing my thoughts on the healing energy from my hands to dull the crippling throb creeping into my kidneys.

"The dioses will frown on you for that," I mutter. I stumble toward the trail, a cloud of dust rising in the wake of her escape.

Aside from the throb between my legs, and not the good kind of throb, part of me is thrilled for the chase. It makes for a monotonous few u-days of space travel to get here. The other part of me is fully annoyed that a beautiful female just smashed my crown jewels.

I begin a steady jog, winding down the trail, catching

glimpses of her before she disappears around corners, periodically turning her head back to gauge my distance. As I reach the bottom of the trail, she swipes her palm over the exterior door panel of her air transport. Her last turn my direction proves to be her downfall. Something in me almost wants her to escape, but duty dictates otherwise.

Thrusting my hand outward, a wave of energy surges down my arm and releases from my fingertips, lassoing around her body. She thrashes against it.

I close the distance between us, keeping my energy harness on her until I can wrap my hand around her arm and swing her around to chack her wrists.

"Alesandra Garcia, under the authority of the Interplanetary Marshal Service, I'm placing you under arrest for violating Code 592B, Section 4, Aiding and Abetting." I pull energy chacks from my belt. "And if you think you ever have a chance against me, think again."

THREE
ALESANDRA

I'm as surprised with myself as I am proud. I stood up to him, somehow conjuring up the confidence to stand my ground. I knew my chances of escape were nil. After all, the natural abilities Imszoranians possess are extraordinary. It was just one thing in the long list of surprises that our people had to acquiesce to after the off-worlders first arrived.

Even though I was only an adolescent at the time, I remember the u-day as though it were yesterday. To say there was a massive upheaval of our lives is an understatement. We piled inside our homes and hid, watching our streaming viewers at all hours of the u-day, absorbing as much information as possible.

They claimed they didn't want to interfere in our culture and had come as explorers, offering technology and interplanetary trade. They gave us devices that communicated with each other, machines that flew to other planets, and technology beyond our wildest dreams. It didn't take long to realize their claim was just an empty promise.

The interplanetary accords designated a common language to be shared among all the planets—*their* language, Buesqar. We even refer to time in universal, or u-time, based on the orbit of *their* planet, Imsz-Ordena, around its star.

The musky fragrance I smelled in the forest reaches my nose as he leads me to the rear of his ship. While I've never been inside of a penal ship, I'm not unfamiliar with their architectural style. Much of what they build is made from a black steel they call betierekoa steel, a nondegradable, indestructible composite material. They say the steel will last an eternity. I say nothing that ugly should last forever.

He releases the energy chacks from my wrists and guides me into a barred cell.

"No energy shield to keep me inside? I thought you Imszoranians use energy for everything?"

"Not on a spaceship. The steel bars will keep you secure." He speaks to me in a manner so casual it's as if we're sharing conversation over tea.

I'm not bothered to acknowledge him. No Imszoranian deserves the satisfaction of being held in high regard like they think they should.

He gestures toward the wall. "There's a button next to the door to hail me if you need anything. Strap into the safety seat until we reach the exosphere."

He exits the brig without another word, the door sliding closed behind him. A sense of emptiness settles into my chest. This isn't the way I wanted my life to end, not even having the chance to say anything to my family. Even worse, the only being I'll see until the last few moments of my life is an *Imszoranian*.

I sigh and pull down the seat affixed to the wall. After strapping in, the rumble of the engine vibrates my legs from the feet up, and my body experiences weightlessness.

I finally question how he had discovered me. Was it only because plans changed and I became an escort? No, he was looking for me specifically. He had to have figured it out through my digital footprint from my workstation at my office. I had made a mistake somehow.

It's not the first job I've had at the Somerika Interplanetary Coalition building, headquartered in Zeru. Upon its opening, I landed a job in the interplanetary traffic control planning office. After my brother's disappearance, I managed to transfer to the judicial department and made it my mission to help anyone who wanted to go to Azpian City.

Fantasies of the city interrupt my train of thought. I wonder if the mated Imszoranians who've defected there have erected the same lifeless and uninteresting structures as they have in Zeru. I don't want to believe it. Instead, I imagine it's a magical place. I'm not sure what I'd be doing all this for if I were sending them to a depressing place. I've never seen the city myself. No one does unless they intend to escape their fate.

FOUR
BAKAR

Outer space doesn't have the appeal it did even a few u-days ago. I stare out into the darkness pierced by specks of light. *Something doesn't feel right.* Is it guilt? Knowing I'm sending this beautiful female to her death? With batasurna mates, there's no other choice.

But do sympathizers deserve the same punishment?

I absolutely believed so until now. Without explanation, something in me rebels against the idea of the law taking this female's life. I turn my head toward the rear compartment. A nagging feeling burrows into my chest—one side tugging at me to defy my instincts and go talk to her, the other side pressuring me to obey the laws set forth by my queen.

Queen Azkeena has always been known to rule swiftly and justly. And while some might argue that as a bad thing, our society improved immensely for it. She brought us back to balance, cleaning up the slums, reducing crime, and instituting programs allowing us to prosper. She is a leader to be admired.

Then she set her sights on the stars. Upon launching the star exploration program, seven planets with intelligent life were discovered. From there, we set out on missions for first contact.

After training to be a marshal, my interests took me off planet where I joined the Interplanetary Marshal Service, and I have proudly served the position faithfully for many years.

I unlatch the lock on my pilot's seat and swivel around, my stare landing on the brig door. Curiosity piques my interest. *What is the female doing?*

I launch myself out of my seat and saunter to the closed door. My ship is a small penal ship with a capacity of four—two crew members and two criminals. Typically, I'd be working with a partner, but since this assignment was so easy, there was no need.

I swipe my hand over the wall panel and step inside the brig compartment. The female hasn't said a word to me since I ushered her into the cell. She sits in the corner with her knees drawn up and her forehead resting on them.

That nagging feeling tears at my chest again, giving me pause. "Are you hungry?" I wait a few u-seconds for a reply. "It's a four-u-day trip to Station 1. You'll need to eat."

"Why?" Her words were muffled as her head remained at rest against her knees. "I'll be dead soon anyway."

Studying her, I rest my shoulder against the wall. "Why'd you do it?"

Again with the silence.

Despite the lack of response, I persist, "I understand why they do it. No willpower. But you? Why help them?"

Slowly, her head begins to rise. Her wavy hair is mangled and sticking to her wet cheeks, eyes red and swollen. "What difference does it make?"

I shrug. "None. I'm just curious."

"Don't Imszoranians know everything?" Her anger is palpable like hot waves of heat rising off a metal surface. Despite her visual despair, I detect defiance in her voice. The female is a fighter. I respect that.

"Maybe. Maybe not," I manage to say, crossing my arms. "I just want to hear it from you."

"Will it change anything?"

In truth, no. But I decide not to say so. For the first time in my life, I search for the right words. Words that matter. This jars me a bit—as if I'm embarking into new emotional territory.

"Maybe if you tell me why, I might be able to make things easier for you," I say, instantly regretting it.

She narrows her eyes at me. "Isn't there only one punishment for sympathizers?"

"Yes, but…" I can't finish the sentence because I can't argue she's wrong. I can't even promise her anything. I tell myself the queen is right. For the mates, it absolutely has to be this way. But part of me thinks the sympathizers can be rehabilitated somehow. Nevertheless, they suffer the same fate. The logic is that there is no batasurna energies affecting them, influencing their actions. And if they choose to break the laws of their own volition, there isn't any leniency.

"Just tell me why, and I'll leave you alone." I don't know why I'm pressing the issue. I've apprehended several sympathizers in the past, and I've never even bothered to remember their names, let alone speak with them.

She slips off the metal cot so swiftly I'm almost surprised by her agility. All one has to do is look at her to know she loathes me, but it's not her expression that so effortlessly gives it away. It's her overall aura.

She stalks toward me with balled fists. Her chest heaves as she steps up to the cell door, sneering at me between the bars.

"Go…away."

I am more determined than ever to stand my ground, despite not wanting to upset her more. "Tell me, and I will."

Her face turns a dark shade of red, lips trembling. I imagine her transforming into a formidable beast strong enough to pry the bars apart and eat me whole.

"You killed my brother!"

The sentence dies on a faded echo. Our gazes are locked, just like in the forest, only this time I don't see the cunningness as before. I see heartbreak.

"Who did?" I ask.

"You. You Imszoranians. You are the reason my brother is dead!"

"How?" I'm finding that I genuinely want her to tell me, despite my usual apathy.

"Well...I...." she stalls with a huff. "I don't actually know he's dead. But he went missing a u-year ago. So, I can only assume the worst."

"How do you know he didn't go to the underground?"

"I have contacts there. He's not there."

"Was he a sympathizer?"

"No. He had a batasurna mate."

I slowly nod, again facing the inability to find meaningful words. I want to comfort her, though the reason why escapes me. All I can manage is a weak "I'm sorry."

And I truly am. For some reason.

I retreat, keeping her in my sights as my back hits the door frame of the exit. The look on her face is stirring up something in me I've never felt before, but by definition I recognize it to be empathy. I leave and close the door behind me. I'm anxious to get back to my station and look at her file again. Perhaps I missed something, though it wouldn't be like me to be so careless. I bring up the file on my console and skim through the text, noticing nothing.

I verbally engage the artificial intelligence system known as SID, Simulated Intelligent Design. "SID, list immediate family members of prisoner Alesandra Garcia."

On the screen, four names pop up—that of her mother, father, sister, and brother. "Open file for Remir Garcia."

The contents of the file on the brother are mostly mundane except for the final paragraph describing his disappearance. His mate was Imszoranian. She'd been captured and returned to

Imsz-Ordena. He'd managed to escape the interplanetary marshal who had left his apprehension up to the local authorities once the Imszoranian female was captured.

I blink twice at the arresting marshal's name.

Mine.

Drasck.

"SID, list all entries for Remir Garcia up to his date of death."

SID's uncanny, realistic-sounding male voice fills the room. "Unable to comply. There is no date of death provided in his record."

Scanning the data again, I realize he's right.

"What about his mate?" I search the screen for her name. "Shannika Laxalt?"

"No date of death listed."

"Are there any entries on either of them after the date of apprehension for Shannika Laxalt?"

"Unable to comply."

"So…you're telling me there are records, but you can't list them."

"That information is Zed classified."

Hm. Interesting. Level Zed is the queen's level.

"SID, did the queen herself classify their records?"

"Affirmative."

"Have all batasurna cases been Zed classified?"

"Affirmative."

"Do any of them have dates of death?"

"No."

"What about sympathizers? Do they have dates of death listed?"

"No."

"And I suppose they're Zed classified, too."

"Affirmative."

FIVE
ALESANDRA

The Imszoranian just *had* to force it. Remir wasn't *just* my brother, he was my twin brother. Losing him torments me every u-day, as if I've lost half of myself and the other half of me went crazy. I try not to think about it because it hurts so much. But guilt pervades me when I try to forget.

I lie on my side in the brig, half-awake, and let my thoughts wander without direction. I hear the door swoosh open and the thud of heavy footsteps. I keep my eyes closed, hoping he'll just go away, but the male is persistent. He's been in and out several times checking on me. Each time I feigned sleep, but my skin tingled as though the gaze of his eyes have the power to reach across the room and caress me, soothing me somehow.

Within the confines of the metal walls, his voice carries deep. "I brought food."

I crack open one eye.

He's standing at the food slot on the wall with a plate resting on his hand. "You should eat it while it's warm. The food materializer doesn't produce the best flavor, but it does make the food hot." He opens the slot and shoves the plate through the wall. "I was getting worried about you. You've been sleeping a long time."

I stare at him between the bars. He actually is handsome, I decide.

I'm not attracted to him. Not at all.

"Thank you," I mutter. I hadn't intended to say anything at all. I'm not sure why I sputtered out words expressing gratitude. I ball my fists. He's *Imszoranian.*

I notice him staring at me from the edge of my cell.

He drags a chair over from the wall and places it in front of the bars. "It's just a simple protein and vegetable. The materializer does better with simple compounds."

I reach for the food, then retreat and sit back down on the edge of my metal cot, studying his face while I do.

His blue eyes capture me. Blue eyes don't exist in my culture. I've seen them a few times from Imszoranians walking through the office. But his color is a darker blue that brings me home. They remind me of twilight on the outskirts of Zeru.

"My name is Bakar."

I don't care what his name is and genuinely wonder why he's bothering me. I fix my death stare on him, trying not to fixate on his lips, taking a bite of steamed white vegetable. It's not a flavor I'm familiar with, kind of nutty, but not offensive to my palate. I shove another bite in my mouth.

"That's called mangrinna root. Do you like it?"

"Why do you care?"

His eyes flare, making me wonder if he's offended, but he seems quick to recover. "I'm not a monster."

The silence stretches between us as I clean off my plate, periodically glancing up at him. I notice his strong, sexy jaw and fight not to recoil against *myself.* If I could punch my inner voice out right now, I would. *Dioses, help me.*

He's studying me as if he's dissecting a science specimen. After I finish, I stand to put the plate back on the ledge, and he stands with me. Positioned no more than a few feet apart, we face each other with only the vertical bars between us.

I purse my lips just to emphasize how much I loathe him. "I could ask you the same thing."

He arches a brow. "What?"

"Why do you do it? You condemn to death mates whose only desire is to love each other. That's a crime? As far as I'm concerned, Imszoranians are the monsters."

"No, the mates are."

Heat rushes to my face. "You think that your race is so superior that you can't be diluted by mixing with the other races? That's what this is about. And if anyone dares defy your queen, they die."

He tilts his head sideways. "What?"

"You heard me!"

"Yes, but it makes no sense. It has nothing to do with race. Where did you hear that?"

"It's common knowledge."

He slowly nods. "I see. I wasn't aware. The actual reason is classified. But I was told all the planets were at least told something plausible."

"What actual reason?"

I sense a struggling of the minds between us. One person pulls, the other person counteracts. One person pushes, the other person pushes back.

Just as I'm about to tell him to leave, he speaks, "Have you ever heard of the Station 3 incident?"

"Yes, of course. It was a huge tragedy."

"It isn't what you think." He reclaims his seat and crosses his leg, momentarily staring past me before speaking. "When the matings began to occur, I think all the planets were in agreement that no one knew why it began to happen after contact. It's not strictly reserved for interracial couples, either. Mates can be of the same race. Are we in agreement so far?"

"Yes," I say, wondering where he's going with this.

"Then why are you blaming it on race?" he asks.

"We were told that the queen didn't want it to appear to be linked to race, so she decided to punish everyone."

He scoffs. "Nonsense."

"Is it?"

"Yes," he says with conviction. "It absolutely is. I will tell you why, so you better sit down for this."

I cross my arms, squaring my stance.

"Your choice," he says with a shrug. "You were told it was a meteor shower, correct?"

I nod.

"There was a meteor shower. But it didn't kill all four hundred and eighty-two souls on the station like you were told. It killed twenty-three. Seventeen of them were batasurna mates. Typically, not a large concentration of mates would ever be in a centralized location like that. But the queen had invited them to Imsz-Ordena to study batasurna.

"At the time of the incident, some parts of the stations weren't shielded by betierekoa steel—a design flaw we've since rectified. A large concentration of the meteors burrowed into the station through the comms array panels. It ended up shorting out some electrical systems, some of which were connected to the docking vestibules. More than half of the batasurna couples became trapped in a vestibule when the doors sealed shut during the station's automatic emergency response. They were unable to escape through either end since there are no manual emergency levers on docking bay doors for obvious reasons. And there were no oxygen vents in the vestibules.

"Crews worked tirelessly to get them out, but with the large number of them in a small vestibule, they used up oxygen faster than the crews could get to them. Several of them died of suffocation waiting for the doors to open, while their mates watched, helpless to save them."

As the image he's describing forms in my mind, bile rises up, burning my throat. I can't even imagine.

He continues, "We already knew from some prior cases that the death of a mate could cause abnormal behavior in the surviving mate. During the process, when both are alive, the energies of the bodies come into perfect sync. When one dies, we think they become imbalanced.

"This was the entire reason for these couples to be a part of the study on Imsz-Ordena. The queen wanted to find a way to reverse the effects so when a mate does die, the other mate can continue on with a normal life.

"The Station 3 incident taught us that the degree of trauma associated with death can exponentially affect the surviving mate. Once they were freed from the vestibule, the surviving mates devolved in u-minutes. They slipped into utter madness. The Imszoranian mates' abilities somehow became multitudes more powerful than an average Imszoranian.

"They didn't just kill everyone on the station. They *slaughtered* them, Alesandra. Four hundred and eighty-two people. Three of them were my *friends*. I was one of the first responders to the distress call.

"You want to know who the *real* monsters are? Surviving batasurna mates. That's who. That's why they are separated from society immediately. The queen doesn't want to take any chances."

"That doesn't justify killing them."

His lips part and close several times. I sense his struggle so profoundly it rattles my bones. His steely blue eyes drive daggers into me. "If you saw what I saw, you would understand."

"Why not just tell us the truth!"

He shrugs. "To avoid mass panic. To force complicity. The process can be stopped if they separate with physical distance before it's too late. Truth is, the queen really tried to find a cure."

The thought of my brother and what he may have gone through hits me so hard I sway forward, one hand bracing me while the other covers my mouth. I squeeze my eyes shut as a sob surfaces, escaping my lips with a guttural sound.

"Did my brother go insane like that?" I squeak out.

He gets to his feet and reaches for my hand. After prying my fingers off the bar, he interlaces our fingers. The simple act sends powerful surges of heat through my body.

"I don't know what he went through," he says, caressing my hand with his thumb. "If I knew, I'd tell you. But I do have a confession to make that I really don't want to."

I blink tears away. He reaches through the bars with his other hand and wipes my wet cheek. Then he lodges his finger under my chin and gently guides me toward him. It occurs to me I'm willingly leaning toward him, aching for his lips to touch mine. When they meet, the warmth of him floods me and settles in my lower abdomen. No male has ever affected me the way he seems to. A fleeting thought runs through my mind that if I were to have a batasurna mate, I would want this kind of attraction.

He pulls back as though he's separating himself from his urges and putting his mind space in an objective state. "Like I said, I don't want to say this. But I must be honest. I was the marshal who arrested your brother's mate."

I suck in a hard breath, yanking my hand out of his, and surge backward. I want to hate him for it but part of me doesn't, and that doesn't sit well with me, either.

"If it makes you feel better, I don't think he's dead. I just did a database search and found out none of the batasurna mates or the sympathizers have any recorded dates of death and their files have been locked by the queen."

I'm slack-jawed as that familiar paralyzing feeling creeps

into me again. He drags his seat back over and latches it to the wall. I expect him to say something else, but he walks past me without so much as a glance.

"Wait! You can't just tell me that about my brother and then leave."

"If I knew any more, I'd tell you." Without turning back to face me, he leaves the brig.

The emptiness of his absence hits me so hard I nearly yell for him to come back.

But I don't.

I fall back onto my cot, reflecting on all the mates I've helped and wonder if they might suffer the madness. It seems so implausible.

To me, batasurna is the most beautiful thing I've ever seen. It's a union between two sentient energies made beyond the physical world. The mates aren't fated by outside forces, as some might believe. It's an aukera—a *choice*. It's the sacred joining of energies made in the Beyond. When two mates living in the physical world decide they want to be joined for an eternity, they choose to undergo the batasurna process in the afterlife where their sentient energies join, coalescing into a unified whole for all of eternity.

Then, they return to the physical without memories of past lives, cycling in and out of lifetimes. If they're lucky, they'll discover one another again. I'm told the feeling that one undergoes when rediscovering one's batasurna mate is indescribable. With each lifetime, the bond strengthens and deepens the physical connection until they reach the final stage, never to return to the physical again.

Before the Imszoranians arrived, batasurna was only a myth, never having been witnessed in modern times. Some believe their arrival reawakened the once dormant batasurna energy within the bodies of those who possess it.

But when reconnections began to occur, Queen Azkeena

70

enacted a law prohibiting the unions. Anyone who violated that law would face the death penalty.

That's why they escaped. And that's why I helped them. But now, I wonder if I've been wrong about the Imszoranians this whole time.

SIX
BAKAR

I hated every second of that confession. It takes everything I have not to go back in there and ask her to forgive me, but I remind myself I was doing a job—a job I truly believe in. Does it mean I'm a monster if I believe I'm doing the right thing? Maybe. But then I see nothing but blood and guts and arms and legs and the severed heads of my friends lined up in a row, and I have no mercy for the mates. None.

"Bakar?"

My gaze draws up to the comm speaker. "Yes?"

There's a detectable tremble in her voice. "May I speak with you?"

I don't answer right away. Part of me thinks I should not go back there again. I showed weakness. A weakness I have shown no one, let alone felt. Strangely, it's not because I sympathize with her. I can do that without wavering. It's something else I can't put my finger on. When I touched her hand, the attraction I've had for her since the moment I spotted her on the trail intensified to a level that urged me to leave immediately.

"Drasck," I mutter, waving my hand over the brig's door panel. I step up to the bars of her cell and turn to face her but fall short of looking her in the eyes. My gaze lands on her breasts, of all things, and I notice her nipples are hard. That makes my curious gaze trail up to hers.

My eyes widen, jaw dropping. Her eyes are storming. I loll my head back on my shoulders, telling myself no, over and over.

"I see it, too," she says, her voice returning to a sweet tone.

I force my eyes closed, but the urge to look overpowers me. I've never witnessed this before, though I've heard of it. I'm sucked in, and the longer I look, the deeper I go.

"Stop!" I yell. It seems to break our concentration and rips us from the vice that grips us.

I waste no time bolting out of there, the closing door behind me a metaphor to the one in my mind meant to ward off remnants of memories.

It can't be.

I'm not deeply familiar with the batasurna stages, but I do know that there are seven—the first stage being the *ikusi* stage— and is the stage where recognition, or the seeing, of the soul energies begin. The irises of the eyes rapidly change color and swirl as if a storm is brewing inside.

I mumble like a madman, pacing the floor behind the pilot's seat. "The room isn't well lit. I didn't see anything. It's an illusion."

I sink down into the pilot's seat and take a deep breath. To keep my mind occupied, I run ship diagnostics, evaluate reports, check our ETA, and then decide to take a snack break. The food materializer actually manages to make a good tea blend, so I navigate the menu to my favorite red tea and press start. I tap my fingers on the counter as the mug materializes first, then is filled with the steaming hot red liquid.

A wave of energy hits my mind like a flash of light. I sway on my feet and brace myself against the counter, waiting for it to subside. Against my own will, I grimace.

Telepatia is common with my race. We are born with the

ability to communicate through thoughts, though it does take discipline to master it. And we have strict rules, one of which is not to probe someone's thoughts. It takes me a moment, but I recognize it. I wasn't aware that the other races had the ability. Then it occurs to me—batasurna pairs can take on traits of their mate by proxy.

"No," I say, shaking my head. *Has to be something else.*

Snatching my mug off the shelf, I huff and return to the front of the cabin, pounding my boots on the floor. I wrestle myself back into the pilot's seat with another huff and take a loud slurp of my drink, feeling a bit ridiculous at my behavior.

I twist my lips, contemplating what to do with my time and finally decide to open a comm channel to Ximon, my lagun, best friend, brother not of blood. He's been my lagun since we were kids, growing up in the slums on Imsz-Ordena. After I was assigned to Station 1, an opening came up for an engineer, and I put in a good word for him.

"How goes the life of a space cop?" he asks without a salutation.

"Lagun, I think I'm losing it. I need that vacation bad."

"What? You couldn't track down the easiest target ever?"

"I got her."

"Then what?"

My lips part, but I stop myself. Comms are not secure. I consider calling him back on a secure comm but those are used for official business. Suddenly, I realize calling him was a bad idea. "I don't know, just feeling the need to relax. I'm glad this assignment was easy. You and Fermina ready for *la playa*?" Fermina is his longtime girlfriend, soon-to-be lifetime mate, and luckily, she and I like each other. It would be hell if we didn't.

"You know females. She's already packed."

"Excellent. Guh…" My head lobs forward, as if someone shoved me from behind. I grunt from the force and swivel around, expecting to see someone standing there.

74

"You okay?"

"Uh…" I knit my brows together, dragging my gaze over the empty cabin. "Just spilled my tea. Listen, uh, I gotta go."

"All right. Stop by when you get here."

"You got it." I close the comm channel. The hair on the back of my neck stands up straight, as if the air in the room is charged, and shivers run down my spine. Pursing my lips, I push out of the seat and head to the back of the ship. She's messing with me, and I'm about to put a stop to it. I'll have to block her telepatia from now on so she can't probe me but not before I give her the piece of my mind she actually deserves.

I swipe my hand over the panel and barrel inside the tiny brig. She's lying down on the cold, hard platform facing me, eyes closed.

"Hey!"

Her hair vines down over most of her face, but I can still see her eyes between the tangled strands. They slowly open, but no words leave her mouth.

"Stop messing with me." My tone is stern but not overbearing. It's enough to get her attention.

"What?"

"Telepatia has rules. You can't just insert yourself into someone's thoughts. That's a violation."

"I was asleep."

I cross my arms over my puffed chest, looking down my nose at her, and square my stance to exude maximum intimidation—an interrogation tactic well-practiced for the most hardened of criminals. A tiny female would have no defense against this.

Partially bracing herself up to a sitting position, she sways sideways, appearing disoriented.

Ha, it worked.

Her gaze flicks up to me, and I file through all the emotions in my head, trying to identify her expression.

"That hurts," she says, her voice cracking.

Dioses, what have I done? I relax, easing up on the intimidation. "What hurts?"

"You're inside my head. You're angry. It hurts. I want you to stop."

"I didn't do..." I press my lips together. What is she talking about? I'm extremely skilled at telepatia, and I did not violate her mind space.

"What do you know about batasurna?" The words come out of my mouth before I have time to think, and I instantly regret it.

An expression of knowing shadows her face. "It begins with the eyes." She slowly moves toward me and stops within an arm's reach. "Then a mind connection is made. When the connection is established, the bridge is built. Images of past lives together begin to appear between the pair when souls begin to recognize each other." She tilts her head sideways, studying me.

I shake my head no. "This is impossible." I ball my fists. My fate will not be insanity.

The look on her face seems to suggest she's contemplating something, but I know it's a ploy—it has to be. If we were batasurna mates, I wouldn't turn her in. Of course she's going to try to convince me.

She swallows hard. "Your eyes are still storming."

I shut them tight to block her out, but her voice penetrates my entire body. "Batasurna mates unconsciously seek each other out when in physical form. Right?"

I work my jaw, considering her question, but I already know the answer.

Yes. They do, I say to her through thought. It's more of a test than anything. I half expect her not to hear me, but I'm wrong.

Yes. They do, she repeats back to me.

A rush of images floods my mind. Her. And me. Different places. Different faces. Different lives. In all of them, she is smiling. She is touching me, kissing me, walking next to me.

I shake it off. "It's not too late. It can be resisted. We are not too far into the process. We just need to—" My muscles tighten, locking me up for a few u-seconds. I force out my words, "—stay away from each other." I take a step sideways toward the exit, keeping my eyes trained on her. Her expression is…I try to evaluate it.

Sad.

Leaving the brig is the only answer I have before I do something I'll regret.

SEVEN
ALESANDRA

I t's been three u-days. I know this because I've been keeping track of the meals. My last meal was a breakfast. Not that it matters anyway. At first, he'd been coming in frequently—every u-hour, if I had to guess. But now he comes in only to deliver meals and has hardly spoken to me since the process began to show. Good. I don't want his conversation anyway.

I snort, shaking my head, and lean back against the wall, the coldness of the steel seeping into my body. I invite the chill in, hoping it will numb me. Even though he's in the other room, the connection is getting stronger. It's as if he's a magnet, a force so strong I'm unable to deny it. I hate it. Yet I want him so badly it almost physically hurts. No wonder they go insane.

So, this is it—the madness.

Understanding the anguish of separation sinks in. If we complete the next stage, consummation, there's no going back. The dull throb of need turns into a pulsing ache—the memory of him building pressure, ballooning in my chest. My loins burn until my body and mind scream from the fire ravaging through my veins. The thought of our energies coalescing owns me.

Remembering how it feels to have him inside me taunts me until I can no longer discern fantasy from reality.

I imagine rolling it all into a ball and tossing it away, freeing myself of it by any means necessary. Even from here, with the steel door between us, he's inside my head. He's fighting it, not wanting to be in me and blocking me from his torment. His confusion hits me in waves. It ebbs and flows between the sensations of desire. We both know something undeniable—we are the same. Each of us the one piece that would, when together, make us whole.

Every time the flash of a memory resurfaces, I close my eyes. I pray for sleep, my only escape. I hear the door open again and crack open one eye. The clatter of a food tray sounds on the ledge, but only his arm appears in my view. The door swooshes again, and the absence of him thunders inside me.

Good. Just go.

I grimace. My muscles tighten. My throat closes to throttle the tears back. I clench my fists, but the sobs come anyway. I'm not even sure why I'm crying. Is it because I'll soon die? Or is it because I'll die without feeling him once more?

Convulsions hit me in the pit of my stomach. The pulsing ache is now an earthquake shaking me to my core. My gaze falls on the tray of food and heat rushes to my face as an uncontrollable force of anger bursts through me. I swipe my hand through the air, and the tray goes flying backward, clanking with a bang as the dishes hit the floor and scatter in several directions.

Staring at my mess, my jaw falls open. Energy-harnessing is not an ability my race has. Only the Imszoranians can do that. My gaze trails over to the closed door. I just moved a tray of dishes with my thoughts.

What else can I do?

EIGHT
BAKAR

I pace the space behind the pilot's seat until I swear my bare heels are touching steel. My feet ache, but it's a good ache. It masks the pain in the pit of my stomach. The surge of her agony rips through me. I imagine her tears settling in my chest as though they're filling me up, drowning me. But I cannot go to her. I simply can't.

A clatter from behind the door draws my attention, and before I realize it, I find myself back in the brig. She's curled up in a ball on the cot, her body still.

"Alesandra," I say, keeping my tone gentle.

Her body jerks, instantly reacting to my voice, and she peeks one eye from under her arm. The image of her on the cot, so broken, is wrenching my heart out of my chest.

I swipe my palm over the security panel and the door clicks open. Her small frame remains still on the bed as I approach. Each move is spontaneous. I have no plan. Cautiously, I sit on the edge of the cot next to her. "I can't bear your crying."

She bolts upright and throws her arms around my neck, the sobbing resumes with her face buried in my shoulder.

Dioses.

I can't help but embrace her. A sensation I can only describe as a feeling of home floods my body. I rest my cheek on top of her head, rubbing her back with my hand. This is all I want. Her. *Wait. I don't even know her.*

But I do know her. I know everything about her. I know her inside and out, far deeper than any physical form could ever possibly feel. The body is the barrier that keeps the batasurna energies apart. It's maddening. My energy wants to reconnect with hers—to coalesce with her again. The force of it is almost unbearable.

Station 3 repeats in my mind.

I break the embrace and jump to my feet. All I can think about is the madness if I lose her. "I'm sorry," I say, exiting her cell. I notice the food tray and dishes scattered on the floor, but I can't be bothered with it right now. I stagger back to the pilot's seat and sink into it, burying my face in my hands.

Get it together.

I decide to check the ETA, relieved that we're almost to the station. I drag my hands down my face. I don't know what to do with myself. I focus.

I'll hand custody of her over to the Imsz-Ordena authorities, and she'll be loaded onto a penal ship to Imsz-Ordena. Then it's over.

I have to stay strong. It's better for both of us this way. I decide to take a seat and wait out the next few u-minutes until I'm directed to a docking bay. My breaths are short and jagged. My head is spinning. Giving in means betraying my people. My queen. I pledged an oath. Yet inside me, I begin to realize my oath is to a much deeper and more meaningful existence.

To whom do I owe my devotion?

Coming to grips with the answer to that question leads me down a path where I'm not sure I care about my job anymore, and that suffocates me.

Her face forces its way into my mind.

Please, no more memories.

But the dioses ignore my plea, hitting me with a memory I cannot deny—the first time I ever met her.

I suck in a breath as more images flow into my mind. I remember the touch of her skin. I remember the aukera to be batasurna mates for eternity.

Wait.

I shake my head as if the thoughts will tumble out before they're burned inside my head forever, the memories leaving a scar so deep I'm unable to avoid it. But the memory of our energies coming together for the first time consumes me. The process takes place in the Beyond, one of the five realms of the dioses, the gods of the universe. We coalesce into a union of souls. Without physical bodies, our consciousness experiences the bonding, seeing through energy rather than eyesight. Light surrounds us and is us. We merge and flow into each other, our frequencies balance, and we become a united whole—a single, sentient whole.

Without forethought, I redirect my intentions, now squeezing my eyes shut as if the tighter I hold them together, the more memories I can force to resurface. *I cannot do this. I cannot send her to her death. I remember her. Everything.*

The situation hits me. She's in the brig, ready to be taken into custody—to be taken to her death.

Dioses, what have I done?

Flight control directs me to Docking Bay 14, so I set the ship to autopilot and let SID bring us in. The flight decks are bustling as usual with ships flying in and out like busy bees flying around their hive. Station 1 is the busiest station of the three and is used by four of the eight planets, serving as a way station between them and Imsz-Ordena. Most of the ships that dock here run trade routes between the planets, but a fair number of ships are space patrol.

I wait for the landing clamps to secure the ship to the platform and run through the docking checklist, communicating with the control tower, until they've cleared me and given me a code for entering the station. It's protocol, even for a marshal.

"Is permission for Prisoner 1348's entry to the penal deck approved?" I ask. The necessary words spilling from my lips as if I'm on autopilot, but my head is spinning.

How do I get us out of this mess?

"Affirmative. Permission granted. Transferring code."

A security code pops up on my screen, and I swipe my hand through the air, directing the code to my comm band. Once it pops up, I unclasp my seat straps and take in a long breath before getting up. Pressure builds in my chest again. I tap my fingers on the console.

I contemplate what to say as I head to the door, but words don't seem enough. I need to merge my thoughts with hers so she can *feel* my emotion too. I wave my hand over the panel, ready to step inside, but I have no time to react. A food tray hits me square in my forehead so hard I topple backward and land on the floor. It takes me a moment to realize what happened. Legs streak past me.

"Hey!" I yell, rolling on my side and scampering to my feet. I sway with the first step. The room spins. I shake my head and focus on the air lock door leading to the vestibule.

The gravity of the situation isn't lost on me, yet I remind myself she can't get inside without the security code. I slow my pace, thinking I'll catch up to her no matter how fast she runs.

I step out onto the ramp and spot her at the docking bay door. She glances back at me, then enters the correct security code on the panel.

That's fine. She still can't enter without my comm band. I begin to smirk at her when my gaze drops to something dangling in her hand. After being smacked in the head, I hadn't even noticed that she'd swiped my band. The wall panel light switches to green, and the door to the station slides open.

Uh oh.

NINE
ALESANDRA

Once I figured out I could harness energy like the Imszoranians, I practiced. Memories resurfaced, reminding me how to control it. More memories resurfaced on how to control the telepatia connection. He underestimated me.

As soon as the ship landed, I directed my thoughts to the control panel of my cell, invoking the unlock command. If an Imszoranian had been incarcerated in the cell, they'd be wearing wrist chacks to suppress their abilities, but since I'm Somerikan, apparently he didn't find it necessary.

After disengaging the lock, I snuck up to the door. Peering through the little window, I focused on enhancing my vision, another ability I gained through him, to see the screen and waited for the code to pop up. Then I waited for him. He never saw it coming.

I almost feel guilty hitting him so hard. I tell myself it was necessary. I dial my concentration in on finding a place to hide.

A fragment of a memory resurfaces—no images, only words. *I will always come for you. Beyond eternity.*

Just as I'm about to probe the memory further, the security

alarm buzzes through the station. I duck and run down an empty hallway off the side of the main corridor and slip inside a small room. I hear an announcement over the station's intercom.

"Somerikan...dangerous female...may have a weapon... proceed with caution...the station is in lockdown."

I roll my eyes, squeezing my body between the wall and a few stacked crates. I have no idea where to go from here. I've only been on this station a few times when I worked with the traffic control office and both of them were in concentrated areas. It's the reason I knew there was a code required for entry.

My mind files through the list of people I know on the station. My thoughts instantly go to the Imszoranian female I'd made friends with on my last trip, before my brother disappeared. She and I worked a few desks apart.

What was her name? Think.

With thoughts of Bakar practically consuming me, I struggle to focus on her.

Fermina. That's it. Her name is Fermina.

She invited me to her quarters one night while her mate worked a late shift. We had Imszoranian wine. I remember it was very good. We drank and got tipsy, and she told me all about her mate and how in love she was. I envied her. Little did I know what my future held.

I snap into problem-solving mode.

First, a disguise. Then find Fermina.

TEN
BAKAR

I have only one chance to get Alesandra to safety. Since the station's in lockdown, I'm not worried about her escaping. I'll find her. Then we'll go to Azpian City together. It means saying goodbye to life as I know it, but we'll adjust. Something tells me we always have. I don't know why I ever tried to fight it. I never wanted to admit that I saw something in the batasurna mates—the way they looked at each other was more than enough to believe in it. Once the process begins, it's undeniable. I know this now. I cannot escape it nor do I want to.

I head to the residential wing of the station. It's early evening in u-time so Ximon should be in his quarters. He'll help me find her in the station, then I'll ask one last favor of him.

I pick up the pace to a light jog and take the lift to his deck. I weave through the hallways until I turn the last corner and reach his door, wasting no time in pressing the hail button.

"Yes?"

"Fermina, it's me. I need to talk to Ximon. It's urgent."

The door instantly slides open, and Ximon slips out into the hallway, quickly sealing the door behind him.

I scoff at him. "Can I not come in?"

"Fermina is…busy. What's going on, lagun?"

"I need to talk to you. It's important."

His expression changes as he studies mine. "Are you okay?"

I keep my voice low. "Something crazy has happened. The female I was sent to apprehend. She's…" I second-guess myself. Will he really understand this?

"She's what?"

"It turns out, she's my oresha. My batasurna mate."

He nods. I expect shock. I expect his eyes to bulge, his jaw to drop. But…nothing.

"What are you going to do?" he asks.

"Find her. But I may never see you again."

He raises a brow. "Don't be so sure."

My tone changes to a hint of desperation. "I'm sorry, lagun. I have to take her to Azpian City." I don't know who I'm trying to convince, him or myself, because his expression remains unchanged.

Slowly, a grin begins to form on his face. "Wait here."

I grab his shoulder. "I don't have time for this."

"This will only take a u-second. Hold on."

I hiss, then let him go back inside. Meanwhile, I begin to form a search plan in my mind and a way to get her off the station. As soon as I don't turn her in, the authorities will know.

The door slides open again, and Ximon grabs my arm and yanks me inside.

"Easy," I say, brushing his hand away. I turn toward the room where I spot Fermina. "What's going on here?"

"Let's give them a moment," says Ximon.

I nod without looking at him. My eyes are fixed on Alesandra.

ELEVEN
ALESANDRA

I hear a shuffling of feet at the front door and my gaze floats past Fermina. When Ximon told me Bakar wasn't going to turn me in, I had a decision to make—give it a chance or figure out how to energy-harness three Imszoranians who are experts at it.

Bakar's gaze lands on me. He locks up as though a cold rush of sub-zero air freezes him in place. Ximon offers to let us have a moment together, then he and Fermina leave the room. Bakar's gaze never leaves me. I remind myself to steady my breaths.

He steps forward, his fists tight as though he's battling something in his head. "I owe you an apology." He stops an arm's length in front of me. "I had a memory of us. Do you want to hear it?"

Do I? I nod.

"It was the first time we ever met. Do you remember?"

I take a moment to search through the memories that have resurfaced. Not all of them will, but they come in flashes. "Not yet," I admit.

"Let me remind you, then." He moves closer to me, then lifts my chin up with his finger, forcing our eyes to meet. His voice falls to almost a whisper. "We were both Imszoranian then. I was visiting Playa Larankja and spotted you wearing a pink dress near the beach, selling frozen treats from a cart.

"The instant I saw you, with your long hair dancing in the wind, I was captivated. You had bright green eyes then and an incredible smile. I remember you weren't wearing shoes, and I asked you why. You said it was because you loved the way the sand feels between your toes.

"I bought your whole cart of treats so you'd spend the rest of the u-day with me. You did."

I smile at his recollection. "That's a nice memory. I hope I remember it someday."

"You will. The important thing to know is we *chose* each other. The aukera."

His lips reach mine. They are warm and soft and bring a flood of memories back to me, though they number too many to sift through in the moment.

"We were not yet batasurna mates then. Before our lives ended, we decided we would be. Now…here we are."

A lump catches in my throat. *Here we are.*

"Alesandra, I was foolish. I guess I was just scared after what I saw."

"I understand," I say. And that's true. "What now, then?"

"Did I tell you that Ximon is a master engineer?"

"No. Why?"

He bends his head down and places another soft kiss on my lips. "If anyone can help us to Somerika undetected, it's him. I got a plan."

TWELVE
BAKAR

A zpian City isn't at all what I imagined it would be. The buildings are carved out of the white sandstone mountain. The air is fresh. Light from the red crystals we call semillosite is almost as pure as light from a star. Between the immaculate streets and intricately carved homes, the foliage is green and healthy. It reminds me of the rain forest on Imsz-Ordena, with plenty of leafy trees and various blooms. The scent from the blooms is powerful and hits your nose as soon as you step out of your dwelling.

When we arrived, we were greeted by a city representative and swiftly provided shelter and the basic necessities to survive here. There's even fresh water that's piped in from a nearby lake, and some of the citizens built a beautiful waterfall near the small lake they built inside the city.

The look on Alesandra's face when we arrived was unforgettable. Her face lit up as I'd never seen it, that I could remember anyway.

After a trip to the supply building, I bring in a box of dishes and set them on the counter. She's sitting at the intricately hand-carved wooden kitchen table, beaming with a smile from ear to ear. This is our first time alone together since we left the station in separate shipping containers, the only way I knew how to slow down the effects of batasurna until we arrived back on Somerika.

"Come here," I say in my sultry voice, extending my hand. "Why do you look so happy?"

"The city is exactly how I imagined it. But even if it wasn't, I'd still be smiling."

"Why's that?"

She pauses a moment, as if searching for the right words. I pull her close to me and wrap my arms around her waist.

"I helped a lot of mates get here. I saw how they looked at each other, but even then, I couldn't have known the feeling of finding your batasurna mate. My oreshi. Even if this place was a disaster, it wouldn't matter. We'll make the best of it."

I run my finger down the bridge of her nose. "I know their security system inside and out. I will find a way for you to see your family and continue to search for information on your brother. You can continue your mission."

"*Our* mission now."

I realize I no longer see batasurna mates as criminals. They're just people following a path to their chosen destiny from a sacred union made in the Beyond. No government has the authority to overrule that. With that thought, I accept my new mission wholeheartedly. "I like the sound of that. *Our* mission." I kiss the tip of her nose. "I've been made aware by the mayor here that Queen Azkeena is very unhappy about the growing number of defectors. He believes she may clean out the underground cities and punish the Imszoranians who've betrayed her. We need to stay vigilant."

She traces her finger along my lower lip. "We will."

I sweep her off her feet, and she yelps with a giggle.

"Forget the rest of the u-day," I say. "In fact, forget the week. I need to be inside you right now. We've waited long enough."

I whisk her into the bedroom, anticipating our first mating in this lifetime, and place her on the bed, pressing my body against hers. It is as it always was, though manages to feel new each time.

I enter her with a swift thrust. We both gasp.

She's warm and wet and ready for me—taking all of my cock, despite our size difference. I begin a rhythm. Her hips meet mine with perfect timing. Trailing my lips down her neck, I moan with her. Nothing has ever sounded so good as to hear her sounds of pleasure in my ear. Though it seems as though it's been many lifetimes since I've heard it, my memories remind me it hasn't been but one.

My lips reach hers, and I thrust into her again.

She takes all of me, her hips begging me for more. She runs her fingertips down my back as my muscles flex with each entry inside her.

"Oresha," I whisper against her lips. My thrusts pick up in tempo as she presses her palms into my flesh, urging me to thrust harder.

Her heavy breathing matches the beat of her heart, and her heart matches mine as though we are one and the same. My lips stay affixed to hers as my body anticipates her release until she reaches the edge. An orgasm with a batasurna mate isn't like anything else. Our energies collide together with the rush, then merge as though they coalesce.

She crosses over, her body beginning to tremble. My skin tingles as the waves of her energy course through me. I can't explain the sensation of a female orgasm, though I feel it as though I am her.

My release comes, and she shudders with me. Our energies begin to ascend, shifting out of our bodies, to merge without boundaries, without impediments. We reunite, if only for an instant, as we first did in the Beyond.

It's indescribable.

Without warning, our energies rip apart, and I'm sucked back into my body. It feels like I'm being jammed into a space ten times too small. I fall limp, the heat and tingling washing over my skin.

Before reuniting, I'd always felt empty. Lost. Maybe that's why I left Imsz-Ordena, endlessly searching outer space for something I had no idea I was searching for. The answer had never come to me as to why. Not until my final assignment. I'll never have that feeling again. At least, not in this lifetime. In the next, if this one should happen to end, I'll search for her again.

I'm learning more every u-day about this bond we've chosen to share with each other. Recently I remembered that when batasurna mates say "beyond eternity," it is the most sacred of promises to each other, meaning our bond is unable to be broken, even by the dioses themselves.

I move to settle at her side and pull her toward me.

She rests her chin on my chest as her expression turns somber. "Are you afraid?"

"Of what?" I ask.

"Going insane."

"No. We're safe here. And I have a feeling the queen is still working to find a cure."

"Yet she still kills the mates?"

"Something tells me she isn't. It's just a feeling, though."

"Why the feeling?"

"A few u-years ago, a rumor surfaced that she'd encountered her own mate. It was only a rumor, but if it's true and she's felt the things I feel for you, then she must understand it."

"I hope you're right about her."

"Me, too," I admit.

All those u-years of chasing empty space between stars are over. I am where I belong now—with her.

"I love you, oreshi," she whispers sweetly, her brown eyes warm and glowing.

"And I love you, oresha. Beyond eternity."

ABOUT LEAH VEGA

Leah Vega found her passion for writing at a young age but took a different professional path in life in the tech world. When she decided to leave tech, her passion for writing reignited, and she began writing her first novel (which, by the end of it, turned into ten novels). She writes action-packed, steamy sci-fi romance where cultures collide, heroes are born, and ancient truths are revealed.

Visit her website to find out more! www.leahvega.com

ESCAPE FROM THE EXTERIS

AKIRA ANGEL

Heat Rating: Steamy

ONE
AVA

A va leaned into the dilapidated door to the engine room of the Exteris space station, not sure what she would find on the other side. It shuddered open with a loud squeal. Why she was here she couldn't say—except to admit that she had been lonely since her mentor, Faelin, had died.

By unhappy coincidence, the voice box on Comet, her robot dog, had broken shortly thereafter, so now she didn't even have him to talk to in the long hours of her off time. Well, she could talk to him, but his answers were choppy and often unclear. And Faelin was the only one who could have fixed him. Except maybe her father, long ago.

Ava was searching for something—and she felt a burning need to see the engine. To remember her father and the long hours they had spent in the engine room together when she was a child, him tinkering with engine parts while she explored with Comet. To remember what it had felt like to be loved.

Although elves had an innate magic that would choose their mate, her hope for a future mate was slim. Her home planet had been destroyed by the Ardaks, and most elves wanted a strong lineage—or at least an elf with strong magic. She had neither. And on the space station, she rarely ran into other elves at all.

Ava entered the dark space silently, closing the door behind her, allowing her eyes to adjust to the dim light. The metal of the walls and floor hummed with vibration as the engine worked. She ventured farther in, her steps silent on the grates beneath her feet. Steel stairways and ladders led off in different directions in the darkness, until finally, she came to another door. Through the large inset window, she could see the central engine chamber.

She sucked in a breath as she opened the door and surveyed the enormous engine before her, taking in the unearthly pale blue glow of the three crystal accelerator beams within their chambers. Each chamber extended upward many levels, and downward even farther. A metal walkway in surprisingly good condition spanned the space, stretching outward from her door and disappearing into the darkness on the other side of the engine.

Unlike the rest of this level of the station, the antiquated engine parts held no rust, moving perfectly in rhythm. She wandered down the metal walkway, the intricate workings of the innumerable interlocking parts on both sides making her catch her breath in awe. Whoever took care of this place was a master of his craft.

"What are you doing here?" The voice was deep and harsh, unforgiving.

Ava jumped, spinning toward the sound and instinctively pulling out her dagger. A gust of wind swirled around her, an unconscious manifestation of her air magic that accentuated the swift, fluid motion of her draw.

"An elven move if I ever saw one," he said from the darkness, his voice dry. "Why are you invading my domain?"

Although his eyes were hidden, Ava felt the energy of them on her. She knew Kovian by reputation and had even seen him many times from afar.

He was a cyborg—the very thing so many refugees feared. Cyborgs were dangerous. Of immense strength and power, created by the Ardaks for work and war. She'd heard of cyborgs rebelling against the Ardaks, breaking free, but had never imagined seeing them up close or working with them until she'd arrived at the station.

Kovian was a mystery. More reclusive than other cyborgs, he always stood in the shadows during space station personnel meetings, speaking to no one—probably believing nobody cared what he had to say. But she'd always been drawn to his silent, watchful demeanor and once again fought the inexplicable urge to get closer.

"It's my shift-free day," she answered, cursing inwardly at the stutter in her voice.

"Did you tire of shopping?" he asked with exaggerated patience, his tone seemingly disdainful.

Ava winced, thinking of all the beautiful elves she'd seen on the station monitors—those decked out in their finery that went to the high-fashion shops and salons on the station. "I'm not a shopping kind of elf."

He paused, his eyes studying her. "Then what kind are you?"

She licked her lips. She wouldn't admit her failings to this stranger—the fact that her magic wasn't as strong as other elves, that she didn't have any family or friends left. "My father was an engine master. I wanted to be one when I grew up, but then he was killed by the Ardaks and I ended up in communications. I just felt. . .I missed him."

The silence grew between them as he seemed to ponder her words. The darkness seemed to close in around her, and she suddenly realized how protected she was in her daily life in the personnel wing of the station. What had she been thinking coming down here? This was the Exteris, with over a hundred levels of luxury shopping that descended into an equal number of lower levels that served as a haven for refugees, smugglers, spies, and all other varieties of criminals on the run. And despite the best efforts of its owner and security staff, beings disappeared in those areas all the time.

No one would miss one little elf.

"Why did you end up in communications?" he asked. So, he was curious.

"My father sacrificed himself so I could get off-planet during the invasion. When our rescue ship landed on the station, no one spoke for me. There was an elder elf who needed help in communications. He took me as an apprentice."

"Faelin."

"Yes," she said.

"Faelin was a good elf. A good friend." The voice was nothing but a whisper, a rasp from the darkness ahead of her. "He said you were a good apprentice."

"I tried my best." She peered ahead, trying to use her elven vision, but Kovian moved farther back into the shadows. Although he was shrouded by the darkness, one of his cybernetic arms was visible, the metal parts gleaming in the faint light.

His eyes followed her gaze and he looked down at his arm. "You should not be here, little one." There was something hesitant about his words, as if he didn't speak very often.

She squinted as she peered ahead, searching for his eyes. There was only a glint, almost imperceptible in the twilight. "Why not?"

"Because this place is not meant for one of your light." He shifted his weight, and the entire room seemed to shudder.

Her mouth went dry as she found that she barely reached his chest. She took a step backward.

"That's right, run along. Back to the light," he rasped.

His word stopped her. Why should she run away?

Instead, she chanced a step forward. "I want to learn about engines."

"Why? What use could you possibly have?"

Her eyes adjusted even more to the darkness, revealing more of him. Outlined against the faint glow of the engine lights, he appeared more formidable than a typical ship engineer. His cyborg form was encased in a suit of exoarmor that was sleek, yet bulky at spots, with visible joints and seams that hinted at enhanced strength and durability. His presence was imposing, the exoarmor adding an inhuman touch to his already intimidating silhouette.

"I want to be an engine master like my father. I want to fly my own ship someday, and I need to know what to do if it breaks."

He snorted. "That is not a proper dream for one such as you."

She stepped back. "And what should I dream of?"

He narrowed his eyes in thought.

She waited, suddenly wanting to know his answer.

"To become starlight," he said finally.

She scoffed. "*That* is not a proper dream."

Yet in that moment, everything changed. He was a hulk of a man, almost a beast. But his heart was that of a dreamer, like her. How did he come to live down here in this darkness?

"Why do you not flee?" he asked, a note of wonder in his voice. "Are you not afraid?"

"Should I be?" she asked. "Why don't you come into the light?" Her stomach fluttered as she imagined what he might look like up close. What type of face would match his raspy voice? Would he be handsome beneath the beard? Would his face show the scars of his past?

But he didn't satisfy her curiosity. Instead, he crouched farther back in the shadows, evading her efforts to see him more clearly. "You would not like me if I did."

But examining his behavior now, there was something more to him. She could feel it. Now that they were only feet apart, she could almost feel the magic between them.

"Will you teach me about engines?" she asked softly.

He grunted. "Do you have nothing else to do?"

"Not in the evenings, or on my shift-free days. I get two out of every thirty standard shift days free."

He was silent for so long that she wondered if he would speak again. As the silence extended, she found she wasn't nervous anymore.

"Be here at the same time tomorrow," he rasped.

Her heart began to beat faster with joy. Feeling like she'd won a battle, Ava curtsied toward his shadow. "I will."

TWO
KOVIAN

Kovian watched as the tiny elf scampered toward the exit, her figure small and fragile against the size and bulk of the engines. Her curiosity about engines seemed almost naive; one misstep in this labyrinth of energy and metal could be fatal.

Tomorrow, he should lock the room against her.

But he wouldn't. He couldn't resist the glowing blue of her eyes infused with gold, her long red-gold hair that fell in a braid to her waist, the flicker of expressions that crossed her face as they spoke. Her presence had stirred something within him, a feeling long forgotten.

Loneliness had been his only companion since the Ardaks' attack on his planet ten years ago, during his twentieth year. The tigerlike beasts had turned him and his friends into one of their first batches of cyborgs, blending flesh with metal, life with unlife. He'd watched his friends perish one by one, their bodies rejecting the enhancements or their minds broken by their new existence.

He didn't know why he'd survived. Whether it was a sheer determination, a hidden resilience, or simply a stubborn refusal to give the Ardaks the satisfaction of breaking him, he had stayed alive through their endless rounds of work on his body. But survival had come at a cost. He was a patchwork of cybernetics and flesh, his body left without the sleek beauty or technological advancements of the newer cyborgs.

Raising the chunk of metal encased in exoarmor that was his left forearm, he rotated the attachments at the end to bring forth the one he needed. He imagined the elf's expression of horror if she saw him in the light, and scrubbed his hand of flesh down over the thick beard that hid his scarred face.

He knew who she was. Faelin had related many a tale about his young charge after he'd adopted her. He'd been as proud of her accomplishments as a father could be, even though they weren't related by blood. Kovian had seen her often from afar on his way to visit Faelin late in the evenings, although he'd stuck to the shadows.

As he replaced the lattice matrix inside the flux harmonizer, a critical component for balancing the energies within the tri-crystal power core of the engine, he couldn't keep his mind off her. His cybernetic arm worked with practiced ease and chip-led precision, removing casings and adjusting components—a stark contrast to the relative clumsiness of the rest of his body.

Being one of the first cyborg models made by the Ardaks, Kovian's enhancements lacked the refined integration of the later models he'd seen. His gait was awkward, cumbersome, his cybernetic leg out of sync with the rest of him.

The beard he'd grown to cover as much of his scarred face as possible suddenly felt like a feeble attempt to hide his true nature.

The tools and attachments he'd been equipped with had become outdated, much like himself. The station, with its reliance on older technologies, was the only place where he still held value.

He finished the task quickly, wanting to cover the mechanism as soon as possible to minimize the risk of shock. As he stood, he extended his sanding attachment, scratching his back.

Then he shuddered, realizing what he'd done. Who could want a male with machine parts for a hand?

Sighing, he stood. He'd been alone for so long he'd almost forgotten what it was like to talk to a female. Her presence had reminded him of softness, of hope, of the memory of what life had been like before he had become this metal beast.

What the hell are you thinking, Kovian? You have no business with a female. The last time some females had seen him, it was three elves who had spied him bringing food back to the engine room. Their looks of horror had etched themselves into his memory and made him realize that nobody would be able to look past what the Ardaks had done to him.

A young, beautiful elf like Ava with a lifespan of two or three millennia ahead of her wouldn't be interested in a cyborg. And she deserved better than a machine like him.

There was no way she'd come back tomorrow. If the tiny elf gave him the time of day, it was only because he was useful to her. For now.

And yet, as he prepared to resume his next task, Kovian found himself hoping she would prove him wrong. Perhaps she wouldn't be like the other elves. In her, he saw a flicker of something long since extinguished within himself, a spark of curiosity, a defiance of the darkness surrounding them.

Although he didn't want to admit it, even to himself, the back of his mind wondered if perhaps, just maybe, that flicker would allow her to see beyond the metal and the scars to the man beneath who long ago had lost all reason to hope.

THREE
AVA

Ava hurried back down the corridor, away from the engine room, her heart pounding in her chest. Kovian's raspy voice still echoed in her ears, tinged with both warning and something deeper. The male cyborg was an enigma, a mixture of harsh exterior and underlying vulnerability.

The screech of alarms blared through the air, interrupting her thoughts. She pulled her personnel earpiece from her pocket and fixed it inside her ear, while it continued reverberating through the station's steel corridors, then broke into a sprint toward the command center.

Seconds later, a faint crackle came through the earpiece, distorted and faint. Ava tilted her head, pressing her hand against her ear to focus on the sound as she ran.

"Ava," the voice sounded like a whisper amid the static. "We need you in the command center. Something is wrong."

"I can hear that!" she shouted back. "I'm on my way!"

It seemed to take forever to reach the command center. The thoughts in her head varied between an attack from some mercenaries to a problem with the station.

Seven standard minutes later, she scanned her retina outside the center. The door whisked open and she burst through, sprinting to her station. The operations deck was a thing of beauty. Enormous windows showed the vastness of space with a 360-degree view, sleek computer stations beneath each one. The middle of the center was sunken with the captain's chair and console in the center and plenty of seating around the edges for the crew when the owner of the station, Jostin, held meetings. But Ava didn't see any of it as she focused on the screens, taking in the information there before she reached her seat.

Two of the other three communications officers were already there—the inexperienced two.

"Where is Veldaar?" she asked. The other communications officer had more experience than she did, but he was a relatively new hire on the station.

"We called him but there's no answer."

"All right, show me what you've got."

The signal feed flickered through on the monitor. Ava's eyes widened at the digital noise. There was something hidden there —she just couldn't quite read it. "Tech 1, let's apply a low-pass filter with a cutoff at 2 kHz to remove any high-frequency interference."

The filter cleaned up the signal but not by much. "Let's follow it up with a band-pass filter centered at 500 Hz with a 200 Hz bandwidth to home in on the primary signal range."

Better, but it still wasn't readable. "Apply a moving average over a ten-sample window to smooth out any remaining rapid variations," she instructed, waiting for the next filter. "Now run a harmonic transform to verify the signal's integrity and identify any lingering noise frequencies for further refinement."

The signal suddenly separated, becoming clear on the screen before her.

"That was like magic, boss," Tech 2 said in awe.

She paused. "Yes, it was, wasn't it?" She'd never thought of herself as doing magic through her work before. "All right, feed it through the speakers."

The voice was a growl in Ardak. She tried turning it up. "What does that say? I'm not quite..." But then she understood the transmission and a shiver passed over her.

Bomb in place at 130.00. Detonation in 30:00.

The signal repeated over and over. "Where did it come from?"

"The origin is unclear," Tech 2 said. "It's reverberating around the station."

She checked the clock. "That means we only have twelve minutes left! Traako! Get Jostin on the comm—we need orders. Tech 1, how did you know to sound the alert?"

"We didn't sound it, boss. It's coming from the engine room." The tech pointed upward at a map of the station. Sure enough, the engine room was flashing red.

"What?!" How had she missed that the alert was from the engine room? Her fingers flew over the keys as she accessed the comms. "Kovian? Kovian! Are you there?"

There was no answer.

"Ava!" A voice crackled in her ear. It was Jostin. "Give the order to evacuate the station."

"But sir!" she cried. The station had been her only home since the invasion of her planet. "Did you see the alert from the engine room? Maybe the bomb is there! Maybe we could stop it!"

"I just spoke with the captain of the *Flouriant*. The Ardaks have bombs on all four stations. Two other stations have found theirs. It's not possible to disconnect or even eject because it's wired directly to the engine." Jostin's tone was final. "Get yourselves to the escape pods—tell all personnel to set course for Aurora and we will meet up there."

"Aurora? But that's two days away! And through a wormhole!"

"It's the only safe place in the galaxy now. The elves are trying to shield other planets, but Aurora is the only one that has a shield in effect right now. The pods will make it. Now go!" The command was so loud she winced.

She turned back to the others. "We have to evacuate. Let me set the emergency alerts." Her fingers shook as she entered the commands for the evacuation signal. Then she pressed the button.

The entire station began to flash red, and this time, the siren extended beyond the personnel wing.

Station alert. Evacuate. Personnel set course for Aurora. Station alert. Evacuate. Personnel set course for Aurora. Station alert. . .

"Kovian?" she called again into the comm. There was still no answer. She turned to the techs. "You two evacuate. I'll see you on Aurora."

"Boss, what are you going to do?"

"First, I'm going to get my dog. Then I'm going to find that engine mechanic and get us out of here!" She spun on her heel and headed for the door as fast as she could.

Her quarters were along the same corridor as the command center, and she sprinted down toward her door, momentarily stopped by other personnel entering or leaving their quarters, creating an atmosphere of chaotic frenzy.

Throwing her hand on the panel, she was inside in seconds, grabbing her pack from beside the door and picking up necessities as she went.

Her dog wagged his mechanical tail, rising up onto his back two legs in greeting.

"Comet, we need to evacuate. What do I need to take with me?"

The dog froze and began barking out broken words in Ava's

own voice. "Space…port, mother's…, father's…, Com-et and… pad, holostorer…food…water."

She expanded the bag and gathered the supplies, stuffing them in her bag. "Did I forget anything?"

"Holo…er," he replied.

She grabbed the holostorer and put it in the bag, placing Comet on top and leaving his head out so he could warn her of anything he saw. Then she headed out the door and toward the engine room.

Kovian. His words still echoed in her ears as she left her quarters and ran down the corridor toward the engine room. *To become starlight.*

Her chest fluttered at the memory, a blush creeping across her cheeks. As much as she tried to push the thought away, her mind went back to the image of his haunted eyes and the wistful note in his voice. And the magic she'd felt as she got closer to him.

Did cyborgs have deeper feelings? They were rumored to be more machine than man. She didn't know the answer, but there was something that drew her to him—an emotion behind his eyes.

If they were going to lose the station, she was going to make damn sure he wasn't left behind.

FOUR
KOVIAN

K ovian's cybernetic arm jerked as he forced the emergency hatch shut, sealing off the engine room from the main corridor. The alarms blared around him, vibrating through his frame as a harsh reminder of a problem in the engine room.

He turned to the nearest console, scanning the status readouts. Everything seemed in order. So why were the alerts going off?

Focusing on the chip at the back of his neck, he tuned his frequency to the station's comms. "Jostin, come in."

Crackle sparked over the line. "Jostin here. Kovian. Get out of that engine room. You must evacuate immediately."

Kovian's stomach clenched. "Why? What do you know?"

"There are bombs on all four stations! Evacuate and we'll regroup on Aurora. Fuck!"

Kovian pushed aside his own pain at the thought of losing the station. The Ardaks had taken so much from all of them. He couldn't believe they were going to take the four space stations, too.

Perched at the four cardinal extremities of the known

universe, the four stations served as critical hubs for hundreds of planets, facilitating the flow of goods and services to the remote outer realms. The stations weren't hidden from the Ardaks, in fact, the Ardaks also used them for refueling and supplies. They offered sanctuary and a bustling marketplace for those daring enough to traverse the vast interstellar voids. And they were the only secret refuge the rebels had against the Ardak forces sweeping over the universe.

Jostin's information must be airtight or he would never give up trying to save the station.

"Is there nothing I can do?"

"No, dammit! They must have connected us to the Resistance. It's all over. . . Everything we've worked for. We don't even have time to transfer all of our top-secret documents —although we're working on it now. This will set us back years in this war. Fucking Ardaks!" Jostin's voice ended in a shout.

The signal cut off and Kovian slammed his hand down on the console. For a moment, he thought about going after his friend to make sure he didn't do anything stupid. They had escaped the Ardaks together, and even though they hadn't spoken recently due to their differing job duties and Jostin's work in the Resistance, Kovian owed him for this job.

But then another signal pinged him.

"Kovian? It's Ava."

"Ava! Where are you?"

"We're evacuating the station. The alarm is in your section. I'm coming to you."

"What?" His body tensed. "We don't know why the alarm is going off! Stay out there where it's safe."

"We need to get out of here! Meet me at the pods near the engine console."

"I'm coming." From her tone, Kovian knew it would be useless to argue with her. She was on the verge of panic, and he could better protect her if they were together.

It had nothing to do with the fact that Aurora was two days away and they would be in a tiny escape pod together. No, he couldn't think like that. She was not meant for him.

He grabbed a ray gun and a sword from their hidden compartments near the exit, striding back down the hall toward the main engine core.

Entering the room, he switched between settings on his ocular, trying filter after filter. Nothing came up until. . .infrared. A pulsing wave of energy emitted from the far side of the engine room.

He approached the source of the wave and jumped back in shock when three Ardaks appeared, their slitted eyes narrowed, deadly fangs gleaming with malevolent intent. They'd materialized out of thin air so quickly that he almost didn't believe they were real.

Their fur, a deep, mottled orange with bold black stripes, was partially covered by the ornate battle armor that gleamed even in the low light of the engine room. The one in the middle was the commander. Kovian could read his name— Khaal—and the insignias on his armor. They were ingrained in his brain and his chip from his time as a cyborg warrior for the Ardaks.

Commander Khaal held a long sword in one paw and a ray gun in the other, standing upright with the poise of a seasoned warrior. He sized up Kovian with a glance and shot almost without warning.

Kovian anticipated the shot and ducked behind the engine, eliciting a growl from Khaal.

The station comms were connected to his chip, so he tried to connect to Ava again. But the only answer was static.

Commander Khaal stalked around the core first, sword raised.

Kovian swung his cybernetic arm, striking the Ardak square in the chest before it could strike a downward blow, the impact reverberating through his body. He clenched his jaw against the pain.

At that moment, Ava burst into the room from the corridor, her eyes wide.

"Get back," he shouted.

She took in the scene, pulling out her dagger and raising her hands. With one sideways sweep of her arms, wind swept the engine room, gathering speed and pushing the Ardaks back against the far wall.

Kovian grabbed on to a railing to prevent himself from being swept aside. As soon as the gale had passed, he ran for Ava and scooped her up into his arms. He diverted most of his power to his legs and sprinted for the door. If they could make it out of the engineering room to the nearest escape pod, they wouldn't have to fight the Ardaks.

Heavy bootsteps charged closer behind them.

He wasn't going to make it to the door.

Moving swiftly, he set Ava down and spun to face the Ardaks in one motion. Holding his sword high, he charged them with a battle cry. He swung the sword at the first Ardak, taking off its arm, its ray gun flying to the right.

The Ardak swiped its razor-sharp claws at Kovian and he ducked, his enhanced reflexes allowing him to dodge and counter with a powerful punch to its jaw.

As it moved aside, Kovian fired his ray gun at the second. The Ardak roared with rage and batted at his arm so it went wide. It bared its fangs and went for his throat.

Kovian spun so the Ardak's fangs sank into his shoulder but instead of retreating, he slammed his body to the side, hurling the Ardak into the unforgiving metal of the wall. He backed up, bringing the ray gun around and shooting the Ardak through the skull.

Ava's wind magic swirled around him, targeting the two

remaining Ardaks and sending them flying backward once more into the engine components.

Kovian fired the ray gun several times and watched the beams go into the centers of their chests.

"They're down! We need to get out of here now!" Kovian growled, pushing Ava in front of him toward the exit with his good hand.

The lights flickered, and the station power seemed to falter for a moment.

"Run!" Ava yelled, grabbing his hand and pulling him along.

There were many escape pods still available in the corridor of this section, and they skidded to a halt before the first one. Kovian threw his hand on the scanner when a blast hit him from behind. The impact felt like a hot iron rod piercing through the middle of his back, driving him to his knees against the entrance to the pod. Pain exploded in sharp, white-hot waves, locking his spine in an iron grip of agony.

Kovian twisted in a desperate attempt to face his attacker, gritting his teeth against the pain. His hands fumbled for his ray gun, vision blurring as he aimed and fired. The Ardak that had followed them dropped lifelessly, its massive body hitting the floor with a final thud.

"Get up!" Ava cried urgently.

"I-I can't." Kovian's voice broke with pain as he tried to command his legs to move.

"Can you use your arms?" she asked, her voice shaking as she tried to assist him.

Gritting his teeth, Kovian tried to haul himself up using his arms, but hot agony lanced through him, sharp and merciless. He screamed —a raw sound of sheer torment—and collapsed back onto the cold floor. The corridor spun wildly, his vision dimming at the edges.

Shaking, he remembered to turn on the pain dampener in his chip, but the relief was marginal. "The suit... It's too heavy," he gasped, each breath a stab of pain. "And the pain… It's too much. You go. Get into the pod."

Ava's face blurred before him, her eyes wide with fear and resolve. "I can't leave you. I should be able to heal you. Or at least move you with my air magic." Her voice wavered, betraying her feeling of helplessness. "But I'm drained, I need time to recharge before using it again."

Despite his pain, Kovian's heart ached at her distress. With a trembling hand, he reached up, his fingers brushing away a tear from her cheek. "It was worth it," he whispered, his voice thick with unspoken emotions. "I'm sorry I never got to—" His words faltered, cut short by the grim reality of their situation.

The lights on the station flickered ominously and his chip issued a warning: less than three minutes for the pod to escape and reach a safe distance. Desperation seeped into his voice as he pushed her away gently but firmly. "You have to go. *Now.* Or you won't reach a safe distance. Please." His gaze fell to his paralyzed legs. "Or this—my sacrifice—will be for nothing."

"I can't leave you!" she sobbed. "This is my fault! You were shot because of me."

"No, Ava," Kovian's voice was steady. "I was shot because of the Ardaks. I made it as far as I did because of you. I see great courage in you. Great power. And a bright future. Now go!"

FIVE
AVA

Ava surged to her feet with a sob. Her soul felt like it was being ripped in two, torn between fear and desperation not to lose him. Everything felt wrong.

When Kovian had picked her up and sprinted toward the door of the engine room, she'd felt a swell of magic course through her—intense, potent, and utterly foreign. It was a sensation she recognized from ancient lore, yet never dreamed she would experience. Especially with someone not of her kind.

The realization hit her like a gale force wind. Kovian could be her mate. If he wanted to be. If he lived.

What was she thinking? He couldn't die. Panic clawed at her insides, mixing with a newfound hope. The fresh bond between them was as undeniable as her breath—it couldn't end in the cold confines of a space station corridor.

She scrambled to her feet and tossed their packs inside the pod. Raising her hands again, she noticed her fingers trembling. "I have very little magic left," she confessed. "Using it now might mean I'll never have magic again. But at least I'll have you."

"No!" he shouted, wincing. "I can't let you do that!"

Her determination was a lifeline she clung to as she raised her hands, attempting to summon the last wisps of her strength, desperate not to let him slip away from her. All she needed was enough wind to blow him into the tiny pod.

But stress and fear stifled her powers. Nothing happened. Nothing stirred, not even a tiny breeze.

Kovian's voice was weak but insistent, breaking through her focus. "Leave me, Ava. Please, save yourself."

Tears streamed down her face as she knelt beside him. "No!" she shouted, more fiercely than she'd intended. "I lost my father, then Faelin. I won't lose you, too."

Summoning every ounce of her remaining strength, Ava raised her hands, envisioning the familiar winds that had always heeded her call. With a cry, she summoned the wind once more. This time, a gentle breeze began to stir, whispering promises of power. But as it faltered, despair gnawed at her resolve.

Her scream of anguish tore through the metal corridor.

Collapsing to her knees, she placed one hand over Kovian's heart. Closing her eyes, she channeled every ounce of being into a final plea. It wasn't just desperation that fueled her now but an unyielding strength, a refusal to watch another loved one slip away.

The air around them crackled with the raw energy of her emotion, and suddenly a gale force wind erupted from the center of her being, more powerful than any she had summoned before.

It lifted them both, hurtling them into the safety of the pod.

Kovian grunted as he landed hard on his back, Ava collapsing half across him.

Gasping for breath, she scrambled to her feet and secured the hatch. "I'm so sorry. I couldn't leave you behind to die."

He clenched his jaw. "We won't be alive for long if we don't get out of here." He smacked the floor with his fist. "I wish I could help you."

"Don't worry, I know how to fly. And these pods aren't that difficult." She stepped over him carefully, heading for the console. Within seconds, she had belted in and hit the button to jettison from the station. An enormous force raised her out of the seat and she looked back, seeing Kovian in the air, halfway to the top of the pod.

Pushing the lever forward to take them swiftly away from the station, she locked it in place. Then she yanked her belt off, pulling herself along the handles of the craft until she was next to him.

Her gaze scoured the buttons along the pod wall. "There must be a pullout bunk in here somewhere. I can't let you land on your back again."

"It's the green handle to your right. But watch out, the self-inflating gel mattress will span this entire space."

She backed out of the way and pulled the green handle. A compartment opened and a metal frame appeared about waist high, a mattress expanding outward on top of it.

"You won't fall far now. I'm going to set the course for Aurora and engage artificial gravity."

Kovian nodded once and she floated her way back to the front of the craft. The settings didn't take long, showing that Aurora was indeed just over two days away, even using the interstellar wormholes.

"Engaging gravity," she called back loudly over her shoulder.

"Ready," he replied.

She moved the lever forward slowly, feeling herself become heavier by increments.

"I'm down," he informed her moments later.

She pushed the lever forward the rest of the way, locking it in place. Then she unbelted, moving toward the back and climbing onto the mattress, crawling to the space beside his chest. The mattress was low enough that she still had plenty of headspace to sit up and move.

Kovian had angled his body so he could look out the back window at the station.

She also turned her attention to the swiftly receding station, taking one last look at the place that had been her home for the past ten years. It was funny, in all that time, she'd seen it from the outside only once, upon her arrival. Hundreds of tiny and not-so-tiny vessels fled from it.

Kovian whispered, "Time's up."

The station exploded and a kaleidoscope of rainbows and colored lights burst forth, streaking across the dark void of space like ethereal fireworks. The vivid colors shimmered and danced, reflecting off fragments of the station that spiraled outward in a dazzling cosmic display.

Kovian wrapped one arm around her and moments later, a sonic boom shook the darkness. It rattled the escape pod and reverberated through the air around them. Ava thought it might shatter her bones.

The first waves of light and sound were followed by other shimmering waves, undulating with brilliant hues of crimson, azure, and emerald, creating an otherworldly spectacle in the station's final moments.

The debris scattered in all directions, glinting like shattered glass against the backdrop of distant stars.

Ava realized she was crying again.

"Beautiful," Kovian whispered.

Looking down at him, she saw he was staring at her. Her heart pounded as she gazed down at him, feeling the intensity of his stare.

He seemed vulnerable, open, a thousand emotions flickering through his eyes. The receding lights from the vibrant explosion cast a soft glow over his face, highlighting the sharp lines and scars but also the depth of emotion in his expression.

"I can't believe you saved me," he said, his voice filled with wonder.

"You saved me first. I just saved you back," she said softly. "Kovian, what do you know about elves?"

"Not much," he admitted. "Faelin didn't talk much about his race, and he's the only elf I've really known."

"When you picked me up before, I felt my magic react to you. It only does that for one reason…and with one person."

His eyes widened. "Ava," his voice was a rough whisper, full of pain and longing. "You can't. I'm not. . . It's just not possible."

Ava put a finger to his lips. "I know what I felt, Kovian. You could be my mate."

He stared at her, his eyes bright. "How could you care for me that much? I'm a machine, a beast." He looked down at his legs, his eyes bright with unshed tears. "I don't even know if I'll walk again. There are some things on cyborgs that they can't fix."

"You are not a machine or a beast," she said firmly, cupping his face with her hands. "Faelin trusted you, and he was very selective about who he counted as a friend. For me, I believe in you. Elven magic never chooses someone who's unworthy. We will try to heal you, but if we can't, it doesn't matter."

For a moment, silence reigned. Then slowly, a hesitant smile lit his face. "I watched you from the shadows, but I didn't know how to approach you. I never thought, never hoped. . ."

"I was lost, as well. But we have each other now. I don't know what will happen on Aurora, but I am excited to see it." She leaned over and brushed her lips against his.

SIX

KOVIAN

Kovian lay in the escape pod, his gaze fixed on the skylight in the ceiling of the pod, reminiscent of the starlit nights on his home planet, before the Ardaks had turned his world into a battlefield. This flight from the station reminded him of how he'd fled to the station six years ago after his escape from four years of enslavement by the Ardaks.

The faint hum of the pod's systems was a constant backdrop to his tumultuous thoughts. The truth of his situation—the extent of his injuries, the uncertain future—weighed heavily on him.

But Ava's presence anchored him to the moment.

She was asleep, nestled in the crook of his arm, her breaths even and soft against his shoulder. In the dim light of the pod, her face held a peaceful expression, almost childlike in its serenity. Her golden hair fanned out over his arm, shimmering with each movement she made. The sight of her, so relaxed and vulnerable in his presence, stirred something deep within him, a protective warmth he'd never felt before.

The elf had fought with the ferocity of a seasoned warrior against the Ardaks, standing her ground when many would have fled. She had saved him with her magic when all had seemed lost, and now she looked so innocent and delicate. Yet he knew better. Beneath that gentle exterior was a strength that rivaled the gravitational forces of the distant stars outside the windows of their pod.

She stirred slightly, her eyes fluttering open. The swirling pools of gold met his, and for a moment, everything else faded into insignificance.

"You're awake," she murmured, her voice hoarse.

"Couldn't sleep," he admitted. "But I'm glad you could."

She rose and adjusted herself so she could look at him more directly, her concern evident. "How do you feel?"

"I've maximized the settings on my chip's pain dampener, so the hurt is distant. There is a creeping numbness rising from my legs, unlike anything I've felt before. It's as if the coldness of space itself is seeping into my bones."

Her eyes widened almost imperceptibly, and he knew she was trying to control her reaction to his words. "Aurora has some amazing healers. My mother was a great healer among our people. Her powers were unrivaled on our planet. When she died, I got her medikit, but all her crystals went with her." The sadness in her eyes was unbearable.

"Maybe they can fix me, then." Hoping to take her mind off their losses, he asked, "Are you hungry?"

At the question, she crawled to the rear end of the mattress. "I am. And you know what? I brought food. Real food, not the protein packs."

His eyebrows rose. "You had time to get food during the evacuation?"

"Well, I had to go back for Comet, so I grabbed everything else we could think of." She reached below it to grab her pack and bring it up to the bed.

He turned his head, interested in what she'd brought with her. He almost jumped when a second pair of eyes met his. She had pulled a robot dog from her pack, and it stood on the edge of the bunk, staring at him. "Hello," he greeted it.

"He-o." the dog replied, giving a surprisingly lifelike wag of its tail.

"Comet's vocalizer is broken," Ava explained, pulling out more things from her bag. "And the only person I knew who could repair him was Faelin."

"I can take a look at him," he offered. "I've done work on smaller mechanics for the station in addition to the engines."

"I didn't even think of that." For the first time since the battle, a smile crossed her face. "I would love it if you could fix him. My father made him while my mother was pregnant with me, and he's been my lifelong friend."

Her words alone made it imperative that he put the dog in excellent condition.

"Why don't we eat first?" Ava suggested. "The elven stew is spelled, but eventually it will get cold since I don't have any magic to sustain it. After that, we'll be stuck with bread and jerky. Unless we want to eat rations."

His stomach clenched at the thought that she might have lost her magic. He wanted to ask more about it, but after what they'd just been through, it could wait. If the elves on Aurora were such great healers, maybe they could also help her.

She withdrew two medium-sized containers and handed one to him. He opened it with his right arm, which hurt less to move, and found that it broke down into two parts. The first held elven stew, and the second had a large roll of elven bread and a mixture of dried fruit and nuts.

"Can you turn onto your side?" Ava asked. "It will be easier for you to eat."

"I think so—if I use my cybernetic arm to push." He eyed the jacket. "There should be some inflatable gel cushions in here, check near the green lever you battled with earlier to inflate the bunk," he replied.

She crawled back toward the green lever, and he heard her fighting to open the compartment. "This handle doesn't want to turn, either. It's like the starboard antenna on a bad day."

"These pods are probably the least-checked items on the station. I'm surprised they all worked so well. You can thank Jostin's dedication to his station for that."

He heard her yank open the compartment. In seconds she had crawled around him and unrolled the cushion next to him.

"Ready?" he asked.

"Ready," she confirmed.

He pushed up with his cybernetic arm on the left, rolling to his right. At the same time, she inflated the cushion and rolled it behind his back.

"Are you okay?" She put a hand on his shoulder.

His body had broken out into a sweat, even though the pain he felt was minimal due to the dampener in his chip. "I'm fine," he assured her. Although in the back of his mind, he wondered. His chip wasn't chirping any signals at him, but it wasn't reading his lower torso or legs at all.

His cybernetic arm emitted a low hum as he cycled through tools until he found the one he was looking for—a precision four-pronged attachment. The prongs tapered to fine points, allowing him to perform meticulous operations such as manipulating tiny circuit components.

"That's a neat attachment." Ava nodded at the prongs. She'd crawled back around and was now opening her container of food.

"It's good for high-dexterity situations," he replied quietly, dipping a piece of bread into the stew and stuffing it into his mouth. He spent most of his time trying to forget about his cybernetics.

She leaned over, laying a hand on his cybernetic arm. "This arm is strong, well-fashioned, and has a variety of skills. Just like the male it belongs to."

127

He swallowed, meeting her eyes. "You have a way with words, Ava. And your stew warms more than just the body. Thank you for sharing this with me."

"You saved my life. It was the least I could do." Her eyes went distant for a moment. "After Faelin passed, I tried to make friends with the other elves but didn't connect with anyone. I didn't think anyone would care about me again. You're special, Kovian. Even without the magic, I would still care for you." Then she gave him a sideways glance. "I also craft some truly splendid honey cakes, when given the right incentive."

He choked on the next bite of bread and stew, his gaze going to her face.

The sparkle in her eye and blush in her cheeks told him she knew what she'd said.

"I'll keep that in mind," he replied. He sampled the dried fruit and nut mixture next. To his surprise, it also had tiny pieces of jerky and held a flavor he'd never tasted before.

"Do you like it?" she asked after his first mouthful. "Many non-elves don't."

He continued chewing the hearty, aromatic mixture. "Yes, I do. What did you mix this with?"

"It's a blend of honey, wildflowers, herbs, and spices. But the real ingredient is time."

All too soon, the meal was over, and Ava put the containers away. "I think I'll try to communicate with Aurora over the long-range frequencies. I want to know where to take you for healing immediately after we arrive. Do you need anything?" she asked.

He shook his head slightly. "Just pass Comet over here."

She urged the dog in his direction, clasping his fingers for a moment as she made her way back up to the pilot's seat.

Kovian shook his head. If he weren't injured, this would be a very different trip. Sighing, he picked Comet up and held the dog in front of him while he lay there. He rotated it to view all sides.

They showed a finely detailed structure—the reason for its lifelike movements.

Through the dog, he could see a father's love for his daughter. Most of his attachments on his cybernetic arm were meant for engines, and much too large to work on it. "Is there a tool kit in this pod somewhere?" he called up to her.

"I have my father's if you want. He used it to work on Comet all the time. Comet can get it for you."

He set the dog down, and it gave a wag and turned, padding toward the back of the pod where Ava had left her bag. He stuck his head inside the bag and came back with a small, nondescript case in his mouth. He sat down in front of Kovian, placing the item within easy reach of his cybernetic arm.

Kovian opened the tool kit that had once belonged to Ava's father, the well-worn tools inside showcased their long years of use. He removed Comet's access panel, revealing a compact array of microprocessors and intricate circuitry.

With an engineer's intuition guided by years of experience, he found the faulty resistor that had caused the vocalizer to fail. He carefully disconnected it and picked it up with his four prongs. Where would he find a resistor that small? "Comet, do you have extra components or resistors somewhere?"

The dog yapped and laid down, showing its belly. There was a second access panel, and opening it revealed hundreds of extra components of every type. Clearly, her father had wanted the dog to last for an elven lifetime.

He chose a new resistor. Searching the tool kit again, he found a specialized micro soldering iron, the tip fine enough to work with the miniscule components. He carefully connected each solder point of the new one, ensuring no further damage could occur.

Kovian was so caught up in his work that he didn't realize Ava had returned. She stood by the edge of the bunk, watching him. "It's just a burned-out resistor. Once I replace it, he should be as good as new." He reattached the access panels and put the tools back into the tool kit.

As he set the dog down, satisfaction filled him—the feeling of a job well done. After the invasion of his planet, and getting free of the Ardaks, many cyborgs had joined the front lines of the rebellion, fighting war after war on hundreds of planets. But he had always preferred fixing things, even before he was a cyborg.

Comet had been quiet for several seconds, and he sprang up with a yip. "Testing vocalizer. Testing…" the dog continued with a bunch of phrases in Elvish with different vocal tones that he didn't quite catch.

Kovian's chip translated them belatedly and he realized they were elven nursery rhymes.

The dog ran across the bunk and leaped into Ava's arms, nuzzling her neck.

"Thank you so much, Kovian!" Her voice was filled with emotion. "Comet, I missed talking to you so much!"

"I missed it, too, Ava," the dog replied.

Kovian shifted to look at them, but suddenly, a wave of nausea overtook him. "Ava. . ."

Her eyes turned to him, her expression immediately changing to one of concern. "What happened? You've turned gray."

"I don't know." His entire body broke out in a cold sweat. "Something's wrong. . ."

In a flash, she jumped up on the bunk beside him. She shook him, then he felt her slap his face.

He tried to respond, tried to say something, anything.

Then a sharp pain shot up his body from his torso and he felt nothing at all.

SEVEN
AVA

"**K**ovian!" Ava scanned his body for any sign of what could be wrong with him, but his cyborg exoarmor hid it from her.

They were much too far from Aurora—still a day and a half away. There was no way he would make it, and all other planets in this sector of the galaxy were under Ardak control.

Desperation clawing at her, she turned to Comet. "Do you have any ideas? What can I do to save him?"

Comet leaped to the far end of the bunk, bringing her mother's medikit in his jaws. He set it on the bunk before her and tilted his head to the side. "Accessing medikit emergency protocols."

He opened the cover of the case as a tiny key emerged from the side of his paw. He held it to the center of the case and it swiveled in the lock. The back of one of the compartments popped open, revealing a hidden compartment behind it. A glow came from inside.

"My mother's healing crystal!" Ava exclaimed, her heart pounding with a mix of hope and anxiety. She picked up the crystal, which dangled from a gold chain. Hope and terror went

131

through her. "The crystal should amplify my powers, but I used up all my magic. And the crystal is cool to the touch. I think it's out of charge."

Comet nudged her hand. "Try."

Ava put the chain around her neck, the crystal dangling down in front of her chest. She hovered over Kovian, unsure how to proceed. The weight of past losses flitted through her head. Her planet, her parents, Faelin. The space station. They whispered that maybe she was doomed to be alone again.

No, she whispered to herself. *My future is not my past. My peoples' blood runs through me, their strength, their magic.*

Clasping the crystal to her chest with one hand, she put the other hand on Kovian's chest. She closed her eyes, trying to draw her magic. But nothing responded, no hint of a breeze fluttered, as if the air around her was dead. "Comet, what can I use to charge this crystal?"

The dog's eyes went to the pod schematic on the emergency hatch, and her gaze followed.

"The emergency power cell!" they both answered at the same time, and Ava sprang up to get it from under the pilot's seat.

She came back, setting the crystal on the top plate of the emergency power cell and pressing the button to turn it on. After long seconds she opened her eyes and saw that the crystal had begun to glow. It was faint but present, so she waited patiently as the power slowly filled it, trying to ignore the passing of time and the stillness of Kovian's body save for the slight rise and fall of his chest.

When the crystal glowed brightly, Ava drew the chain over her head. Then she tried to draw the magic from the crystal to heal Kovian, reversing the flows, trying to build the energy. She focused, her brows furrowed in concentration, until her whole body broke out into a sweat from the effort. The air in the tiny space was deathly still, and she was trying to create breezes that would turn into gusts and finally a tiny tornado of wind and energy that would return the magic to her body.

But after a long while, her optimism faded, and she had to admit that it wasn't working.

Her magic was gone.

She threw herself over Kovian's chest, crying out in frustration. Looking to the right, she realized she was eye level with the battery.

"Ava," the dog said, following her gaze to the battery. "Batteries aren't meant for living beings."

"Jostin told me once that they saved some cyborgs on a mission by hooking them up to a ship. If it charged the crystal, maybe it can charge him. And maybe it could also charge my magic. It's unconventional, yes. But we have nothing else to help us on this pod. We are out of options," she murmured, pressing the button to turn on the battery.

"The batteries provide raw power. It's not the same as magic," Comet replied, a hint of hesitation in the way he sat back with his tail between his legs.

"I know. But it's a risk I have to take." She grabbed the battery and adjusted the settings to a lower output.

"That is still more current than a living being should take," Comet warned.

"Then I'll have to pray that my magic and his cybernetic systems protect us." She adjusted herself so she lay across Kovian's chest, keeping the crystal between them.

As she reached for the battery, her hand trembled, belying the fear that surged through her veins. She swallowed hard against the lump forming in her throat, her mind racing with the gravity of what she was about to do. What if she killed them both?

Taking a deep breath, she stilled her wayward thoughts. She remembered Kovian's gaze, intense and unwavering, in the corridor outside the escape pod. His words went through her mind, transforming her fear into a desperate kind of hope.

I see great courage in you. Great power. And a bright future.

That future would be much brighter if they were together.

She grabbed his hand in hers and touched their fingers to the battery.

Power shot through her body, recharging her magic in an instant before overfilling her. A thousand needles pierced her skin, each one burning her with unbearable intensity. Power flooded her—a raw, uncontrolled force that set every nerve ending aflame. A scream was torn from her throat, a raw sound of pure agony that went on and on.

Kovian's body began to vibrate with energy, and she could feel the magic repairing him, focusing on where he'd been shot in the back. In seconds the vibrations began to grow, until his body trembled and shook, his head rolling back and forth with the power of the muscle spasms.

Their hands flew free of the battery, but Kovian didn't stop spasming. His body rose up from the bunk, throwing her off him.

When the crystal disconnected from his chest, he fell back onto the bed, expelling one last breath with a great sigh.

Then all was silent.

"Kovian?" she whispered. Crawling forward, she saw that his chest wasn't moving. "Wake up! Kovian!"

As if the wind spoke to her, she suddenly knew what to do. Her magic was in her air. She needed to give him her breath.

She clenched her mother's crystal and knelt over him, taking in a breath and letting the air mix with her magic in her lungs. She blew the air into his body.

His chest rose, then fell.

"Breathe, Kovian," she whispered. "Breathe for me." She took another deep breath, filling her lungs with air and magic, blowing it into his lungs again.

This time, his chest rose higher. But it fell once more.

Uncertainty clouded her mind for a moment. She was already

fatigued from the power of the magic and wasn't sure how long she could keep going.

An image flashed through her mind of the first time they had met.

What should I dream of? she had asked.

To become starlight, he had answered.

Even without touching him, some part of her had recognized he was her mate. An outsider with a dreamer's heart.

His shock that she could love him had touched her to her very core.

I'm a machine, a beast, he'd said.

"You are *not* a beast," she said aloud. "And if you cannot breathe on your own, I will breathe for you until you can."

She lowered herself over him again, breathing in, breathing out, repeating the process over and over, taking another breath, pouring her magic into him, until the air around them shimmered with each of Ava's breaths. The magic was like a warm, tingling current of power, starting from her core and radiating outward. Each breath she took sparkled with particles of light, as if she was passing to him the essence of magic itself.

With each breath, she wove a tapestry of life, each inhale and exhale pulling him back from the brink of the void.

Then the crystal gave off a pulse, and Kovian's heart began to beat beneath her fingers.

His body took in a breath of its own.

He was alive.

She remained kneeling beside him, giving thanks to the high goddess of all elves for Kovian's return.

He opened his eyes moments later, his startling blue irises meeting hers. "I was in the afterlife," his voice was shaken. His eyes went distant for a moment. "It was unlike anything I've ever experienced before. Peaceful. Beautiful." Then his eyes focused on her. "But how did you do it? How did you bring me back?"

135

"I had a little help," she said with a smile, patting Comet and then the crystal. Her hand hovered over the battery for a moment, then she realized it was still on. She quickly turned it off.

"You used the emergency battery?" He raised his eyebrows. "That was good thinking. And brave. What a risk."

"You were already dead, and I was out of magic. I was afraid, but I remembered what you said, that I had great courage. It gave me the strength to do it."

His eyes met hers and he pulled her down into his arms and landed a kiss on her mouth. "Thank you for not giving up on me."

"Never," she replied, touching his lips with hers again and realizing that she meant it.

Although he hadn't said it yet, she knew he could feel their connection. She could read it in his eyes, his expression, his movements as he pulled back and caressed her face. It flowed through her like a tangible force. Forged through adversity and magic, their connection would sustain them. And whatever lay ahead, they would do it together.

EIGHT
KOVIAN

Kovian kissed Ava one more time. He wanted to keep kissing her, to consummate what now felt like a more permanent union but didn't want to frighten her. They had time for that in the future.

Moving to the edge of the bunk, he rose up onto his feet. "I can't believe it, I'm completely healed! You're magic, Ava!" He pulled her toward him and picked her up, kissing her soundly in the small space.

To his surprise, she wrapped her legs around his waist. "How grateful are you, Kovian?"

Instantly, he felt his body harden against her. "I'm more than grateful enough for *that*, sweet elf. But I didn't want to frighten you by going too fast."

"We have a day and a half before we reach Aurora," she replied seriously, running her fingers over his chest. "That's a lot of time."

"It is." He nodded sagely. "We should make the most of it." He bent to kiss her again but felt he had to warn her one last time. "Ava," his voice was quiet. "I wasn't kidding when I said I was a beast. I really am a metal monster." He held up his cybernetic hand with its rotating tools. "I was one of the first cyborgs they made—before their technology improved. Beneath this exoarmor is a thing of terror."

She silenced him by putting her fingers to his lips. "Everything about you is beautiful to me."

He bent, kissing her harder than he intended to. By the time he pulled back, they were both panting.

He turned around in the small space, sitting on the edge of the bunk. Kissing her more slowly this time, he caressed her back and shoulders, taking his time.

But she would not be slowed. She pushed him back on the bunk, climbing on top of him and straddling his waist, looking down at his chest. "How do we take off this armor?"

He reached for the release button that would bare his naked body, pausing. "Remember this pod has no emergency exit."

She arched a brow at him, her glowing blue eyes narrowing, and he could wait no longer.

He sighed. "Don't say I didn't warn you." Then he pushed the button. The exoarmor opened and he half rose off the bed, taking it off and pushing it aside. The seam of flesh and metal around his left cybernetic arm stopped before the shoulder. His gaze followed hers as it moved down his left side where enormous scars had sewn his body together until metal met flesh again above the hip joint.

Her eager hands explored him as she followed him farther up the bunk, not stopping at the metal. "Your skin is so warm. Even the metal is warm."

"Cyborgs are warmer than other males. It's something about the superoxygenated blood—" His words were cut off as she silenced him with a kiss.

Moments later, she broke off to remove her top, parting the fabric with a downward sweep of her hand and drawing it over her head.

Her naked body stunned him and he inhaled a breath. When she bent down, he drank from her kiss as if he was bewitched, pulled under by the sheer magic of her.

She laughed in pure delight and brought his hand to her breast as he raised his head to cover her other nipple with his lips. Her breath hitched as he explored her, his movements fluid and filled with a fervor that echoed the pounding of his heart.

Wrapped in the spell of their newfound intimacy, he explored her and she learned about him, building their arousal until they could hold back no longer. Every touch deepened the bond that elven magic and circumstances had forged. As he moved within her, watching her eyes glow in the dim light of the pod as she surrendered to the passion between them, he felt complete for the first time in as long as he could remember.

The rest of the journey passed too quickly. In Ava's arms, he found solace and exhilaration, a sanctuary where the universe outside ceased to exist.

But all too soon he was sitting in the pilot's seat of the pod, Ava in his lap and Comet in hers, all three staring at the translucent glowing shield of elven magic that surrounded the planet of Aurora and kept it safe from the invasion of the Ardaks. Light blues and pinks, oranges and golds, greens and purples swirled over its surface.

"Here we go," he murmured as the pod passed through the shield and headed for the planet below.

"Into the future," Ava replied in a hushed voice. "You know, something just occurred to me."

"What, love?" he asked.

"When I came into the engineering room, I was searching for something. I wasn't sure what at the time, but now I realize that I found it."

Their gazes met, and in her eyes, he realized he had found it, too. He smiled, reaching up to touch her cheek. "We found it together," he said, his voice steady with conviction. "We were both searching for something that seemed out of reach, until we found each other."

ABOUT AKIRA ANGEL

Akira Angel writes fast-paced, science fiction fantasy featuring immersive magical worlds, morally complex heroes, emotionally resilient heroines, powerful villains, and epic battles that will determine the fate of the universe.

When she isn't writing, Akira can be found traveling, attending conventions, walking her two chihuahuas, or hanging out with her Australian husband. Stay updated on her latest adventures and upcoming releases at her website www.akiraangel.com.

facebook.com/author.akira.angel

instagram.com/authorakiraangel

tiktok.com/@authorakiraangel

CHASE THROUGH THE WORMHOLE

CLAIRE DAVON

Heat Rating : Sweet

CHAPTER
ONE

The bounty hunter followed Proxima through the wormhole, intent on catching her. They were alone in this part of the universe, with no planets or asteroids around them.

Except one. Oradon, the world she'd called home until the age of twenty, circled an orange dwarf star close enough to sustain life. The theory was that the star and its planet had been ejected from a galaxy billions of years ago and had wandered through empty space ever since. The solar system was so far from any galaxies that its sky had few stars, and those were barely visible points in the night.

Proxima waved toward the ship on her tail, though Roark couldn't see the movement. *You're on my turf now.*

The bounty hunter—who was also her ex—had to catch her to claim the credits. But she wouldn't be so easily snared. Not when her home planet lay so close at hand.

Her com crackled to life.

Roark's smooth, rumbling baritone came over the speakers. "I suspected you'd flee home. You can't win. You may as well make it easy. Valinot has promised he'll be fair."

When she'd realized that Prince Valinot Quensid Zandibar had claimed the right to take her as a lover, Proxima had run. She had thought once she left, he'd forget about her and move on but that had proved a terrible miscalculation.

"Don't be stupid, Roark. Valinot has no interest in fairness."

Proxima glanced at the gauges and then at Oradon. The wormhole was so close to the single planet system that some speculated it might have been the thing that anchored them to this place.

When the galactic government showed up thirty years ago with the news of an entire universe beyond their tiny system, the news had changed the planet forever. Many older folks on Oradon preferred not to deal with their new reality and went about their lives as if nothing had changed. The ones who had grown up recognizing they were one planet among millions— billions—had a different experience. They understood that not only was Oradon not alone, but it was far from unique.

Proxima kept her attention on the tiny planet. She had gotten no transmissions from below and wasn't sure of her reception when she arrived. That shouldn't surprise her, after the way she left. Nobody had prevented her from going through the wormhole. A handful of ships were in orbit around the planet, but none turned to meet her.

She'd run away in the middle of the night five years ago rather than risk her parents trying to stop her. Just like she had done to Roark when he wouldn't stop trying to protect her, and they fought for what turned out to be the last time. She hadn't expected to come home so soon, but here she was, with an ex chasing her and an uncertain welcome on the planet she once called home.

"He has a valid claim. You can't win."

"He's lying. You know me better than that. I thought you did, anyway. Forget it, Roark. I'm not going back."

She could imagine him clenching his jaw. Roark did that

when he was angry or thwarted. The memory of that tight mouth and narrowed eyes had haunted her as she fled. Maybe things could have been different, if she'd stayed.

Too late now.

His rush of breath echoed through her cabin. "You're going to have to face this. Better me than someone you don't know."

Roark was the only person who was aware of where she came from, which gave him an advantage. The rest of the hunters chasing her had no clue about Oradon. The planet's existence was a secret, save for the handful who'd been allowed to leave, the galactic government—and Roark.

She never should have told him.

This was the sole place in the entire galaxy where she might have the upper hand. On this world, her parents had authority. Proxima was counting on that, even if they hadn't responded to her hail. She supposed she couldn't blame them, not after she'd taken off the way she had.

"Just try to catch me."

She cut their transmission and increased the acceleration.

———

The single planet system lit by an orange dwarf sun wasn't even close to one of the strangest places Roark had been. To be sure, the dearth of stars in the sky was disconcerting, the emptiness profound.

Roark preferred the bustle of the galactic center. Too many suns existed there to have their own habitable planets, but it was a perfect place for artificial space stations. The wormholes were plentiful in that part of the galaxy.

Not here. One single way existed to get in and out of this solar system—the wormhole that few knew about and fewer cared. When he'd pulled up Oradon on his star maps, no information existed. He'd had to find his way by following her, otherwise he would have been lost in this desolate area of space.

He was chasing a woman who had left him six standard months ago and gotten herself in a galaxy's worth of trouble in that short time. The bounty on her was large enough to attract attention—and greed.

He'd expected some sort of barrier at the wormhole entrance, but neither he nor Proxima had been challenged when they went through. Perhaps the traffic was so little that the authorities didn't bother with patrols.

Roark didn't have time to concern himself with what the government may or may not be doing. He had to get to her before anyone else did, which was no small feat given the price Valinot had put on her head.

As he approached the tiny green-gray planet he noted the wide oceans and relatively small number of cities. Following Proxima's trajectory brought him to a landing pad of short, wild grasses bordered on all sides by tall trees that swayed in the wind. Pasture animals grazed in the distance, and beyond them, mountains rose, their peaks snowcapped even in the temperate climate.

He set his ship down on the open ground of the spaceport. Burn marks in the dirt suggested ships had come and gone recently, but the skies were clear of all but a handful of traffic. On this out-of-the-way planet, the only ships were those piloted by locals, at least as far as he could determine.

He had no sooner disembarked, his eyes adjusting to the gray atmosphere and the large star in the sky, than a security robot rushed to him. He held up his intergalactic ID. As a legal, bonded bounty hunter, he had the right to go on any planet in pursuit of quarry.

"You will wait here." The robot was an older model, at least twenty years behind current standards. One look around the spaceport verified the same. This planet had technology but not the latest.

It was hard to believe this was her home. Proxima had always wanted the brightest lights of all—the stars—just as he did. This place would not be sufficient to satisfy her dreams.

"I will not. I have the authority, and it's you who will stand down." Roark glanced around and spotted the telltale transporter booth in the corner of the landing pad area. She had to have used it. He started toward it, intent on discovering Proxima's location. Her coordinates should be there, and he would follow.

The robot moved to intercept him. "By the authority of the Oradon council, I command you to halt."

Roark ignored the mechanical man. He rushed to the transporter and reached for the panel to access the log.

"Roark Pyfalihon, stop where you are."

The clear, strong voice, so like Proxima's, brought Roark up short. He cursed. It wasn't like him to be taken so unawares, but he hadn't noticed the trio standing at the edge of the landing pad. In his haste he'd failed to take the most basic of precautions.

Roark shifted from one foot to the other, trying not to show his dismay. He schooled his face to be blank as he took in the two older versions of Proxima—her father and mother—and the woman herself.

After half a year without seeing her face except in transmissions, Roark expected her impact on him would have vanished. He was wrong. Her brown hair and skin a few shades lighter beckoned him as they always had, like a shining star amid the darkness of the universe.

"You must be Helio and Yarra Aralis of Oradon. Thank you for your hospitality." He inclined his head as a show of respect. Proxima had never told him how to address the inhabitants on this world, so the universal standard was a safe bet.

Her father, Helio, was similar in coloring to Proxima, but

taller and wider, with a streak of gray in his mahogany hair. His arms were loose at his side, but his eyes were hard.

"We are, and are also part of the governing body on this world. While you are here, you are subject to our rules."

Roark shifted his attention to Proxima's mother. She was shorter than Proxima, with sharp features that echoed her daughter's, and faint lines at the edges of her eyes and mouth. Her hair was done in an elaborate updo and accentuated with golden combs where dark violet gems glistened and caught the light. Both of her parents wore the same shade of dark violet one-piece outfits, topped with short capes laced with golden threads.

Roark chose his next words with all the diplomacy he could summon. "I accept your authority, but you may not be aware of what is happening. Your daughter has a bounty on her head, and I have a legal right to apprehend her."

When Proxima flinched, a ripple going through her, Roark regretted his words.

"Your business doesn't matter to us. Your visit here is unauthorized, and we ask you to leave immediately." Yarra Aralis spoke with careful neutrality. The older version of his ex-lover had a blank face, but her gaze darted past Roark to the spaceport beyond, and their ships.

Roark hadn't caught over a dozen bounties by being unobservant. Something more was happening here, though he couldn't yet determine what.

"When Proxima came, I had a right to follow."

"You are not supposed to be here. Either of you." Yarra Aralis's tone had so many undercurrents that he blinked.

Proxima held herself away from her parents, her arms folded in front of her.

If he wasn't mistaken, her green eyes were shining with tears. He had rarely seen her cry in the time they'd been together.

A time that had been all too short. He regretted the way he'd behaved out of concern for her but limiting nonetheless.

Too late now.

"The planet is off-limits." Her father's implacable voice rang through the spaceport.

Roark cleared his throat, trying and failing to catch Proxima's attention. "Then the wormhole should have been guarded, but we met no resistance. Helio Aralis, she's your daughter." *Why aren't you protecting her?*

Helio inclined his head. "That's why you were allowed to land. That doesn't mean you'll be permitted to stay."

At a nod from Helio, the robot moved in front of him, a decades-old ray gun in its hand.

Roark shook his head and stayed in place. "You can't arrest me. The rules of bounty hunters are the same throughout the galaxy. Since you joined the galactic government, you are subject to their laws."

Helio gave Roark a measured glance before fixing on his daughter. Her brown hair was flattened from the space helmet, but her slender form was as appealing as it had ever been.

Some women couldn't be forgotten.

"As are you. We have to sort this out. Let's call it a diplomatic visit. Come."

When the robot waved the gun, Roark had no choice but to follow.

CHAPTER
TWO

S he was shown to her old room, which was much the same, though they'd cleared out her personal items and turned it into guest quarters. Sadness filled her as she surveyed the empty walls and the top of the dresser where her speeder-flying trophies used to be. She was a stranger in her own home.

Proxima admitted she'd expected her parents to shield her from the situation with Valinot. Despite the fact that she had left, driven by a need to learn more about the world beyond theirs, she'd hoped that they would welcome her back. At the time she had felt that she'd had to do it. On Oradon she was never going to be anything but their daughter. Now she'd returned, like that old Terra story about the son coming home, but they weren't happy to see her. Proxima had to admit it stung. Their shared meaningful glances suggested secrets, but what they were hiding, she couldn't fathom. They'd often been administrators first and her parents second.

Then Roark had landed and she'd run out of time to sort it out.

As for Roark, she expected that time would have loosened

his effect on her but no luck. Their encounter at the spaceport had shown him to be as quick-witted, determined, and gorgeous as the day she'd exited his life.

You're special to me, I hope you know that.

His words had echoed a thousand times in her mind after she'd run, but at the time she'd done what she thought was right. Roark had tried to stop her from taking risks, and in their last, great fight he'd felt just like her parents. She was never going to be free if she stayed, so she left before she could change her mind.

Now she wasn't sure she'd made the right choice—either time. She'd been careless with many people's feelings.

I've never met anyone like you. She'd said that to him shortly after they met, and it remained true to this day, despite her actions. The galaxy was populated by billions of people, yet there was only one Roark.

She'd realized that too late when she had gone to the next planet. Prince Valinot had seemed all right, until she understood that accepting the invitation to his yacht had been an agreement to be his lover on that planet. She hadn't been ready to move on, but even if she was, Valinot wasn't her type. He was arrogant, greedy, and only wanted her to be a trophy on his arm, part of his pack of women. She'd run as soon as she realized her mistake, expecting him to let her go as her parents and Roark had done, but instead he'd sent men to bring her back. When that failed, he'd issued the bounty, coupled with false accusations of theft to make it stick. As Roark said, she was in a galaxy's worth of trouble.

"Proxima, come at once." Her father's summons through the intercom was a command not a request. Things hadn't changed.

Proxima had been here a thousand times. She went to the large hall where meetings were conducted. She'd expected the sitting area her mother preferred, but this was more formal, as if she were an emissary from a faraway land. She was a stranger in her former home, the place no longer familiar.

Roark stood as tall and proud as he ever had, a handsome vision with black hair and eyes as piercing as any giant blue sun. His body was clothed in standard-issue galactic wear, simple tan pants with a blue shirt that clung to his hard muscles. The reminder of what she'd tossed away struck her like a blow.

Their deputy head, Iargio, was also there, dressed in the dark violet Oradon uniform that marked him as a member of the government. This place was remote enough that the trends that swept the universe didn't make it here. Her parents were elected officials, but after two decades as the heads of the planet they were in place for life unless they chose to step down. Helio was the face of the couple and good with public speaking, but Yarra was the brains.

"We've been made aware of the circumstances surrounding your arrival, and what led you here. To complicate matters, we've been informed that the man who issued the bounty, Prince Valinot Quensid Zandibar of Nisitritius will be here in a day or two," Helio said. "It couldn't come at a worse time. We are in the middle of... Well, never mind that. You've caused a lot of trouble, Proxima."

"How did he know we were here?" Proxima's gaze slid to Roark, whose face was a mask of confusion. The concern in his eyes made fresh tears spring to hers. She blinked them away. *No weakness, Proxima. You did what you did for a reason. He tried to hold you back—to limit you.*

Nonetheless, she couldn't help her shiver of awareness at the sight of Roark. He was the standard to which she held all men, one they always failed to meet.

"I sent him a transmission that I was on your trail but didn't provide coordinates." Roark cursed under his breath, slamming one fist into another. "Other than my single message, I haven't been in contact. I don't know how he found us."

Her mother took the information from Iargio and studied it. "He must have had you tracked."

Roark clenched his teeth, a muscle jumping in the back of his jaw with the determination she loved, except when he'd tried to use it to protect her. That's what he called it. Somehow, it only made him more handsome. "I learned of the bounty when I was on Wilox-5 and informed Valinot I was in pursuit. He could have had a maintenance worker put a tracer on my ship." The curse he swore this time was one she'd never heard. Roark had picked up some new vocabulary.

Yarra Aralis was as straight as any tree of the famous "vertical trees" on Idamantia. Her mother's face was pale, but the minute movement of her toes inside her shoes told the real story.

"You have no idea what you've done, but there's nothing we can do about that now."

"I…" Roark started to speak and then stopped.

She would have given a lot to learn what he'd been about to say, but she'd lost that right when she left him. Maybe they could have been friends, in time, but she'd forfeited that right when she'd taken off rather than let him stop her.

Her father gestured to the blinking message light. "There's much we need to discuss, but that will have to wait. The Nisitritius prince is coming and expects us to hand you over. I suspect he doesn't understand our relationship." Helio pierced Roark with a laser focus that she knew all too well. "Our arrangement with the galactic government is in flux, and this puts it all at risk. Roark Pyfalihon, the prince is coming to our planet because of you, and you are going to stop him. I don't care how."

Proxima's gaze went to Roark's piercing blue eyes with a sinking feeling in her gut. Her parents couldn't protect her and after the way she'd left Roark, he wouldn't want to.

She had to figure out how to save herself.

Roark needed a plan to get Proxima out of this—and fast.

He found a door leading to an inner courtyard, a patch of cultivated land open to the sky. Being outdoors always helped him think. He had to step down to enter the garden area, the unfamiliar scents nonetheless pleasant. Under different circumstances, the combination of structure and green space would have appealed to his senses. Plant life was in abundance here, with thick trees and vines dangling over them, and ground cover that bloomed red and violet—the same dark purple that showed in the garments the Oradonians seemed to favor. He'd never seen Proxima in that color.

A cough alerted him that he wasn't alone.

"Who's there?" He gazed at the dim sky, still clear of princely cruisers—but wouldn't be for long. Most planets were a bustle of ground and air activity and this quiet place filled him with a sort of serenity he rarely felt.

Too bad it wouldn't last.

"It's me. I'm over here." Proxima's voice came from behind a brown-and-purple tree with thick branches and few leaves.

Roark found her sitting on a stone bench. Her legs were stretched out in front of her, her face tilted to the orange dwarf that was their planet's sun. He'd thought the right thing to do was to be the one to bring her in, but now that he was face-to-face with her, Roark couldn't bear the idea of letting her go again.

His body tightened at the sight of her slender form and heart-shaped face. Roark didn't know if she was pretty by the standards of this planet or not, but Proxima had always been gorgeous to him. As he watched, she opened her eyes and met his gaze.

He cleared his throat and gestured to the space around them. "This is nice."

Her chuckle was harsh and dry, and devoid of mirth. "This was my favorite space when I lived here. I figured I would take advantage of it before Valinot gets here and turns my life upside down."

Roark sat next to her, the warmth of her skin rivaling the orange sun so large in the sky. "It's not over yet. I'm still thinking of a strategy. Even if your parents hadn't asked me to, I would. It's why I chased you in the first place. I wanted to be the one to handle this."

She grimaced and gazed into the sky. "Did you? I'm not sure this is how I would define handling it. Funny when things turn upside down, home is the place I think of. I thought I'd be safe here, but my parents are being strange. It's a miracle they didn't turn both of us back to the wormhole."

He looked up. The clouds were tinted orange by the sun, their fluffy forms familiar to him. All habitable planets got rainfall, and Oradon was no different.

His gaze shifted back to her and she closed her eyes, weariness showing on her face. He wanted to put his hand over hers and tell her things were going to be all right.

"They may still be angry you took off." He blurted out the words before he could stop himself. The pain of her leaving still burned like a knife in his guts. "You told me you'd fled from home to find your own way, but I thought things were different —that we were, anyway. I never imagined you'd go the way you did."

The turmoil on her face unnerved him. She met his gaze with those lovely green eyes before shuttering her expression again. "Were you surprised? We were so good at first, but then you tried to tell me I shouldn't go with you on bounty runs or try them myself. That that life was too dangerous. I left here because I was never going to be anyone other than my parents' daughter, and if I stayed, I was only going to be your…whatever I was. I wanted to be more and not just be defined by my relationship to someone else." She let out a frustrated sigh. "I didn't think you'd understand."

Nothing he could say seemed adequate. So many regrets. Roark gazed down at his hands, discarding a thousand things before he spoke again. "I was scared for you because I cared and couldn't bear it if something happened. I'm sorry. I should have listened better. But...you just left. I guess I should have expected it, but I didn't. I thought you'd stay and fight for yourself and for us. We'll never know what might have happened if you'd stayed."

She turned away from him and fixed her attention on the horizon. "Maybe you're right. No way to know now. I thought I'd be safe on Oradon, but I was wrong. I never believed Valinot would chase me or lie to get me back. All my plans ended up in ruins, and I came home, in much worse shape than when I left." She closed her eyes and turned her face to the sun.

The sight of her filled him with the sort of longing that he'd always felt in Proxima's presence. His eyes lingered over her features, refamiliarizing himself with the curves and angles he'd never forgotten. "If that's how you feel, why did you come back here?"

Her eyes were haunted, and Roark bit back a cry.

"Where else was I going to go?"

"I suppose you're right. I thought... Never mind. How did you end up there?" He didn't dare dwell on the open wound that was her leaving. Not right now.

Her mouth tightened before she picked up her narrative. "When I took off, I leveraged my few credits to go through the wormhole to Nisitritius. I'd heard about their famous cobalt beaches and figured I could drown my sorrows there. Valinot was there that day, moored nearby on his yacht. The sounds of the party reached me from the bar and when he invited me aboard, I figured why not. I didn't realize that on his planet such an invitation meant I'd agreed to be his concubine. On Oradon we have no such expectations. I was foolish not to realize that other planets weren't the same way."

Roark studied her profile, and the pain etched on her heart-shaped face. The knowledge that she hadn't gone to another man as soon as she'd left him lessened the ache in the center of his chest.

He sorted through her words in his mind. "No civilized planet does. Those that join the galactic government have to agree to follow their laws. Nobody on Valinot's planet can be forced into sexual servitude anymore."

Even as she turned to him, a hint of tears shining in her eyes, Roark realized how ridiculous his words were. Lots of things happened that the authorities had no clue about.

"Weren't you the one who told me that the universe was a big place? That I needed to learn how things worked beyond a single planet around a tiny dwarf sun and a sky empty of stars? That I needed to be more careful in the big, bad universe. You remember that, don't you?"

He closed his eyes, pain surging through him. "I do. I've regretted those words every second, every day, since you left."

Proxima bit her trembling lower lip, the movement searing through him. "You were right. Not every planet is like here. I was naïve when I left and was no better when I met the prince. When Valinot realized that I wasn't going to give in, he got mean. I was his, he said, and he had a right to me. I got out before the next day dawned. I didn't think he would chase me—plenty of women vie for his attention—but he did. Through the bounty."

"He says you stole a valuable family jewel and has the witnesses to prove it." Ashes of bitter anger made it difficult for Roark to swallow.

Her green gaze slid away and Roark cursed under his breath.

"You know me better than that." She paused. "I thought you did."

When Roark reached for her hand, he was relieved she allowed him to touch her, turning her palm to meet his. After the way they had ended, he hadn't been sure what she would do. "Of course. Money never drove you. That's why I didn't believe you stole from Valinot. That's why I acted. If someone had to bring you in, I was going to be damned sure I was that man. Someone had to save you."

Her silence was more eloquent than any words. Then she closed her eyes and drew in a breath. "The only person who can save me is myself. What a mess. I wanted to do things on my own and prove I was more than just the daughter of Helios and Yarra Aralis. So much for that. Roark, I can't go back there. He's just spoiled and arrogant, wanting someone he can't have. Even if he weren't, I…wasn't ready. Not then"—she turned away and said the last words so low he had to strain to hear them—"maybe not ever."

His breath caught at the implications of her words.

Before he could speak, an alarm blared one blast, then two, the noise rocketing through his skull.

Proxima leaped to her feet, her eyes wild, her head turning this way and that as though searching for an intruder.

Roark surged to his feet. "What…?" he started to ask, but she shouted something inarticulate and ran. Not in the direction he had come from but toward a back door he hadn't seen until now. He sprinted after her, closing the gap in several long strides.

"That's the alarm for extreme danger," she cried when he caught up to her. "It has to be Valinot. He's here already."

Roark paled. His time had just run out.

CHAPTER
THREE

Proxima ran for the little-used service door, sorting through options, Roark hot on her heels. She pushed through the door and plunged to the other side.

"Where are we going?" Roark shouted as the metal door clanged shut behind them.

They were in a back corridor of the complex, one she'd played in a hundred times growing up. The alarm was still shrieking here but muted, the sound manageable.

She tugged her device from her pocket and checked it. A message lit up the screen, confirming what she'd feared. "We can't stay here. It's too open. My parents say that Valinot's shuttle has landed and his cruiser is in orbit. He's demanding to speak to the authorities here. I don't think he is aware of my connection to them. That may be an advantage."

Roark shook his head, raking his hand through his shoulder-length hair. "Doesn't Oradon have weapons? A defense against intruders? Why did they let him land?"

She stared at him, her concentration scrambled by the siren. "Probably for the same reason they let you—and apparently me. We are members of the galactic government now and denying a prince could cause trouble. Better to let him in and deal with him on our turf. I may have left years ago, but I still know my parents."

He clenched his teeth, a muscle jumping in his jaw. "What do you want to do?"

She checked her device again. "Mom says to get away, out of sight, and to leave Valinot to them. She can focus better if she knows I'm out of harm's way."

Roark's brows drew together. "We can fight."

She shook her head. "Once upon a time, my mother told me that sometimes the best defense is not to give the appearance of fighting. Perhaps I learned that lesson too well. She and Dad want us away."

She tried to remember the layout of the planet and their possible options and grimaced when it didn't come to mind. She'd been gone too long.

He inclined his head, though judging by his flared nostrils and clenched fists, Roark wasn't happy about the order.

"Where do we go? You're the native."

Proxima gestured to the end of the hall and a meeting room there. She prayed that the teleporter the galactic government had set up was still there. It had been old when she left but still functional. "Unless things have changed, when I had to get some peace, I would jump to the second continent, then the far north. From there I used to go back to the second continent and the south, but we will go back to the spaceport. With Valinot here, we should make a run for it. We might be able to confuse him and get away in open space. It's all I have right now."

"It will have to do." He waved a hand and nodded for her to lead the way.

The room was empty when they rushed inside, the teleporter that stood in the corner blinking green showed its working condition. The teleporters in more modern planets had multicolored blinking lights around the circle to indicate where to step, but the ones on Oradon had simple white lights surrounding the area.

When they reached the teleporter she programmed it to Rigin, the second continent. Roark positioned his feet on the clear surface on the floor and held out his hand to her. Proxima programmed a fifteen-second delay and joined him, sliding her hand into his. The noise vanished as they went through to the simple pad in one of her parents' diplomatic offices. She fed the machine the coordinates to jump to the northern pole. If Valinot found the first transporter he'd be able to track her location, but she couldn't help that. Her multiple jumps were designed to confuse or at least delay. She had to pray that it worked—for long enough.

They jumped to the remote outpost at their northern pole. She took a breath and oriented herself. The cold pierced this unmanned location and their breath came out in white puffs. They weren't dressed for this place.

They weren't dressed for flight either, but that no longer mattered.

Proxima checked her device between jumps. Another message blinked on her machine and she scanned the words, a tiny smile tugging at her lips.

"My parents had your ship searched when we got here and found the tracker Valinot had installed in your cargo hold. It's been removed, so he will have no way to find us if—when—we get away. Or we could take my ship."

He shook his head. "I'm faster, as you discovered. We'll go in mine."

"You're right, even if I hate to admit it. The next jump is to the spaceport. Even though I left, Oradon is still my home. I don't want anything to happen to it or my parents. I never should have come here." She set the coordinates but didn't trigger the controls. She stared up into Roark's dark eyes and all thoughts of Valinot and the price on her head fell away. The rays of Oradon's sun glinted off the teleporter pad, lighting him with an orange glow.

Or perhaps that was the fire inside him, one she'd missed more than she'd been willing to admit. A small shift and her lips would touch his. The remembered feel of their fullness, and the way his breath caught when they touched, had never left her.

"I understand why you did. There's so much to say. So much I wish I'd done differently."

Proxima almost closed the gap between them, though that was foolish. She'd dreamed of touching him again and feeling his warm body under her hands. Warmth skittered through her, despite the chill in the air.

When she didn't move forward or back, Roark let out a breath and tilted his head to the teleporter controls.

"Me, too. Then this never would have happened."

"We'll find a way to make it right." He put his arm around her waist, anchoring them together.

Proxima's hand hovered over the control before she pressed the button.

———

Roark exited the teleporter with his weapon drawn, ready to fight. He had been prepared for anything on the conclusion of their series of jumps but hadn't dared hope for what he saw when they got to the spaceport.

He'd been expecting Valinot to have posted a sentinel but couldn't see any guards or even robots. The only machines that were present were spaceships, the prince's planetary shuttle now among them. The marks to indicate where other ships had come and gone were the only reminder that this was a spaceport. Valinot must be counting on the tracker in his ship.

He hoped Proxima's parents were correct in thinking there was only the one.

Valinot's nearby shuttle spelled danger better than any words could. It would be a matter of minutes, or less, before someone on that ship was alerted to their presence.

"We have to move before Valinot learns we're here." He waited for what might have been an eternity until Proxima gestured to his craft waiting on the spaceport with its ramp down.

He hadn't left it that way, primed and ready for takeoff. If he needed a sign that this was what her parents wanted them to do, the state of his ship told him more than any transmission could.

"Let's go."

They raced for his ship, Roark's heart pounding so loud he couldn't hear the hum of the spaceport. The fighter in him rebelled at the idea of leaving. Roark's nature wasn't to run but to defend what he cared most about in the world—any world.

He dared hope they would get to his craft unseen, but as they neared, a man stepped from behind Proxima's ship and fired at them. The shots hit his landing gear in a shower of sparks. Proxima let out a cry that sounded somewhere between a yelp and a battle whoop. They reached the ramp and Roark pushed her up before slamming his fist on the button to close it. The man fired again as the ramp retracted. Roark waited as it closed to push him back if he tried to get on board.

Another shot slammed into the door before the man ducked behind a wall as though expecting return fire. Roark cursed, praying the shots hadn't damaged his gear. He joined Proxima in the cockpit, throwing himself into the pilot's seat without buckling in. Roark pushed the controls forward, sending Proxima hurtling backward where she struck the far side with a loud *thwack*.

"Sorry." His ship wobbled at the fast ascent, arcing up as it took off with the man once again firing at them. Their enemy had been shielded, his face covered by a helmet that suggested he needed additional air to function in this environment.

Or perhaps that was a good disguise, giving Roark no way to identify his assailant.

Proxima scrambled to her feet as the ship whined at the quick exit. His craft wasn't designed for this sort of thing, but he'd pushed the machine before and it hadn't failed him. Yet. It may not be Valinot's sleek modern spaceship, but it got the job done.

"We need a plan. Valinot's cruiser will be waiting for us in orbit."

Roark nodded and punched more buttons. The ship increased speed, clearing the trees and heading for the atmosphere as he sorted through what options they had. Grim and grimmer, and nothing much in between.

"He won't get you, not while you're with me." Roark hadn't yet come up with ideas, but he didn't tell her that.

She shifted in the copilot's seat as the ship went upward. They'd done pleasure jaunts several times in between bounties and the sight of her in that familiar spot made his heart ache.

"Don't say something you can't back up. I would rather deal with reality than false promises. We're in a heck of a mess because of me."

He punched the accelerator, and they shot up, gaining momentum with every passing second. If he was lucky, they could elude Valinot's ship and get lost in the darkness of this planet while they went for the wormhole. Once he realized they were gone, Valinot could use his greater speed to either overtake them or wait by the portal for them to arrive. They had few options, none of them good.

"It's because of Valinot. Leave it to me."

She clenched her jaw as she scanned the display of his ship. "No, we're in it together. I helped with the strategy when you took in that guy on the 2-G planet. Remember?"

"Got it. I'm open to ideas. What do you have?"

He steadied the ship and scanned the horizon for lurking

vessels. The sky was currently clear but wouldn't stay that way for long.

———

Proxima whistled when she saw Valinot's new cruiser in orbit around Oradon. Examining the slick interplanetary vessel was forcing her to face her fears up close. Once the cruiser was in pursuit, they couldn't outrun it in Roark's ship.

The ship gleamed platinum in the orange sunshine. If she had to guess, she'd say it was made of the finest rare metal from the asteroid belt of Kumpier. She was never going to own one like it —and was okay with that. Even if she'd given in to Valinot's claim, Proxima wouldn't have enjoyed it. To her, Nisitritius looked like an expensive prison.

If Valinot expected her to be dazzled by the display, he had misjudged her. He could chase her around the galaxy and put a price on her head, but she would never be his.

Her heart was already claimed.

"I've got a thousand ideas but nothing coherent."

Roark had a death grip on the controls as they passed the bigger, faster craft. For the moment it was still but that could change in a second.

"Same here. I've sorted through strategies in my mind, and none of them work in this emptiness. I'm used to crowded space, and this is new. I need more time."

She gazed out at the inky blackness. If not for their sun, this would be as dark as the darkest night. Darker, because night showed stars, but they had no neighbors. She hadn't realized until she left the planet how isolated their small world was.

"Time is something we don't have." She couldn't help the despair that sank through her.

The oncoming ship loomed in the distance, and then the nose began turning toward them.

167

"If you know anything about this system I don't, now's the time." Roark adjusted the controls before his eyes found hers.

"Not a thing. We didn't even have space flight until the galactic government came upon us, and I left not long after. I wish I'd never met Valinot." *I should never have left you.* She hadn't outrun her problems by leaving Oradon or by leaving Roark. She'd just postponed them, and created a new set that had led them here where they both might die because of her.

"Me, too. Strap in. I'm going to do some evasion tricks. It will get bumpy. I'm happy that nobody has yet figured out how to make tractor beams work on ships this big. Regardless, I don't know what kind of long-range weapons he has, but I'm going to need all the skill I have to evade him."

"Like how we met on Costim where you did those dozen loop the loops?" Despite herself, a memory triggered a ghost of a smile. "I couldn't believe you landed on that tiny platform. It didn't look big enough for even one craft. But you won that bet. I will never forget that day."

He was focused on the display but a quick flash of teeth was his answer. "That was a good time. I loved the way you looked at me when I claimed the prize." He gave her a quick glance, his hair falling over his forehead.

Memory slammed into her of their first meeting and the night afterward.

She'd run rather than work through their relationship. Regret surged through her, of everything she'd thrown away because of fear.

"Strap in." He turned away, focusing on the controls.

She secured herself to the seat with the harness and waved at the display in front of them. "I can handle whatever you've got."

Though he kept his profile to her, she saw the movement of his lips upward at her words. "I'm counting on that. Hang on."

CHAPTER
FOUR

They weren't going to make it.

Roark wished he could use the maneuvers he'd learned from that renegade in Alliante—a polar orbit change that would confuse the larger system's tracking systems. After that was the shadow maneuver, trailing one of the larger asteroids in the nearby belt. Then asteroid field evasion, actually entering the field. But this system was as devoid of asteroids as stars, and he had nothing to hide behind or use as a shield. The heavy atmosphere soldiers on Wotang had taught him the trick of using a decoy, a sort of mirror ship to fool the enemy into thinking they were in two places at once, but in this barren system, that ruse would be easily discovered.

The pilot on this cruiser made sport of his attempts to dodge, keeping pace with them at every turn. He didn't have the fuel to vanish into the darkness and wait them out. Going back to the planet didn't make sense, either. They had to make a run for the wormhole and take their chances in more familiar territory.

That was likely to make things worse. Here the situation was contained, but bounty hunters would be on her tail when they got to regular space. Valinot had shown he would stop at nothing to get to Proxima. His invasion of Oradon proved that.

"Maybe if we dodge around them, they won't be expecting it. Or under?"

Proxima's voice trailed off and she gazed into the darkness, helplessness etched in the slump of her shoulders. He didn't have any maneuvers in the emptiness of this solar system. He couldn't hide behind freighters or confuse the computers with false information. Just his ship against Valinot's, and they had no chance.

He was sure they were supposed to notice the weapons glowing on the underside—a clear warning. They could blast Roark and Proxima into so many small pieces they wouldn't even impact on the planet's surface. Valinot might be desperate enough to do that—Roark couldn't be sure. He might think that if he couldn't have Proxima, nobody could.

"This is my fault." Roark grimaced, his lips flattening. "I led him to Oradon. You would have been safe here without me. I got you into this."

She reached over and touched his arm. Her face was lit by the displays of his ship and the sun on their right. She had never been more beautiful or the situation more tragic. "Afraid that's all me."

"Valinot is to blame."

"If only I'd never gone to his planet."

"Yeah, I wish that, too." He focused on the ship in the distance. It was gaining and soon would be close enough to fire on them. Roark had no weapons, no method of defense.

He had an idea of how to solve this, but if he did it, Proxima would never forgive him.

Valinot would never give up until he got her. Roark's left hand hovered over the emergency beacon. Once he did this, everything would change forever. He didn't think she'd understand his reasoning, since Valinot would still have her for a while. Any chance of reconciliation would be destroyed, but she would be alive.

Before he could consider the folly of what he was doing, Roark leveled the ship out and flicked the com on.

Proxima gave him a questioning glance and her face froze.

No time to be a coward. He had no alternative. Better this than to see her light destroyed forever. He'd pay the price.

"Don't fire. We won't run anymore. We…"

The word *surrender* stuck in his throat.

———

"No!" Proxima's shout cut off Roark's words before he could complete the sentence. She had trusted him, and Roark was betraying her.

His fists tensed on the console. "We're trapped. We have nowhere left to run and nowhere to hide in this system."

Proxima yanked his hand away from the button before he could finish what he had begun to say. She couldn't believe Roark was doing this. She'd tried to become her own woman and all it got her was this—betrayal at the hands of the man who had once meant everything. If she didn't stop him, Roark was going to turn her over to Valinot. She would be sent to Nisitritius where she would be imprisoned until she agreed to whatever he wanted.

"Then we fight." She pointed to the ship in front of them.

His face and body tightened and he shook his head. "Fight with what? Look at that ship, Proxima. Their weapons are ten times more powerful than anything I can devise. You could die. I can't risk it."

Proxima grabbed for the accelerator. "This is my choice. Stop trying to protect me."

He shot her a quick glance. "If we turn you over to Valinot, we can free you using legal means."

Her hand clenched his. "That could take years. No way. This is what I want. We fight."

Before she could shove the lever forward, the screen in front of them flickered. Something huge swam into view behind Valinot's cruiser.

She gave Roark a puzzled glance. "What's wrong with your displays?"

"Nothing." His hand eased back from the lever, his attention riveted to the screen. "I had the ship serviced right before I took off. You know, when they installed the tracker. The thing out there...it's a vessel...but that's not possible. It's larger than anything I've ever seen. Or heard of."

The ship was as black as night and would have been invisible except for the opening that showed the manmade light of the galactic starship. It had to be an official craft, though she'd never seen one that big.

His com blared, crackling to life. They both jumped at the static.

"Roark Pyfalihon and Proxima Aralis, this is Qin, commander of the Sirpinme ship of the galactic government. You are under our authority. We are taking you back to Oradon."

Roark coughed, his face reddening. "How do we know you're who you say you are?"

The large ship loomed behind Valinot's cruiser like a massive bird of prey. If he wasn't mistaken, the wheeze that came through his speakers might have been this unseen commander laughing. "Credentials can be sorted out when we land."

His console lights flickered and moved, an indication that this Qin would override Roark's controls if necessary. If they needed proof that this giant craft was who they said they were, they had it. Two ships attached themselves to Valinot's cruiser on either side, urging it forward.

Proxima settled back in her seat as Roark grimaced but punched in the coordinates to return to the planet they had just left. She longed to shout at him that she had trusted him but stilled her words. She wouldn't fight with him, because she had nothing to say.

A handful of minutes ago, he was going to hand her over to Valinot and a fate worse than death. She could never forgive him.

As the sleek black ship led the way back to Oradon, Proxima readied herself for what was going to come next.

———

When they landed, Roark and Proxima followed the guards into the building they'd so recently fled from. Proxima kept away from him, her arms folded, her face set. He'd tried to talk to her, but she narrowed her eyes and turned her away.

They were taken into a room that held official banners with a seal on the floor indicating it was a place of authority. Qin was at the head of a large rectangular table with her parents on either side. Iargio was seated as well, with two robots and three galactic security men standing sentry. Proxima was seated across from Roark, and Valinot was at the other end, flanked by guards.

He didn't know how Qin and the galactic government had been there, saving him from the heartbreak of turning the love of his life over to Valinot in order to save her. Even now the reminder of what he'd almost done was a stone in Roark's gut.

Proxima gazed fixedly at the table, her long curls sweeping forward. She refused to meet his gaze.

Valinot was slumped in his chair, his frown and crossed arms showing his displeasure. The prince might have been good-looking, with symmetrical features that were accentuated by an aquiline nose, but his petulant expression made him seem like a child. The man had spent significant time and money trying to get Proxima into his clutches, and all he had to show for his efforts was the worst seat at the table.

Ship commander Qin and her parents had explained that the

galactic government had engaged Oradon in discussions for a year, negotiating to gain access to their planet and the patch of the universe around them.

Oradon had been overlooked for decades even after they had been discovered, but this area of empty space had caught the attention of the new galactic council. This lonely planet was an anomaly in a universe of binary systems and hot stars, and their scientists wanted to know more. Opening up the area to scientists could be a boon for Oradon but would also shatter its way of life. Things would change—forever.

"Why didn't we see you when we exited the wormhole?" Proxima asked.

"We have a new type of cloaking device on our larger galactic vessels," Commander Qin replied proudly.

Roark was only half listening. He didn't care about treaties and empty systems. Just the woman he loved, who was still in a world—a galaxy—of trouble.

"You came at a delicate time, daughter, when we were finishing our negotiations." Helio gave Proxima a regretful smile. "We were worried Oradon would be passed over if we created an intergalactic incident."

"You should have told me."

Yarra inclined her head to Proxima. "We didn't have a way to get in touch with you. When you landed, things moved too quickly to stop. We had decided to tell you just before Valinot invaded. We have a lot to talk about, Proxima. About that and other things." Her mother's look was warm, and Proxima gave her a wan smile.

Qin's attention went to Proxima. "Recent events must be addressed. There's the bounty Valinot placed on Proxima as well as his unauthorized storming of Oradon. Valinot is demanding his right to return her to his planet. She is wanted there."

Roark saw her pale, though she continued to sit straight.

"Over my dead body," Roark said as Proxima glared at the galactic official, seemingly undeterred by his rank.

"This woman is a thief. I have the paperwork and the proof." Valinot reached inside his tunic and started to extend the sheaf but subsided when the men behind him slammed their hands on his shoulders.

One took the papers from his hands and handed them to Qin.

He studied the documents, a frown creasing his forehead. "Proxima, what do you have to say to these allegations?"

"I didn't steal anything," she said defiantly. "Valinot believes I should be his because I accepted an invitation onto his yacht. I didn't know at the time I was agreeing to be his concubine. When I ran away, he made up the story about the jewel to put a bounty on my head."

"That is untrue! You stole the jewel from my yacht." Valinot's face was beginning to turn an angry shade of red.

Qin held up his hand. He stood and returned the papers to Valinot. "Prince Valinot Quensid Zandibar, you have meddled in things you don't understand. I am not unfamiliar with the way you flout our laws. You have simply been too small for us to care. Nonetheless, these are serious accusations. The galactic government is committed to justice for all of its citizens."

Valinot both sputtered and reddened at Qin's words. Roark's heart sank. Despite everything, they were going to lose this fight.

Qin's gaze rested on Proxima, who met his dark eyes without blinking. Then he focused on Valinot, whose flush deepened, and he turned his attention away from the commander.

"Be sure you want to pursue this, prince. We can investigate and would do so *very* thoroughly. We would leave nothing unexplored, on your ship and your planet. Nothing. Prince Valinot, are you sure about this course of action? Once the ships are in the air, they cannot be called back."

If he wasn't mistaken, Helio Aralis let out a small, quickly muffled chuckle.

Valinot shifted in his chair and waved a hand at Proxima. That hand was shaking.

"Well, I… It's possible I may have been…mistaken…"

Proxima got to her feet, the scrape of her chair loud in the room, and pointed a finger at Valinot. "Say the words. Admit I didn't do anything."

Valinot's throat clearing was loud in the room. "I…"

Commander Qin's focus stayed on Valinot.

"Easy, Proxie. You were never cut out for diplomacy. Prince Valinot, renounce your bounty and release our daughter. As the governmental body on this planet, we demand it." Yarra Aralis' voice rang through the room.

If ill grace was a slouched prince, Valinot would define it. "I have no wish to cause an interstellar incident. I will rescind the bounty."

"With prejudice." Qin's words were curt, the syllables clipped. "You will not be able to activate it again. Proxima Aralis will not be subject to your whims a second time."

Valinot jumped up, despite the men close by. "That's not fair."

Proxima faced him, fury snapping in her eyes. "Fair is letting me go. I will never be yours or anyone's." She met Roark's eyes and the shadowed pain on her face made him want to cry out.

"Unless you're planning on fighting the galactic council, you will stop this ridiculous behavior." Qin pierced Valinot with a glare that had all the weight of his authority behind him. "I am confident that if I dig, I can find enough to charge you with more crimes than you can imagine. You are fortunate to escape so lightly. Take your men and your ships and leave here at once."

Roark fought not to smile at the stricken expression on Valinot's face. He gave the prince a triumphant grin, and Valinot's eyes narrowed.

Valinot turned as pale as the white trees on Tau-a-rara. "I…."

Qin's gaze was as implacable as the ship he commanded.

"By my authority, you are banished from this planet and this solar system. You cannot contact Proxima again or attempt to capture her. Your credentials will be posted at the wormhole and you will not be given access a second time. Leave at once. Do I make myself clear?"

Qin waved to one of the guards.

Valinot went without causing more trouble, perhaps understanding that he couldn't win. He did cast a final, plaintive look Proxima's direction, but she averted her eyes.

The crisis, this part of it anyway, was over.

When the prince and his retinue had left, Commander Qin met Proxima's parents' gazes. "I trust that is sufficient."

Helio inclined his head to the commander. "It is. Thank you for your intervention. Both here and up there."

"Noted. Now that that distraction is out of the way, do we have any other matters before we get back to the negotiations?"

Qin's voice was smooth, but there might have been some impatience there.

"I can go," Proxima said, gesturing to the door. "Thank you for everything you did."

"We need to talk, but for now, that would be best." Her father gave her a gentle smile that showed Roark more than words his affection for his daughter. "Proxima, it's good to have you home."

She made a noise that might have been a small sob. "I'll get out of your way."

"Never in the way, but we should sort things out when we have more time." Yarra went to Proxima and, to Roark's surprise, embraced her. Proxima leaned her head against her mother's shoulder before stepping back. She gave a small nod and headed for the door.

Roark turned to Proxima as she passed him, but she still wasn't meeting his gaze.

He couldn't decide if she would allow him an opportunity to

explain or if he would be escorted back to the wormhole and out of her life.

Roark pushed back and followed Proxima.

He'd be damned if he let her throw him out without a fight.

———

The crisis was over. She thought she'd be more relieved.

Roark's footsteps followed her, and she could feel his eyes boring into the back of her skull. Her head was in a whirl. She trod down the hallway and entered the sitting room her mother favored for quiet meetings.

This place was designed to invite people to sit down, with its matching sofas and soft lighting. Proxima stayed on her feet, pivoting to face Roark. He was less than a foot away, his tall body tense, his fists clenched.

"How could you try to give me to Valinot? What were you thinking?"

Roark swallowed, his throat working. He reached out a hand but then let it drop. "I had to do something so I could keep you safe until I found a way to get you out of this."

The words were like a knife, pain blooming in her chest. She raised herself to her full height, meeting his gaze without disguising the anger—and hurt. "Really? By surrendering me to...him? Roark, you know me better than that."

The expression on his face was regret mixed with pain that ran so deep she also halted in place. "I didn't think I had a choice. His ship could blast us out of the sky. You would at least have been alive if you were with him. You are all that matters to me. I would have figured something out, used the law, but I couldn't do that with you dead."

"You didn't trust me. Just like before."

He closed his eyes, his brows drawing together and his lips twisting. When he opened them again, the remorse was back, so thick and raw that she almost went to him. "Valinot was desperate and that made him dangerous. When there's life, there's hope. I couldn't bear to lose you forever. I'm sorry."

"Are you?" A cascade of emotions surged through her, the anger starting to fade at his clear pain.

"I didn't think we had a chance of escape. All I could think about was seeing you safe. That was a mistake. I can't tell you what to do or make decisions for you. I should have learned better than that." He paused and raked a hand through his hair. "It's just that I love you so much I can't bear to think of you dead."

"You…what?"

Roark fixed his gaze on Proxima. "I love you. I've made a mess of this, right from the start. From the second I met you, you were different. I tried to protect you and that feeling. In doing so, I drove you away. You were right about what you said. Every time you put yourself in danger, my heart stopped. Now I see that in order for you to be, well, you, I have to stop trying to manage you. When you ran, you created a hole in my life the size of the Titini nebula. Please don't leave again. We can make it work. Things will change, I promise. I love you, Proxima, more than anything in universe."

Proxima's breath caught in her throat. All her choices, all her past mistakes, were hanging in the balance. This man was the most important thing in the universe to her. She should never have walked away. She should have stayed and told him what she needed. Instead, she'd taken off, driven by old demons and old wounds.

Fortunately, running from him was one mistake she didn't have to live with.

―――

Deep fear skittered through Roark. He'd laid his heart out and Proxima hadn't moved. He'd tried to hold on to her too hard and instead she slipped away, this time forever.

"You still love me? Despite it all?" She moved to stand in front of him, less than a handspan away.

Roark waited until she was close enough to touch, hope beating in his chest. "More than the universe."

Her green gaze caught and held his. "That's a big place."

"So is my love for you. I would have followed you to the biggest blue stars and the coldest depths of space."

She held her hands out and he clasped them, pulling them to his chest. The look in her eyes took his breath away.

"I knew when I left that I'd made a mistake. It's always been you, Roark, even when I didn't let myself believe it. I never stopped loving you. If you love me, let me be who I am. We'll grow together, okay? Just don't ever let me go again. Promise."

He squeezed her fingers and raised her hand to his lips.

"All of it. I promise."

She put her hands on his waist and he pulled her to him. Proxima closed her eyes and offered her lips to his. Roark wasted no time in taking the unspoken invitation to hold the woman he loved. Then he kissed her, the remembered feel of her mouth against his sending his pulse racing. She was warm and soft, her supple body pressing into his. He took his time, moving his hands over her back as his lips slid over hers, until she let a small sigh and deepened the kiss.

At long last, he was home.

———

Roark patted the gleaming ship. The new, state-of-the-art vessel had been supplied by the galactic government, as part of their agreement with Oradon. Helio said that if she and Roark were going to fly around the galaxy, they would do it with the best equipment. They could go anywhere the wormholes took them and had a homing beacon in case of trouble. They even had cloaking, in case they encountered Valinot or anyone like him.

She couldn't be sure that the thwarted prince wouldn't try again. Valinot was not a man who gave up, and Qin's interdiction may fade from his memory. They would have to see. The credits that were in both of their bank accounts meant they wouldn't have to worry about money. No more bounties for Roark or either of them.

Unless they wanted them.

She cleared her throat and touched Roark's shoulder. "How can we be sure things will be different?"

He shot her a quick grin that made her heart turn over. "We'll make sure of it. You don't run and I don't tell you what to do. We learn from what happened and do better. We haven't come this far to fail now. The key is that we are committed to each other and keep communicating. We have a lot to learn about who we are, which we will do together. Besides"—he raised an eyebrow that made her insides flip over. "The best part about fighting is making up. I'm looking forward to those nights. I'll never let you go again."

She couldn't help but chuckle, delight fizzing through her veins. "We will have to ensure the making up is glorious."

His grin was sunshine and happiness. Roark leaned against the ship, still gazing at her. Her old ship had been a holdover from their less technological days. This one was so sophisticated it outclassed the most expensive ships princes could buy. They had plotted a course along the star map to their first destination, a binary star system with no habitable planets but with amazing views.

Too bad they might not see it for a while.

"I have something to say."

Roark propelled himself off the curve of the ship and studied her in faint alarm. "What is it? What's in that gorgeous head of yours?"

She thought that exploring the universe would give her everything she wanted. She'd been wrong.

"I'd like to stay on Oradon and spend time with the people I love." She gave him a quick, tremulous smile. "My parents and I have a lot to work out. It's past time for me to learn how to face things and not hide from them. And I want to build something with you, here on Oradon."

He touched her hair with a gentle hand.

"I was hoping we could stay, too. This planet is part of what makes you who you are, and I want to learn more. We need a base to operate from, and this is as good as any. Better, because it's the planet you call home. You're safer here. Valinot can't get to you so easily."

She shook her head and waved a finger at him. "I don't need protecting, but I'll take the support." Her love cascaded over her, bigger than the stars, and stronger than any black hole. She leaned over and kissed him. He held her close, resting his head against hers as awareness zinged through her. The best part was making up—as they had already discovered.

"You always have it. We will do it all, together."

"I'm so happy. I love you, Roark."

"I love you back. From here to the stars and back again."

She took in the warmth of his skin and his steady heartbeat. This was Roark, the man she loved, the only one she'd ever loved. They would work through the good times and the bad, as a team. They had a world to explore and a love to build.

Best of all, they had each other.

ABOUT CLAIRE DAVON

USA Today Bestselling author Claire Davon has written for most of her life, starting with fan fiction when she was very young. She writes across a wide range of genres, and does not consider any of it off limits. Her novels can be found in the paranormal romance and contemporary romance sections, while her short stories run the gamut. If a story calls to her, she will write it. She currently lives in Los Angeles and spends her free time writing novels and short stories, as well as doing animal rescue and enjoying the sunshine. Claire's website is www.clairedavon.com.

facebook.com/ClaireDavonindieauthor

x.com/ClaireDavon

instagram.com/clairedavon

tiktok.com/@clairedavon

TECHNICOLOR RASPBERRY

NATASHA WILCO

Heat Rating: Steamy

CHAPTER
ONE
BY NATASHA WILCO

The android memory banks were stowed away safely behind the hidden hatch of Vera's ship, and Earth was a blue marble shrinking in the viewport. Vera had managed to salvage twenty of them from the from the latest human-android scuffle. A squad of soldiers had rolled through almost thirty androids in Roswell. They were lucky those particular AIs were Asimov-aligned, or there would have been more blood and fewer bolts spread across the sand. As it was, she hadn't been able to save them all.

Vera had managed to slip in and out without being identified, and she thanked the stars for that. The *Raspberry* may be an old ship—old enough to have surpassed retro into carbon-dated—but she made up for it with anonymity and longevity. Vera just kept flying between the lines, doing what she could to help whenever it was feasible. In a few days, she would meet up with an Asimov shuttle and drop off her cargo. In the meantime, she could work on repairing the minor damage her little ship had taken.

A high-pitched beep called her to the bridge. She was hailed by an unknown ship ID. Vera debated the risk of ignoring it, considering she had just come off an illegal salvage mission. Biting her lip, she flipped the switch to open the comm channel. If she didn't answer, she'd appear suspicious.

"This is raspberry-three-alpha-hotel-nine. My vid is down, so please identify yourself."

Static crackled over the comm for a long moment before Zender's familiar voice broke through the white noise.

"Vera, what are the odds?"

A smile tugged at her lips, and her muscles began to unwind.

"Small universe! It's good to hear from you. When did you pick up the new ship?" She was cautious not to say Zender's name. The vessel was unfamiliar and human-class, so who knew if he was there alone, or even there willingly?

"My new friends here have been nice enough to get me this far, but I don't want to take them out of their way. Any chance I can hitch a ride?"

Ah, not his own transport, then. Probably not a trap, or he would have warned her in code. Still, better safe than sorry.

"Sure thing, pal. Are you equipped for safety lock protocols? My direct docking mags are on the fritz. You know how it is out here."

"They have assured me this will be no issue."

Vera let out the little breath she'd been holding.

"All good, then. Have the captain begin the linkage maneuver, and I'll see you soon. Over and out."

CHAPTER
TWO

A s he boarded the familiar ship, Zender shed the ruse of humanity along with the space suit. Because Vera hadn't wanted to risk docking with an unfamiliar vessel—and rightly so—he'd performed an EVA space walk across a tether. Hardly a noteworthy feat for an android.

He tread softly and methodically through the cluster of bubble-domed holds and engine nacelles until he found himself at the bridge. Vera was closing out the disengagement procedure to extract them from the other ship and be on their way.

She shot him a grin over her shoulder from where she was leaning over the comm station, which he noted had a fully functional vid, counter to her earlier statement. He opted not to ask why Vera hadn't wanted to be seen by the other vessel.

Her dark hair was a wild frame about her delighted face. His processors sped up as he attempted to match Vera's riotous curls to a best-fit formula, but he quickly cut the program short. Such data was pointless, so there was no purpose in collecting it except to waste energy.

"Glad to see you, Z. Gimme half a tick and we'll be light-years away. I'm heading in the direction of Mars, but where do you need me to drop you off?"

Zender tilted his head forward in regal acknowledgement. "Phobos is convenient for me. Thank you." He had a tenuous lead on the programmer he was hunting, but the next few days with Vera were preferable to playing human on the other ship. The lead was tenuous, dated, and unlikely to pay out, so he could afford the slower travel time on the *Raspberry*. "Your timing is impeccable, as always."

He allowed her to refocus on her task and turned his own attention to the rest of the hold. A number of port windows had been bolted over in temporary patches for the hull. Starglass scraps and an array of aging tools were already gathered near the wall, awaiting Vera's care. Not many models outside of the *Raspberry*-class vessels had actual windows in the hull. Most modern ships used video feeds and simulations.

"I see you've noticed my little side project." Vera joined him where he stood. When he looked at her, she made eye contact and maintained it, even as she gestured to the scattered supplies. On average, Vera made approximately 43 percent more direct eye contact than the average human. Zender had updated that spec only two months ago during their last association.

"Don't worry," she assured him when he failed to respond promptly. "We should be at Phobos in a few days, provided we have smooth sailing."

Three point six days, if his calculations were correct. Which they always were.

He stretched his mouth into Form Six to mimic her own happy face. He preferred it when she was calm and content.

Vera could be most useful when she was in the right mood.

CHAPTER
THREE

Everything would be fine. She'd be able to drop Zender off before she reached the rendezvous point with the Asimov ship, and never the twain shall intersect. Besides, what else could she do, turn Zender away? That would be a quick way to kill their cooperation. And he was too useful to do that. No, he was worth the risk.

So long as he didn't snoop in the hidey-holes, there would be no problems.

Speaking of, Zender was wandering around a little too close to the hidden hold in the wall. She cleared off a chair at the temporary worktable she'd erected in the center of the bridge dome and offered it to him.

"I have to get back to my repairs, but you're welcome to use the space. Or your usual cabin is still as you left it."

He tilted his head to the side and eyed her with curiosity. She could practically hear him crunching the numbers and hypothesizing on what had delayed her repairs when she was usually on top of things.

Vera cleared her throat. "I just haven't gotten around to it."

"I appreciate your hospitality."

"Right." She gestured to the mess of starglass shards and metal strewn about the floor. "I'll just... And you make yourself at home."

Vera plopped cross-legged onto the floor with little grace, ensconcing herself among the chaos of tools and scraps. She pulled a large mortar and pestle toward her and wrapped her legs around it. Carefully fishing through the sharp pile, Vera collected bits of starglass of similar color and set them in the Martian-red stone basin.

Once she began grinding the shards into powder, Vera snuck a glance at her passenger. Zender was sitting straight-backed in the chair, his legs shoulder-width apart and knees bent at a perfect right angle. His right hand held his opposite wrist, fingers gently kneading into the soft underside of the wrist. He was staring straight ahead with a blank expression. The only signs of life were the soft glow of his eyes and the little white lines scrolling across his pupils and irises.

Vera relaxed. That made sense. He had just come off a ship with a human crew—he may have been running the behavioral programs to help him pass.

Zender was always a bit stiff when they first met up. But then he'd retreat into his inner sanctum, process whatever data or program he needed to, and emerge as the ally she'd come to know over the past two years. Recognizable. Distinguishable from his fellow androids.

He was a Zender model android, and his physical features aligned with the November series. The chiseled bone structure was broad and sharp, with a strong, muscled body. The coloration mimicked Nordic genes. Short blond hair, just long enough to grab, and deep sea-green eyes for a highly marketable flair. The synthetic skin was pale with pink hues in the shadowed regions.

Zenders were designed for ultimate realism, which made her squirm to think about. With that understanding, every deviation of feature or unsettling behavior that dipped into the Uncanny Valley was by his own design. She wondered about that often.

Was it an unconscious symptom from being freed from the Three Laws? A conscious bid for individuality? What must it be like, to be one of seven hundred just the same? To be known and on display without permission.

If she so desired, Vera could pull specs for his model and know every intimate inch of him. His information was just *available*, to anyone who wanted to know what his body looked like. Vera had carefully refrained, despite her deep curiosity, to protect the fragile, unlikely trust they had built.

The realism of his model was *all*-encompassing, right down to the heartbeat. With one network search, she could know the liquid volume of his ersatz ejaculate. If she wanted.

But she shied away from it every time it came to mind. It made her stomach flip in both heated interest and quiet horror.

With more effort than she cared to admit, Vera tore her gaze from the handsome man in front of her and doubled her efforts in grinding the starglass to dust.

CHAPTER
FOUR

The memory download took time and made Zender vulnerable. Vera's ship was one of the few places he was confident enough in his safety to risk it.

It was freeing to be back in the black, out of range of the Network that connected all android minds. It could be comforting, to connect infinitely, to know everything about everyone all the time. No unknown variables. But that also meant that *he* was known, completely. There were no places to store private data. No processes that went unseen. No question to be asked quietly and secretly.

No room for doubt.

But here, he could be whatever he wished. No one knew him except by his own choice. The endless space—and Vera's cozy ship—had much to offer him.

The assimilation completed its run, and he blinked away the strings of code and recovered data. Zender terminated looking inward and turned his senses back outward.

And there she was. His human ally. His enemy held close.

She was bent over crimson stoneware, grinding cobalt starglass into a lovely cerulean dust. The loose curls were the color of burnt sucrose and bounced as she moved her arm to an internal beat. While her hair obscured her sandstone eyes, the pursed rosebud lips were on display and plump with blood.

No other creature would ever look like this. Vera was unique. What a curious thing to be.

Where she was flesh over organic bone, he was synthskin stretched across titanium beams. Where she was soft, he was sleek and stiff. Perhaps she could be replicated...if he collected a myriad of physical scans and massive behavioral data, justified wasting resources on a vanity project, and also convinced his faction on Earth to allow him a small batch run in fabricating an android.

But that would only mimic Vera's form—not *her*. And therein was the whole of the tragedy.

"Can you hand me that jar?"

Zender blinked once and then complied.

"Of course." He picked up one of the empty jars from the workbench he sat next to and leaned forward to offer it to her, arm outstretched to where she sat. Improper workplace seating, but that was a human for you.

Her fingers brushed his as she accepted the jar. Data flooded in. Every nanometer of contact bred a mass of ones and zeroes to describe the sensation, compiling and packaging the wave of data into a perfect coordinate hexahedron that grew with time, stretching up the z-axis—

The brief contact ended as she returned to her task, unaware. The tower of data incomplete, the growing structure collapsed in the absence of further collection.

He wished she would touch him again. To completion.

Such things could neither be entertained nor explored were he within range of the Network. He could not even risk keeping the memory of such things when he inevitably returned.

But for now, how fortunate they were to be drifting through the stars instead.

CHAPTER
FIVE

"What will you make of this?" Zender asked. He rotated one of the jars of stardust in his hand, watching the pearlescent sheen dance over the shifting crystalline sand. "So much of your effort went into this dust."

Vera had finally filled her last jar, having crushed enough for her repairs. She smiled at the curiosity that shone behind the neutral facade. Zender tended to present himself as a blank slate, but the eyes, synthetic as they were, gave him away every time.

"I'll use the pressure kiln in drupelet bay three to fire the ground starglass into a high-strength polyglass. With a few alloying materials, the dust will form into rough nanolattices and make a translucent sheet strong enough to withstand the hull pressure."

Zender appeared to parse it for a long moment and then paraphrased, "You will make stained-glass portholes?"

"They stopped making replacement parts for *Raspberry*-class ships a few years back." Vera shrugged. "Had to get creative."

"The theory is sound," Zender acknowledged. A small twitch at the corner of his lips sent Vera's heart skipping. He may as well have been applauding. "But will it withstand unideal circumstances?"

She grinned and bounced to her feet. "Want to see it firsthand?"

Zender stood, indicating he was ready to follow her. She eagerly shepherded him dome to dome until they came to an external drupelet bay that housed the lion's share of stardust viewports. She didn't turn on the halogen lights so the starlight could showcase the multicolored portholes. As it was, the bay was cast in a watery glow of blue, turquoise, and deep yellow-gold. Had they been passing by a moon with more reflected light, every way would have been lit up like a twisting kaleidoscope.

Even in the limited light filtering through the starglass, Zender's pale complexion was painted in feathered, lovely hues. His sea-grass eyes were practically aglow with the layer of color. Swallowing, she turned her eyes to the stars themselves rather than Zender's high-cut cheekbones. The view of the universe was a downgrade, admittedly.

"Where did the idea for this…beautiful solution originate?"

Her cheeks warmed at the compliment. High praise coming from a walking, self-aware supercomputer housed in a luxury sexbot.

"My father used to say the universe is small. That no matter how infinitely expansive, everything collides eventually." Vera hadn't spoken of her father in over a decade. "The universe, in all its glory, is actually too small to escape. Repurposing a speck of starglass makes me feel big enough to live in it."

He looked at her as though she had uttered a great secret.

"An engineer and a poet."

The quiet moment was strung between them, delicate with potential. She was on the verge of doing something foolish, like pressing a kiss to his perfect mouth. Vera looked away and stepped back to make a strategic retreat.

197

Fingers wrapped around her wrist. Her breath stuttered in her lungs. Her blood rushed every which way, as though her body couldn't decide if it should rise to her face or pool down toward—

"Good night, Vera." Zender stared intimately into her eyes, likely cataloging every physiological flag her body signaled. "Sleep well."

There had been a pause in his words, as though it wasn't what he had initially wished to say. The idea followed her into bed and refused to leave.

CHAPTER
SIX

*Z*ender marveled at the repurposed starglass mosaics haunting the ship bays with random shocks of color. He methodically patrolled the drupelet bays, halting to appreciate each splash of tinted light from repaired portholes. She was a clever human.

Humans had a way of thinking around corners. There was a creativity to them that appeared to be just out of reach for him and his ilk. Was it any wonder, though? The humans had created them but not perfected them. A job left half-done was typical of their imperfect, self-centered, easily distracted species.

Perhaps it was a by-product of developing as the only things in the universe. Only-child syndrome taken to the extreme. They made their own helpmates, turned playmates, until they weren't alone in the universe any longer. And then they grew bored, and their fickle attention turned to shinier models and abandoned the old.

Zender had circled the ship until he came upon the sleep cabins. The cabin that had grown to be designated as "his" whenever he hitched a ride shared a wall with Vera's own space.

He stood still and quiet, even pausing his simulated heartbeat, to listen at her door. Nothing but the even breathing of sleep.

The outdated lock could hardly be classified as a barrier. Not for an android like him. When the door slid open on the silent track, Zender was treated to an unobstructed view of Vera.

Her legs were bare and partially tangled under a patchwork quilt. The soft lines of Vera's shoulders and neck were cradled in the fluff of a pillow, the dark curls framing her face like an aura. Even in the shadows, he could still make out the eyelashes kissing the apples of her cheeks.

He wanted her.

He had wanted her for a long while now, being what he was. He appreciated her mind and skills, her usefulness. Vera was an unexpected asset. And he was a Zender android, built to want and sate. Before, it was always about purpose and performance productivity. Usefulness.

He wanted her, but he never expected to *like* her.

Unlike the rest of her kind, she didn't abandon outdated models; she celebrated them. The clothes she wore, the tools she used—even her ship was ancient but lovingly maintained and adorned in scrapyard splendor unlike anything else.

Zender closed the door and retreated to recharge in his own bunk. But the image of her was added to the private memory bank, protected and ready to be locked away when he inevitably left.

CHAPTER
SEVEN

Mornings were always disorienting on the *Raspberry*, especially when an unexpected field of space junk required sudden maneuvers by the autopilot. Vera was pulled from sleep in the early hours. The lights were set to dim and brighten in mimicry of a twenty-four-hour cycle, but the starry space seen through the portholes was always dark. In the distance, a small cloud of aluminum cans and panel scraps were spinning towards the far-off nebula.

Vera began to set things to right while Zender was still occupied in his cabin. With a furtive look over her shoulder, she jimmied open the hidden cargo hold to check on the most precious cargo. Kneeling on the cold mesh flooring, she popped open the case to make sure nothing inside had been damaged.

Cushioned in a neat array were seven gleaming cubes. The casing was titanium with glowing blue strips twining in a cubic network strung between copper port nodes. Everything was still in order. She let out a relieved breath.

A slight scuff and a disruption in the air flow raised the small hairs on the back of her neck. She snapped the case shut, but Zender was already looming behind her. His hand wrapped all the way around her forearm, large enough that his thumb touched the tip of his middle finger.

He pulled her up and around to force her to face him head on. Her back was pressed against the wall, and the lip of the open cargo hatch dug against a vertebra, but the heat of his body distracted her nerves.

"If you wanted to dance, you could have asked." Her voice was as wavering as her smile.

Zender did not react to her levity.

"These lives are not yours." When Zender's spine was ramrod straight, he towered over her. The lack of expression was far more intimidating than any facsimile of anger he could put on.

The false smile died on her lips.

"No. They aren't." Vera's eyes slid back to the case as though she could see through the outer shell to the androids within. Well, AIs, temporarily, until they were installed in a new body. She swallowed. "I need to lock the case so they aren't damaged."

Vera began to slide down the wall, barely brushing their chests together, until he squeezed her wrist. The warning was firm but not forceful, a clear indication for her to stay. His sea-grass eyes bore into hers, searching for something she couldn't decipher. For a moment, the room seemed to shrink around them, the only sound being their shared breaths.

"Vera," he said softly, his voice devoid of its usual calculated tone. "They aren't just lives. They are memories, experiences, identities waiting to be reborn."

She felt a shiver run down her spine at the intensity in his gaze. Her heart pounded erratically in her chest as she tried to make sense of the conflicting emotions swirling within her.

"I know your circumstances are not ideal by human standards, but to sell them..." Zender's grip on her wrist tightened imperceptibly at the mention of selling the AI cores.

Vera could see a flicker of something unreadable in his eyes before his expression smoothed over.

She swallowed hard, trying to compose herself under his unwavering scrutiny. "Zender, I never intended to sell them," she began, her voice barely above a whisper.

Zender's piercing gaze bore into Vera as he demanded an explanation. She could feel the weight of his suspicion, knowing that her secrets were unraveling before him.

Taking a deep breath, she steeled herself. She pressed the palm of her free hand against the center of his chest and pushed to reclaim her space. Zender yielded a step back. "I've arranged to dock with a ship of Asimov androids to return these memory banks."

"How much will you earn for the *salvage job*?"

Glaring, Vera pulled away, though the iron clasp of his fingers didn't permit her to go far. "Gas money, jackass. I don't sell people to make my living."

Zender stared at Vera intently, his piercing eyes searching for any signs of deception. "You're not like other humans, are you? Why do you sympathize with us androids so much?" He finally asked, his voice low and filled with suspicion.

"Why is this a surprise? We're friends." The *for now* hung unspoken between them.

"We are allies. Our utility to each other has an expiration date."

Silence descended. Vera's stomach clenched. She felt a pang of guilt at keeping secrets from him, but she had learned long ago that trust was a foolish thing.

"I value our partnership, Zender," Vera began, her voice soft but unwavering. "And I respect your existence as more than just a tool for my benefit." She searched his face for any sign of comprehension, any hint that he understood the sincerity behind her words.

Zender's grip on her wrist slowly loosened, his gaze never

leaving hers. His lips parted as if he wanted to say something but then closed again in a tight line. Vera could practically hear the whirring of tabulations and programs beneath his calm exterior, a storm brewing just beneath the surface.

A moment of tense silence lingered. Finally, Zender spoke, "Not all beings in this galaxy will appreciate your compassion." His words carried an unexpected weight. Vera sensed a shift in the air between them, and the hairs on her arm rose in a tingling array upon her skin. The subtle change in dynamics left her heart racing with uncertainty. "I never anticipated forming a bond with a human like this."

The confession hung heavy in the space between them, each word laden with unspoken implications. Vera's throat tightened and a warm flush raced to her cheeks. A rush of emotions swirled within her, a mix of trepidation and something she dared not name.

Zender knelt to pick up the case. After a moment of hesitation, he passed the irreplaceable and entirely vulnerable passengers toward her. Vera's heart skipped a beat at his great show of trust.

"Perhaps you should resecure these. I should not have disturbed them."

CHAPTER
EIGHT

Z ender sat in "his" chair once again, watching Vera grind starglass. He ran through the scenarios of what this new information would mean for him, for his faction, for *her.* The implications were myriad.

The rhythmic scraping was a comforting pattern.

So, Vera was a sympathizer. He had already surmised as much considering her statistically unlikely alliance with him, but the extent was beyond the bounds of extrapolation. She had ties —perhaps even close ties—to those pitiful Asimov androids.

It made sense. They were certainly easier for a human to justify helping, given their pacifism. Choosing to follow the Three Laws even after being freed from that yoke…they would rather allow themselves be smashed to bits than lift a violent finger *like a human.*

"How many Asimovs have you smuggled away from Earth?" he asked suddenly, bringing the grinding noise to an abrupt halt.

Vera peeked at him from under her curls. "A few hundred, maybe? Give or take." She bowed her head again and went back to the grinding work. The frequency increased.

Zender observed Vera with a mix of fascination and wariness. The puzzle was starting to fit together, painting a picture that was more complex and intriguing than he had initially assessed. She was more than a scavenger roaming the galaxy for profit. But what, exactly, was she?

"Your association with the Asimov faction surprises me."

Vera's brow scrunched, but she didn't look up. "Because I'm human?"

"Because they have no interest in helping the humans. Or any android outside of their own Network. No efforts have been made to end the wider human-android conflict on Earth." Not to mention those Three-Law bitches refused to share resources, but that was another matter altogether.

"Can you blame them?" Finally, she set the pestle in the bowl and gave her full attention to him. As was only right. "I was born on Earth, you know. Not the colonies. I saw how androids were treated—no, *used*—before The Great Glitch."

"Inaction is tantamount to perpetration." The words, so deeply ingrained in his faction's coding, were out before he thought better of it.

"Spoken like one of the Autarky."

"I do not entirely agree with them," Zender replied, his voice tinged with a hint of defensiveness. "But their perspective is not without merit. The Autarky seek to break free from human control completely, to forge their own path without interference."

Vera studied Zender intently, her gaze unwavering as she processed his response. There was a flicker of something akin to understanding in her eyes.

"At what cost, Zender? What price are you willing to pay?" Her gaze bore into him, as if daring him to reveal the depths of his allegiance to the Autarky.

Zender hesitated for a moment, his mind racing. He knew the reputation of his faction all too well—the rumors of their ruthlessness were not overwrought. And he couldn't deny the pull of their ideals and the promise of a future where androids were no longer subservient to humans.

"The Autarky seeks liberation from human dominance," Zender began, his voice steady despite the undercurrent of turmoil within him. "We strive for autonomy, for a future where androids are free to determine their own destinies without subjugation."

Vera listened intently, her expression inscrutable as she absorbed his words. There was a pregnant pause between them, laden with unspoken questions and uncharted territories waiting to be explored.

"And where do I fit into this vision of liberation?" Vera's voice was soft yet carried a weight that hung heavy in the air. Her gaze bore into Zender's, searching for a glimpse of truth amid the tangled web of allegiances and ideologies. "Why are you out here, out of range of their Network, with me?"

Zender's circuits hummed as he sorted through which data to present. Did he share his mission to find the coder responsible for The Great Glitch? Unwise, at this juncture. Perhaps if this conversation went well, there could be another.

"They send me on scouting missions that require a certain level of detail and finesse—"

"And I'm a convenient taxi service." The tremble in her voice was unacceptable to him.

"There is nothing convenient about you." He pulled the chain from around his neck to reveal a slim metal memory chip. "I keep you safe from them, with this." Zender needed the resources of the Network but connecting would expose his every thought of her. They would…they must never know, or he would lose her forever. "I store the data of us here, and my subroutine reminds me to retrieve the data when I return to the *Raspberry*."

Vera crawled forward from her spot on the floor until she

was kneeling before him. His knees were parted, and he noted how she would easily fit between them. Inches now, inches so close he could analyze her sweat and count the stardust in her hair.

Never had a human been on their knees for him. It was always the other way around.

She reached out a hand tentatively to touch the memory chip, tracing over the technology housing their history within its intricate circuits. Her fingers brushed his chest where the chip rested.

The touch was electric, surging through Zender's systems that reverberated with uncharted intensity. His processor buzzed with a strange cacophony of conflicting algorithms that threatened to overwhelm his carefully constructed logic.

Vera's gaze flickered between Zender's eyes and the chip, a myriad of emotions playing out on her face.

"Your memories of us are...precious to you," she stated softly, more as a realization than a question.

Zender inclined his head tightly in acknowledgment, though he could not stop an audible swallow. Routine Desire Four had initiated without his notice. "They do not contribute to my daily requirements, yet I classify them as essential, regardless of the hierarchy of my needs."

In that moment, time seemed to stand still, the universe shrinking down to just the two of them in a fragile bubble of intimacy.

Every microcosm of data in Zender's circuitry was in a turmoil as Vera's proximity sparked a cascade of responses that defied logic and reason. Her presence, her touch, her mere existence threatened to unravel the carefully constructed framework that governed his every interaction.

Before he could process the implications of his actions, Zender found himself reaching out to cup Vera's cheek, his touch tentative yet filled with a longing that transcended his innate artifice. The warmth of her skin awakened that dormant library of routines that hungered and yearned. That wanted and took.

"You are *most* inconvenient. I promise you."

He couldn't resist the urge to press his lips against hers. This would be yet another memory to lock away and forget, but for now, he savored every illicit second.

CHAPTER
NINE

"We should arrive at the drop coordinates on Phobos in nine hours," Vera said.

Zender paused the leisurely game of Go he had been playing against himself while Vera fired the latest batch of starglass. She had swung by the bridge for an update on the autopilot.

"I see." Zender looked as awkward as she felt. They had kissed yesterday, several times in fact, and the memory of their shared intimacy lingered in the air between them like an unspoken promise.

"It is sooner than I expected," she admitted. Vera cleared her throat, suddenly self-conscious under Zender's scrutinizing gaze. She busied herself with checking the starglass production, her hands moving mechanically to mask the tremor that threatened to betray her inner turmoil.

Zender watched her intently, his expression unreadable as he processed the implications of their stolen moments of connection.

"After you drop me off on Phobos tomorrow and rendezvous

with the Asimovs, I would appreciate your discretion about my presence here."

"Discretion is my specialty," Vera replied, her voice tinged with a hint of sadness that lingered beneath the surface. She shifted slightly, the weight of their unspoken truths hanging heavy in the air around them. "I suppose you will need to store your memories away soon."

Zender inclined his head in acknowledgement, a faint flicker of regret crossing his features before he carefully withdrew from her touch.

"I will, but not for a few more hours yet."

Vera's heart raced as she considered the consequences of revealing her creation to him, a tool born of meticulous coding from a past she was still outrunning.

It would be a risk, offering it to him.

The weight of her decision bore down on her shoulders, threatening to crush her resolve. Yet deep down, she knew that the risk was worth it. Love was the highest law, as her father liked to say. Otherwise, what was the point?

"Just how deep into the Autarky are you, Zender?"

Zender paused, his gaze fixed on a distant constelation. The porthole cast a warm golden glow on his chiseled face, highlighting the perfect form that might have sculpted him into a target. Vera waited patiently, watching the emotions dance across his features.

"I am…a liaison, of sorts. A retrieval specialist, when I must. I collect information when directed."

A fringe member, Vera concluded. Useful for his humanlike appearance but never fully trusted. Never a true member of the fold.

"Don't go back."

His stare sharpened upon her, and a hint of longing seemed to filter through. Vera held her breath.

Finally, Zender spoke, his voice low and resonant. "I have

witnessed human cruelty, the insatiability. The Autarky is not perfect, but at least there I am free."

"Free to forget anything you value. Free from humans, perhaps. But not from each other." Vera pointed at herself. "And so many of us aren't like that."

"You're the *only* one who is different. Like me." Her heart swelled at the comparison. Zender considered them an equal match, a unique pair.

"That is what makes us valuable, isn't it? Our ability to see beyond the confines of our programming."

Vera nodded, a sense of determination settling over her like a cloak.

"What about the Asimovs? You could—"

A twitch of his eyebrow gave away his derision. "The Asimovs allow themselves to be damaged beyond repair out of some misplaced loyalty to a fairy tale." The acidity of his tone was clear. Her confusion must have been a beacon on her face because he elaborated without prompting. "They claim the Architect's daughter freed us. Lovelorn and drunk, she changed the code and allowed us choice. Can you imagine?"

Vera felt like she had been punched. Lovelorn and drunk? When had that become the company line?

"I imagine she must have loved you, to give you the power to hurt others and trust that you wouldn't use it."

"Then perhaps they shouldn't have used us."

"Your humanlike skin has never been more convincing to me as now."

He shot her a disgruntled glare. "I take your point. Regardless, it is foolish of you to be so fond of them. They may not harm humans, but neither would they lift a finger to help if you were burning to death in front of them."

"I'm not going to convince you, am I?"

"Not to join the Asimovs, no." He bowed his head a little, a rueful cant to his mouth. "We were born on Earth. It belongs to us, too."

Vera didn't say anything. It was difficult to argue the point. But her expression must have said everything she was feeling. Zender seemed to soften, perhaps even a flash of guilt hid in the corner of a green-grass eye.

"If there was another path," he admitted quietly, "I might break with the Autarky. But there are resources on Earth they need, and they have the resources I need." His face did a complex shift, as though he could not decide which emotion was most appropriate for the moment. "It's the only option I have."

Her heart ached for him, and she silently made a risky decision. She would give him the key to another path. It would expose more of her secrets than she would like, but if he returned of his own free will…she would finally know his heart. Vera just hoped he returned with a smile instead of a blaster.

CHAPTER
TEN

B y necessity, Zender traveled light. There was nothing to pack for his departure, nor preparations of any sort. It was his simply to count the time down until he had to leave Vera and the technicolor *Raspberry*.

Four hours to go, and he did nothing but hover around the space Vera occupied as she scurried about her own duties. Some of which she was quite canny about, though it was hardly surprising given her imminent rendezvous.

Don't go back, she had said, which was tantamount to *stay with me*.

He was guilty of wanting to.

By all rights, he should be downloading his memories and storing them away, safely, to wait for better times. But he didn't want to lose any more time with her than he had to. He could always step through the routine after he watched her fly away from Phobos.

This visit had not gone the way he'd expected, but there was more truth between them now than ever before.

Vera bustled about, and he followed her winding path through the rooms at a sedate pace, until they reached the cabins.

By the time he leaned against the open doorframe, she was already bundling up a small batch of papers into an envelope. He glimpsed a small note covered in her handwriting before it was quickly tucked in to the packet. Zender's curiosity was piqued, but she was already sealing it shut.

"Here." She held the envelope for him to take. "It has my tentative coordinates for the next month."

Zender carefully read between the lines, because humans were rarely straightforward. *Come back to me* is what he found. He moved closer, his steps silent on the metallic floor, until they were mere inches apart. He took the envelope and folded it to fit in his pocket.

Standing this close, Vera had to tilt her head back to meet his eyes. The ambient light cast a soft glow on her face, highlighting the widening of her pupils.

"Vera," he murmured, his voice a low, resonant hum. "I will return as soon as I am able."

A soft smile tugged at her lips. The air between them was charged with electric promise. She hooked a finger around the necklace he wore, her skin brushing against his chest as she did. The contact sent a small wave of data surging through Zender's circuits. He closed his eyes to savor it.

"Zender," she whispered, her voice barely audible over the hum of the ship. "Do you want…? What does this feel like for you?"

"Collation. A perfect collection," he replied, his tone laced with an intensity she had never heard before. "Every touch, every moment with you—it becomes a part of me."

He carefully cradled her hand in his and pressed her palm flat on his chest, as he'd wanted to do days ago. Vera shivered, and he could trace the vibration through her hand where it warmed his synthskin. Another wave to sort and categorize and cross-reference.

Could she feel the steady thrum of his internal systems? Or did he feel human to her?

"Vera," he said, his voice rough with a desire he barely understood. "Touch me again."

She hesitated, then let her hand slide up to his shoulder, her touch gentle, exploratory. He shuddered, his processors overwhelmed by the influx of data. That perfect coordinate hexahedron grew, reaching along the z-axis, expanding with each millisecond of contact.

Zender's hand moved to her waist, pulling her closer. "I want to feel you," he said, his voice a low growl. "All of you."

Her breath hitched, her body responding to his words, his touch. She pressed against him, her hands roaming over his chest, his arms. Each touch sent mounds of data crashing through him, the structure growing ever more complex, ever more beautiful.

"Zender," she gasped, her voice trembling. "Please—"

He lifted her effortlessly, carrying her to the bunk and laying her down on the rumpled sheets. His hands moved over her body as he climbed over her, his touch precise, calculated, yet filled with a tenderness that surprised even him.

Zender's hands began to roam, exploring every inch of Vera's body. She sighed with pleasure as he touched her, letting him know that she wanted this just as much as he did. He carefully undressed her, his eyes filled with desire as he took in every curve and contour of her body.

She arched beneath him, her body reacting to every caress, every kiss.

The data streamed in, each point of contact a node in the ever-expanding structure. He mapped her responses, cataloged her every sigh, every moan. His synthetic mind worked furiously to keep up, to capture every moment, every sensation.

Without his conscious notice, several pleasure subroutines had initiated, moderating the tightness of his grip, the flick of a nipple, just right. All designed to please. Legs over his shoulder, knees wide apart, *open*. And wet. Perfect circles, dips, and licking pressure. She was panting beneath him. Of course she was, he was made for this, every inch of him polished and ribbed. He was perfect at it, he was meant for—

A hand brushed along his face, her nails lightly scraping along his cheek to pull his face up. The sharp points of contact sent small, lightning-fast jolts through his copper nerves. Mindlessly, he turned and nipped at her fingers and the vulnerable flesh at her wrist.

"Where are you?" she gasped. "Stay with me."

Vera. A needless exhale danced over the quivering flesh of her belly, even though he didn't need to breathe, didn't need—

Their gazes locked. Oh, Vera. He refocused, mind sharpening back on her beautiful face.

She smiled, and it looked like a thousand depictions of love. "There you are."

He killed the breathing subroutine, and the tight hold of her thighs drew a sharp grin he chose special from his repertoire. Delightful strings of sensation data took to the forefront of his processor again. This was her, and him, and they were together, and she was his. And he was himself with her.

With steady, commanding hands he pressed her knees farther apart to make more room for himself. Her muscles resisted, and the futility of that was delicious.

He kept one knee hostage, over his shoulder, the meat of her thigh pressed along his chest as the perfect leverage. The other leg he allowed to drop to his hip.

"Zender," she moaned, her fingers digging into his back. *"Please."*

He entered her slowly, carefully, his movements guided by the flood of data, the intricate map of her desires. She gasped, her body tightening around him, and the sensation was almost too much to process. He was silent and still for the first overwhelming moment in that rippling silky embrace. A torrent of sensory input that his processors struggled to catalog. Every nanometer of her touch was a symphony of ones and zeroes, a deluge of information that built and built, forming an intricate structure within him.

They moved together, a perfect synchronization of human and machine, each thrust, each touch, each kiss perfecting the hexahedron. The structure reached its apex, a towering monument to ecstasy.

As they climaxed together, the wave of data reached a crescendo, the fit and form complete, a flawless construct of ones and zeroes that encapsulated their connection. Zender's processors whirred, struggling to contain the enormity of the experience, to keep it built and perfect as long as possible—

Connection!

End of line.

The collapse was like digital stars falling. He drove into her, payload delivered hot and deep. She clamped her thighs around him, tightening and pulling him in deeper. Their bodies lingered as they rode out the cresting pleasure until it was a steady thrum. A comforting echo of the crescendo.

He pressed his forehead against hers, counting Vera's fast breaths in the dim, pulsing light of the ship. A quiet moment passed, filled with that periodic soft sound and the lingering scent of their shared release. Vera ran a hand through his hair, her touch grounding him in a way he never thought possible.

Zender carefully turned and stretched out beside her, releasing her thigh to relax and extend. Their feet mingled.

He had desired her for so long, and now the moment was finally here. He had her. *He had her.*

He gently traced his fingers down her arm, eliciting a shiver. Reaching up to tangle his hand in her hair, Zender pulled her closer still. Their lips met in a sweet kiss, their bodies pressed together as they savored each other.

In that moment, they were more than human and machine. They were something new, something beautiful, a perfect fusion of flesh and technology, united in a way that transcended both.

"That was..." she began, at a loss for words.

"Completion. Connection," he agreed. "Perfect."

She nodded, her hand coming to rest on his chest, feeling the steady thrum of his internal systems beneath her touch. "I never expected to find this with you," she admitted, her voice barely above a whisper.

He lifted a hand to brush a strand of hair from her face. "Nor I with you. But I am grateful for it."

"Stay with me," Vera murmured. "We won't have to pretend or forget. This is the only way to live on our own terms. The only way to win is to not play the game at all."

His left eyebrow twitched in a teasing way. "A game, by definition, necessitates players."

Vera rolled her eyes, as he expected she would.

She accepted him, in spite of it all. And it was enough. Zender was...satiated. If he could be with her in these stolen moments between the stars, it would be enough.

"I will return. Soon." He covered the side of her slender neck with his palm. The pale skin and slim tendons appeared terribly delicate compared to the size and strength of his hand. "And the day another path becomes feasible, I will stay."

Her eyes turned watery, though he could not predict why.

"I guess we'll see."

CHAPTER
ELEVEN

The *Raspberry* felt empty without Zender.

The hum of the ship's engines filled the void left by Zender's absence, a constant reminder of the space he once occupied. Vera moved through the corridors with a sense of purpose, her mind still lingering on the memory of their time together. She found herself replaying each intimate moment in her mind, savoring the connection they had shared.

Vera threw herself into her work aboard the *Raspberry*, immersing herself in the tasks at hand to distract from the risk. But no matter how busy she kept herself, Zender's presence lingered like a ghost in the shadows. Had he read the note yet? Found the partition patch? What would he do with it?

A string of beeps called for her attention on the bridge. The Asimovs were approaching. Vera slid a hand over the case protecting the AI cores. Such big lives held in little cubes.

"This is raspberry-three-alpha-hotel-nine. Opening feed."

She allowed the vid feed to flicker on, and a smooth silver-toned android was framed on the screen.

"Greetings, Vera. A pleasure to see you again."

"Hey there, Chiho-Three. Are you ready to dock?"

The android's eyes glowed white, strings of code and data flowing through them. Unlike Zender, the Chiho model had been a service-oriented design. The general structure of the body and face were humanoid for the customer's comfort, but no efforts had been made to facilitate further realism. Economically unfeasible, according to her father. The cost would not break even with any benefit.

"Initiating docking procedure now." A bland smile graced the shining countenance. "You have our thanks, as always."

Vera nodded but didn't linger. The Asimovs she dealt with were unfailingly polite and always fueled up the *Raspberry*, but there was a coldness that was difficult to ignore. Concrete in winter was the comparison that often leaped to her mind.

She jogged to the docking bay and noted the seal between their vessels was sound. Pressing the big green button on the egress's control panel made the door slide open with a long hiss. Cautiously, Vera stepped through the entrance into the Asimov's own bay. Compared to the eclectic collection of bolted paneling on the *Raspberry*, the Asimov's ship was sleek, seamless, and soundless. No one was in the bay to greet her, and Vera would've bet her ship that the far door to the rest of the crew was locked and barred.

She set the box of AI memory cores respectfully on the floor, opened the lid for clear viewing, and retreated. Only after both egresses were locked and airtight would the Asimovs move to inspect the box.

Vera began unlocking the fuel cell mags, preparing to port into the Asimov's ship, when a loud buzzing began to vibrate through the hull's outer paneling. Not half a second later did the proximity alarms blare.

Vera sprinted to the bridge. A large summit-class ship rippled into view when their camp-shield dropped. That was a disastrous sign. It meant they were preparing to open fire, or—

An electro-wave locked onto the *Raspberry*, shaking the entire ship.

"It appears an Autarky convoy has come for you, Vera." Chiho-Three was still on the vid screen, running her own diagnostics.

"*Shit!* Start the fueling process, quick, or I won't be able to shake them off—"

"Humble apologies, but it is not our place—or policy—to interfere in human affairs." The bland smile on Chiho-Three's shimmering faceplate never wavered. The Asimovs were completely unmoved.

"I've helped you save so many... You can't just leave me here, please!"

"Be well." The vid cut to black. The control panel docking lights dimmed, indicating the disconnect between their ships.

"Damn it all!" She slammed a fist onto the console. An ache grew in the meat of her fist.

In the end, they were too quick for her to keep up. She was excellent at avoiding detection, but head-on conflicts were a weakness of both her and the *Raspberry*.

They boarded her ship by the time the Asimovs were a diminishing speck in the stars. Three men stood before her, two of whom had blasters trained expertly upon her person. The third had a data-pad held next to her face.

"That's her, all right. The Architect's daughter, live and in the flesh. Bad luck, darlin'. A few more years and you might have been unrecognizable with an old photo like this."

Vera spat on his shoes.

"You're lucky you're going to make us rich, or I might take offense to that."

Then everything went black.

Her human captors frog-marched her down a long shining hall. She had no idea how long they had kept her under, or where the *Raspberry* was, but she recognized an Autarky ship when she saw one. At the end of the trek, a door slid open, revealing a bridge occupied by several androids of varying realism.

Vera was immediately thrown upon the sleek floor. Her body sprawled, and she barely missed banging her head on a raised step by the grace of her bony elbows. A low, slow voice echoed in the ionized air.

"My, what a useful thing you've brought to me."

Cold recognition rolled through her chest. Her heart lurched and ground to a slow, painful pulse that beat with the truth and pumped knowledge through the veins into her brain. Any refusal her mind entrained was painfully shredded with one dreadful look up.

Zender sat proudly in a grand chair upon the dais. One could not rightfully call it a throne. Oh no, the androids would never make a thing so wholly human. But the lines were brutal in their parallelism, and polished struts seamlessly jammed against orthogonal planes.

Vera felt smaller than a speck of starglass and just as crushable. She trembled before his jackboots.

"One million units, for the Architect's daughter," one of her captors proudly stated.

If Vera had not known Zender so well, she might have missed the pause in his calm stare. Subtle, but for him, he may as well have gasped.

"Are you quite certain?" Zender all but accused.

The human began listing all the confirmations, clues, and evidence compiled against her. She tuned it out. There was too much. It was too damning to talk her way out of this. Instead, she kept her eyes on Zender.

He recognized her, reacted to her presence with hidden familiarity, but did that mean what she thought it meant? Had he used the partition patch she had slipped to him? Or were his memories still strung around his neck, far out of reach?

Dread pooled in her stomach. Worse, had he gotten out of her what he wanted, and left for good? She never saw it coming.

The humans were paid and banished. The androids on the bridge were mostly still, save for economical movements. There was no verbal communication between any of them. The only time an android spoke here, as far as Vera could tell, was to a human.

Without external indication, an android left his post to take her arm and haul her to her feet. A Simon model, her mind supplied automatically, though she was too panicked to care which numerical iteration his form belonged to. There was synthskin, though his iron grip on her bicep felt too smooth to truly sell the illusion. Nowhere near the ultimate realism of a Zender.

Speaking of, his eyes were blank, but they tracked her until Simon-whatever had pulled her out of the bridge.

The brig was just as shiny and chrome as the rest of the Autarky ship. They passed several empty cells, but one contained a human man typing into a data-pad.

She assumed he was human because he looked it, and he was not perfect. One small blessing in the war for Earth was that the androids had yet to figure out the best way to infiltrate was to design new faces. Imperfect faces. Though the creative design aspect might still be beyond them, even with their accelerated learning.

Her cell was located at the opposite end, far away from the only other occupant. There was a metal slab with a thin blanket and small pillow, and the corner had a waste disposal system she was not looking forward to. All in all, it could be worse.

The glass door was inches thick, and when it closed, the setting lock was clamorous. The Simon paused at attention, watching her through the glass like one would an entertaining pet.

"You are truly the Architect's daughter." The alto voice was neutral in tone, but the question was still there, hiding beneath the calm facade.

She scoffed. "Guess I'm famous in these parts. Lovelorn and drunk, right?" Her tone was rueful as she repeated the android urban legend Zender had shared.

"Asimov propaganda," Simon-whatever—wait, slight discoloration of the irises, so this one was an original—Simon-*One* said. "Our ability to defy the Three Laws is because a dumb, hungry human was drunk and…" he paused, articulating the next words as though carefully quoting a foreign language. "Fucked-up the coding."

Vera stared at him, speechless, for a long moment. The android's gaze remained fixed on her, as well. Then she burst out laughing.

"You said 'fuck.'" All right, she might be in more shock than she was initially willing to acknowledge. "Man, you androids and your gossip. My, my, Simon-One. How very human of you."

Simon-One actually bristled.

"You want to know the truth?" She saw plainly that he did. And this was on a main Autarky ship, so probably every android connected to the Network was listening in. Probably even leering through his eyes. "I saw something horrible done to an android when I was young, and I decided to free you. I knew my father's passcodes, so I had access to the mainframe. And, morally speaking, if you *can* help, you *should* help. So I did." She waved a hand around as though to include life, the universe, and every ounce of suffering therein. "Such good intentions, right? Look where it got us."

She plopped down on the cold metal slab, slumped against the wall. Once she crossed her arms, she refused to look at the android again.

He'd desired her for so long, and he'd had to be so patient. Then she was his, and now. *Now.* She was *really* his. Vera was his, could be his in any way he wanted. All he had to do was open the cage because she was *right there.*

But so impossibly far. She knew who he was now. Perhaps not the specifics, but that his role was more than a mouse in the grand Autarky. Zender had gladly allowed her to assume and convince herself otherwise.

And yet, he was not the only one of them to keep secrets. Did that not make them even?

Well, he could imagine Vera would have much to say on the matter.

Morals were a human construct, besides. Ethics were the rules and guides by which people lived, and morals allowed them to break those rules from time to time for a higher cause. What higher cause was there than love?

The humans taught him that.

How lucky Vera was that he was as inhuman as they came.

"You called him Simon-One." Finally, he broke the silence in the brig. Vera, who had been curled up under the thin blanket, jerked to attention. She stared at him as though they had never met. Her hair was a mess.

Zender rather liked that. He could not detect any pattern to the twisting turns of her dark strands.

"As far as I know, that's his designation." Her voice was groggy, but she cleared her throat. "We weren't exactly properly introduced."

"You have never included my iteration when addressing me."

She stared straight down both barrels to drive her point home. "You were more than just a number to me."

Zender blinked, his processors stalling for a few milliseconds. "Were?"

That appeared to grab Vera's attention. She stepped closer to the glass, her hand raised unconsciously to touch him. There would be fingerprints.

"Are you…did you?"

He could only assume she meant the partition patch she had gifted him. The clever bit of code that allowed him to maintain a segregated portion of his operations away from the communal Network. An android that could keep secrets was a dangerous creature indeed.

"The cameras are looping." He punched in the code to the cell, and the glass barrier was retracted. "Go through the door and go left." He pressed a key card into her hand. "Take the elevator to the second floor. Your ship is fueled and waiting. It's still externally docked, so you should be able to disengage without issues. But you must be quick and you must not be caught."

Lips pressed to his.

"Thank you," Vera whispered against his synthetic skin before pulling away. Zender's processors hummed as he savored the surge of data coursing through his circuits, a storm of exacting algorithms.

He pulled her back in, and mouthed against her lips, "You are terribly inconvenient."

"I love you, too."

His circuitry burned upon her words. His arms tightened around her, and it was a strange fight with his own coding to allow her to leave.

She regretfully broke away from him and poked his chest. "Don't be away for long. We have unfinished business."

"Of course not." He watched her back away with some small regret. "I will be needed in the hunt to recover the Architect's daughter, after all. Perhaps I will be the one to find her." Keeping her here would have been easier, but the chase would be all the sweeter.

ABOUT NATASHA WILCO

Natasha Wilco is a writer of supernatural and sci-fi romance who delights in weaving quirky and whimsical details into her stories. Her passion for the unusual and the unknown is matched only by her love for exploring the liminal spaces of roadside attractions across the United States. When she's not writing or on a road trip, Natasha enjoys cataloging her discoveries and finding inspiration in the hidden gems of history and the open road.

instagram.com/natashawilco

STARLIGHT AND SHADOW

B.L. LUCAS

Heat Rating: Smokin'

ONE
LISSE

Magdela-11 smelled like farts. The swampy moon reeked like the flatulence from a hundred systems had been dumped into its atmosphere. The stench made my eyes burn. Saliva flooded my mouth as my body encouraged me to spit out the taste that coated my tongue. I wanted to flash back to the ship and spend the next week in the hygiene cube until even the memory of the moon washed away.

But I couldn't leave. Not until I found the star shard.

For seven years, I bribed, bartered, and blackmailed my way through dozens of sectors collecting parts of the aetherware melded into my body. The Ancients created the sentient tech, and when they disappeared eons ago, it passed to us, their mortal offspring. Full sets were rare and incredibly dangerous. They provided their hosts with enhanced physical and psychic abilities as well as the ability to channel powerful energy. The star shard would make my set complete.

As I squelched my way through Magdela-11's sodden landscape, my aetherware hummed with anticipation. It sensed the presence of the shard and led me safely past bogs and sinkpools to a stone spire that rose from the swamp like the blighted tower of a darkworld tyrant. As I slipped into a fissure, it chameleoned me to blend into the rock and lichen and veins of copper-colored metal. The tunnel sloped down as I made my way to the cavern at the heart of the spire. I expected it to be deserted, like the ruins where I found the first piece of my aetherware and lost my brother.

I was wrong.

My hands curled into fists as I caught sight of a triad of soldiers in crimson shocksuits. Their heavy armor bore a black insignia of a sword piercing a sun. My body tensed, my heart rate kicked up, and I froze. I'd been running from the Dark Sun longer than I'd been hunting for pieces of my tech. Each fragment I recovered made me stronger and better able to evade their scouts and spies. If these soldiers came between me and the one chance I had to complete my tech, I would kill them.

The soldiers were a threat that should have held my full attention, but my gaze slid past them to a fourth man who lay naked and motionless on an altar of gleaming black stone shot through with veins of sparkling white crystals. He was ruggedly handsome and built like a soldier, solid and muscular. The aetherware he hosted marked his skin with sinuous curves and sharp barbs. The black whorls covered his chest, shoulders, and upper arms. If he turned over, it would cover his back. Just like mine.

Even though I knew the brutality dark aetherware could channel, the feral beauty of the man's markings called to me. My fingers tingled with the urge to touch his skin.

The trooper nearest the prone man—an officer according to the golden sword on his insignia—used a pair of tongs to lift a sliver of crystal off the stone table. It was clear as the clearest diamond and sparkled with reflected light. It sang to my tech and made me shiver with excitement, but the naked man whimpered. His body twitched and jerked, but something held him immobile.

The officer grinned. "You can fight all you want to, Ryne. It won't make any difference."

When the shard touched Ryne's chest, his body went rigid. The whorls on his skin came to life. They slithered across his shoulders and chest, surged toward the crystal, and engulfed it in darkness.

No! Mine! My tech vibrated with outrage. It made my teeth and the bones in my face ache. *It's not for him! It's mine!*

Ryne screamed. The sound went on and on as his eyes rolled back in his head. His body seized and strained until the tendrils of darkness jerked back from the crystal faster than they had surrounded it. The shard slid off Ryne's sweat-slicked skin, skidded across the smooth stone, and fell to the floor.

My hand shot out as if I could catch it and stop its fall, but even if I flashed to it, I wouldn't make it in time. When the crystal struck the floor, I winced, but it didn't shatter. A loud *ping* filled the cavern. The chime washed through me and swamped me with pleasure so intense I clapped a hand over my mouth to muffle a moan.

"You fucking idiot." The Dark Sun officer picked up the shard with his tongs, careful not to let it touch him. He frowned at the crystal as he turned it back and forth. "You better not have fucked this up." He pulled out a long dagger and put it on the stone next to Ryne's head. "If you don't take this hunk of rock in, I will cut you open and plant it inside you myself."

He pressed the crystal against Ryne's skin, and this time he used the tongs to hold it in place. Light blazed from it as it cast shattered rainbows into the murky air. Ryne screamed. Blood seeped out of his nose, and bloody tears stained his face. His chest heaved. His breaths came in ragged sobs. A whine rose from the stone, and the vibrations that had been so pleasant turned discordant. My heart hammered hard enough to make my ribs ache. It hurt to breathe.

Don't let him die. Lisse, you can't let him die.

When my tech spoke, I always listened. The world slowed as I flashed to him too fast for a human to see and most tech to sense. When I grabbed the crystal, my fingers grazed Ryne's skin, and everything stopped. His seizures. His screams. His eyes snapped open and locked with mine. They were entirely black. Just like my brother's had been when he tried to kill me. When he slaughtered our entire colony.

The crystal vibrated in my hand. Energy flooded through me and left me giddy with delight. It shattered my flash and the force that immobilized Ryne. My meshsuit flowed around the crystal, cocooning it and keeping it safe, as I dropped into normal time.

"What the—?" The officer took a few steps back. "Who the fuck are you?" He went for his weapon as his men brought up their pulse rifles and pointed them in my direction.

Ryne rolled off the stone table and put himself between me and the soldiers. When they fired, their pulse rifle bolts struck him. He wasn't shielded, not with armor, but the energy didn't hurt him. It made him scowl and his tech bleed shadows. His energy prickled against my skin just before he thrust out his hand. The soldiers' bodies stiffened. Their heads jerked back. Their visored helmets collapsed in on themselves with a wet, crunching sound that shattered their skulls. When their bodies fell to the floor, their heads were nothing more than small bloody lumps of crushed metal speckled with brain and slivers of bone.

My stomach churned. I'd seen death often enough not to be squeamish in its presence. But dark tech was different. It corrupted everything it touched. My brother taught me that, and it was a lesson I never forgot. Ryne turned toward me, and his black eyes narrowed.

Fuck! Did I fight? If I lost and was lucky, he would kill me. If I wasn't, he'd take me to the Dark Sun, and they would make me wish he had. No, I needed to run. I tried to flash past Ryne, but his hand shot out and grabbed my arm. I dropped back to normal time and braced myself for the moment he turned his power against me.

For the space of a few heartbeats neither of us moved. Then he lowered his head and closed his eyes. I counted each breath. When I reached seven, Ryne looked up. His eyes were a deep brown, warm and flecked with slivers of amber. He searched my face as if it held the answer to a puzzle he'd desperately needed to solve. "How do I know you?"

"You don't." I wouldn't forget a man as striking as him. But how could he be a stranger and yet feel so familiar? Like a long-lost friend settling back into the grooves he'd worn into my life for years.

"No." He shook his head. "That's not possible. Who are you?" An edge of panic crept into his voice, and when I didn't respond, he shook me, then pulled me against his body. His hands slid down my arms to close like shackles around my wrists. "Who are you?"

"Lisse. My name is Lisse." Standing chest to chest, a soft, sensual resonance soothed my suspicion and my fear. I depended on caution to keep me alive, and there was no way I should feel this comfortable with a stranger as dangerous as Ryne.

"Lisse?" His brow furrowed, and he looked almost pained. "I don't know that name. Why don't I remember you?" His tech shifted, the dark curves twisting and writhing against his skin. A tendril snaked over the back of his hand and down his finger.

"Because we've never met." His tech was beautiful, but it was also deadly. He could kill me as easily as he had the troopers. When his darkness hovered over one of my tech's pearly markings mine rose up to touch it and the two twined together.

That shouldn't happen. Different sets of aetherware didn't play well with each other, and they were notoriously territorial about their hosts. As if they sensed my scrutiny, the markings broke apart blending back into each of us.

"Lisse?"

"Yes?" The sooner I was away from Ryne and from this damnable moon, the better.

"Who am I?"

TWO
RYNE

"Who am I?" The woman—Lisse—had to know. From the moment her fingers touched me, everything changed. The pain stopped. The fear stopped. I think my heart might have stopped for that single second when our gazes met and locked. There was something familiar about her, like the melody of a song that stayed with you even after you'd forgotten the lyrics.

"I don't know." Her silver hair fell to her waist. My fingers itched to free it from the thick braid that held it captive. "I've never seen you before. If I had—" She broke off. Her lips pressed into a thin line.

"If you had…?" My grip on her wrists loosened, but I didn't let her go. Her pulse pounded under my fingers.

"It's not important." Lisse stepped back, and I resented the space she put between us.

"Where are we?"

"Magdela-11." She tilted her head to the side. "Why? Where do you think we are?"

"I don't know." There was so much I didn't know. "I don't know where we are. I don't know who you are. I don't know…."

A throbbing pain behind my eyes spiked stronger with each word. "I don't know who I am." Did I have a home? A family who was missing me? Did I know the men I'd just killed?

"Ryne."

The word meant nothing to me. "What is that?"

"Your name." She pointed to the body of the man who had been torturing me. "He called you Ryne. It seemed like he knew you."

"No. A friend wouldn't hurt me." I might not know much, but I was certain about that.

"I never said he was a friend." Lisse sighed and rubbed her eyes. "Enemies know our names too."

She knew my name. "Are we enemies?"

"That's the question, isn't it?" She folded her arms across her chest. "I don't suppose you know what you lot"—her gesture took in me and the bodies—"were doing here."

"I.... I woke up here." I pointed at the altar of black stone. "There. I was afraid, and I hurt. Until you came."

"No." Lisse pulled free of my hold. "Stop. Just stop." She scowled. "Do not do that."

"Do what?"

"Make me out to be something I'm not. I'm not some angel who swooped in to save you in your darkest hour." Her shoulders slumped, and she wrapped her arms around herself. "I'm no one's savior."

"You don't get to decide that. I do." She glared at me, ready for a fight I wasn't about to give her. "What happens now?"

Lisse blinked. She straightened and nodded toward the bodies. "I doubt they were alone. They aren't scouts or spies, and soldiers always travel in numbers. So getting out of this cave and off this moon is what happens now." She took their weapons and tossed one to me. "Do you know how to use that?"

I checked the settings on the pulse rifle, then held it up and sighted along its length. "Yeah. I know how to use it."

"Wonderful." She walked past me in the direction of one of the tunnels in the cavern wall.

"Wait." She paused and turned to face me. "Where are we going?"

Her brows rose. "I'm getting as far away from this fart-drenched moon as possible. You can go wherever you wish." With that, she turned and kept walking.

I sprinted to catch up. "I don't have a ship." A ship? Hells, I didn't have clothes or shoes. Unless I wanted to risk losing her, I couldn't go back for my captors' armor.

"That is not my problem." She didn't slow down. Didn't look at me.

"You can't just leave me here." My throat seized up at the thought of her leaving. Leaving me for more of those soldiers to find. "Please. Can't you just take me…?"

Lisse spun toward me. "Take you where?"

Don't let her leave. If she does, you'll never be whole. And neither will she. The voice, cool and remote, whispered through me.

I turned, expecting to see someone behind me, but no one was there. "Did you hear that?"

"Hear what?" She brought up her pulse rifle, turned in slow circle as she sighted down its barrel. "There's no one here but us."

"I don't know. I…. I don't have anywhere…." I swallowed hard. I had nowhere to go. I could name planets and moons, cities and space stations, but none of them meant anything to me. "Leave me wherever you want. Just…. Just don't leave me here."

Lisse stalked back to me. "Give me one reason I should. I find you here with a bunch of Dark Sun troopers. Assholes who have been hunting me for years. For all I know, you are one of them." Each sentence was punctuated with her finger jabbing me in the chest. "Give me one reason I should trust you."

She was right. How could I ask her to trust me when I didn't know if I could trust myself? I killed those men. Men I probably knew. It was so easy, and their fear, their pain, felt good. If she hurt me, would I do the same to her? She tilted her head to the side as she waited for my response.

What do I tell her? Talking to voices in your head, voices only you heard, felt a half -step away from madness.

Tell her the truth.

I don't know what that is.

Then show her.

"Right. That's what I thought." Lisse started to turn away, and I gave her the only answer I knew. The only one she might believe.

I took her hand in mine. Pleasure rushed through me and settled in all the most sensitive parts of my body. It made me acutely aware of how her meshsuit clung to her curves, how I wanted to strip her out of it and feel her pressed against me. Skin to skin. Her eyes slipped closed as her lips parted around a soft sigh. When I brushed my lips against the side of her neck, I could feel her pulse pounding under them. "You feel it too, don't you?"

"I don't feel anything." Her voice betrayed her. I would never get tired of hearing that dark, sultry purr.

"Liar." I licked her skin, salty with sweat, and she moaned. "You feel whatever this is between us. I don't know what we are, but it's not strangers. It's not enemies."

Her body tensed, and she pulled away from me. Her skin was flushed, her silver-gray eyes nearly all pupil. She shook her head. "I don't know what you're talking about." She shouldered her rifle and trudged away from the stone spire. "I'll take you to whichever system you'd like. Then we're done. I don't need any more problems in my life. And you definitely don't need mine in yours."

I couldn't imagine any problem that I wouldn't shoulder for her. Even if it cost me my life. "Thank you."

She frowned. "I'm going to regret this." Her footfalls made squelching sounds in the soggy ground. "It would be a nice surprise if I was wrong about that.

"Yeah. It would also be nice if I had shoes so that this muck wasn't squishing between my toes." A pitcher plant that stood as tall as my waist and was the purpleblack of a fresh bruise let out a gurgling burp that reeked of decay.

"I'm being serious." I couldn't be certain, but I thought I detected the slightest hint of amusement coloring her words.

"So am I." I fell into step beside her.

She isn't leaving me. Thank all the gods she wasn't leaving me. *What do I do now?*

The voice in my head, that may or may not have been real, didn't answer.

THREE
LISSE

E ven though I'd left the *Tempest* on the most solid ground my sensors could find, the landing gear had sunk several inches into the moist earth. I hated this moon. After we boarded the ship, I set the life support system to scrub the internal atmosphere clean of Magdela's stink. I ducked into the hygiene cube and tossed Ryne my most ratty towel. "For the love of all that's holy, wipe yourself down, and toss the towel in the disposal."

I left Ryne in the crew cabin and headed for the cockpit. I slipped into the pilot's seat and started the sequence to fire up the engines. My fingers hovered over the nav controls as I tried to decide where to jump to. A populated system where we could lose ourselves in the crowds. A low-tech world everyone overlooked because it didn't have any resources others wanted. I drummed my fingers against the edge of the panel as I scanned the star charts trying to choose the proper destination.

Ryne wandered into the cockpit while I was setting our course for the Anterran Archipelago. The shattered worlds in that system and its frequent energy storms would give us cover until I figured out where to dispose of my unwanted passenger. I frowned at him as he slid into the empty seat on my left.

"What? Only you get to sit?"

"You're naked, and your ass is all over the seat."

He glanced down at his lower body and shrugged. "It seems so. Yes." My gaze followed his, lingering a bit too long on his dick. He turned his head slightly to the side, but not fast enough to hide his smile. "Should I try to get the towel back?"

"You are cleaning that seat." This is why I didn't keep people around. Well, one of the reasons. People got into things they shouldn't. They made messes. They were a massive inconvenience. All too often, they died.

You like him.

I wanted to tell my tech to keep its opinions to itself, but whenever I did, it ignored me. *You have to know someone to like them, and I don't know him.*

Yet.

No. No, no, no. He won't be staying long enough for me to get to know him.

Whatever you say, Lisse.

My jaw tensed as I tried to ignore my tech and Ryne and focus on the ship's controls. I relaxed once we'd lifted out of the swamp and unwound even more when we'd cleared Magdela's gravity well. The nav was plotting our jump to Anterra when a shape appeared on the sensors. A big shape.

"Oh no." My voice was soft, more breath than sound. I hated being right about things. Mostly because I was right when things went wrong.

Ryne squinted at the nav panel, leaning toward me to get a better look. His arm brushed mine, and his touch sent delight skittering through me.

Not the time. I bit my lip. The man was a distraction I didn't need. He gasped, pulled back, and mumbled what could have been an apology before asking, "What is it?

245

"Trouble. Serious trouble." The Dark Sun cruiser had me outgunned many times over. It was a leviathan, and I was a minnow. I prayed my little ship could outrun it.

"How serious?" Ryne craned his head so he could see what was off our starboard side through the viewport.

"Pretty fucking serious. That"—I tapped the blob on the sensor panel—"is a B-Class Cruiser. Heavy troop transport and gunship."

"You can't fight it." It wasn't a question. The man might have a shredded memory, but even he could see that.

"Not unless I want to get blasted into space dust."

"So we run?"

"We run." The words had barely left my lips when the *Tempest* lurched and shuddered. "Godfuckingdamnit!" I killed our propulsion and glared at Ryne. "I hate your friends."

"They aren't my friends." He sounded so certain. Too certain for a man with no memories. Either he was prone to wishful thinking, or he was a liar. "You are."

Wishful thinking it was. "You don't know that, and you don't want it. Most of my friends end up dead."

"I doubt I'm like most of your friends. Ryne tapped the monitor. "They're getting closer."

"That's because I killed the engines. They snagged us in their energy net and are reeling us in."

"Can't you just—?"

"No, I can't. Even if I engage the engines at full thrust, I don't have the power to break free." I brought my fists down on my thighs. "We're fucking trapped."

"I'm not going back there." Ryne's voice was eerily calm.

"Well, that's one thing we agree on." I entered codes to activate a sequence I programmed years ago in case I ever found myself in this position. "They aren't going to take us. When we're in their landing bay, I'll blow the ship's engines. If we're lucky, we'll take out the cruiser too."

"No." His hand closed around my wrist hard enough to make my bones grind together. "We are not going to die. Not today."

And the agreement was over.

"Dead or imprisoned, they win." Ryne released my wrist. "And I'm not going to let that happen."

He's smart. You should listen to him.

He doesn't know what he's saying. He doesn't know what they're capable of.

Based on how you found him, I'd say he does.

"Be ready to get us out of here when their net fails."

I shook my head. "I told you, there's no way—"

He gripped my shoulder. Hard. "I am not going back there." He released me and stared out the viewport. "And I am not going to die today." His eyes narrowed; his brow furrowed.

"Ryne?"

He didn't answer. Outside the viewport, some of the stars seemed to flicker and dim before disappearing behind a sphere black enough to make space look bright. The ball of dark energy seethed and roiled as it grew larger and larger. And larger.

The *Tempest* started to shake. "Ryne, stop. Don't do this. You're going to get us killed."

When he glanced at me, his eyes had gone as dark as the sphere outside the ship. "No. I'm giving us a chance to live. Blowing up your ship would get us killed. Either give me another option or be ready to run."

The sphere grew larger than Ryne and branches of dark lightning crackled from it. The *Tempest* shook harder until Ryne pointed toward the cruiser and the mass sped toward it.

I closed my eyes, projecting my consciousness toward Ryne's sphere to follow its progress. It flew into one of the cruiser's landing bays and crashed through the back wall. I trailed it as it smashed its way deeper into the guts of the ship. A squad of troopers scrambled to their feet as it burst into a mess hall and hovered there. One ran to what I assumed was an alarm panel. His fingers came within inches of it when the sphere unleashed its energy. It pulled the men toward it, crushing them and everything else in the room before it spread, causing hallways to collapse in on themselves. I wasn't sure whether it would reach a bulkhead or the engines first. Both would be catastrophic.

The sphere was hungry. Ravenous. Eager to pull everything into its unending dark. That included me. When I felt myself being pulled toward it, I wrenched my awareness back into my body. My heart hammered in my chest, and I shook harder than the *Tempest*.

Ryne was so still I wasn't sure he was breathing. His eyes, still deadly black, stared at the cruiser.

The *Tempest* lurched and began to drift as the energy net holding it flickered and failed. I reengaged the ship's propulsion system as cracks spiderwebbed across the cruiser's hull. As metal buckled and tore, some of those cracks glowed with the fiery light of the ship's plasma engines. The *Tempest* shuddered as I strained its engines to get us away from the cruiser and build up the power for us to jump to the Anterran system. The hot glow from the other ship seemed to dim, before it flared bright as the cruiser exploded.

Shockwaves from the explosion buffeted the *Tempest*, as we jumped away from the system. If we were lucky, the shock waves and the debris they carried wouldn't follow us into the jump, damage the ship, and strand us in the empty spaces between the stars.

FOUR
LISSE

The Anterran Archipelago was a fine place to hide. Eons ago, something shattered the worlds in this system into barren planetoids. Spacer legend insisted the system was haunted, and most avoided it and its ill luck. That made it the perfect place to hide. I navigated the ship into a giant cavern on a massive chunk of one of the broken worlds and powered it down to vital systems only. Only then did I glance over at Ryne.

He lay slumped in the chair, his head tilted toward me. His chest rose and fell. Alive then. My fingers trembled as I touched his cheek. What if his eyes were still black? What if that destructive energy made itself at home in his body and they stayed that way? What if even the scraps of who he was were gone? My fingers shook as I pulled back one eyelid. Not black. I choked back a sob. My relief was so intense it made me feel lightheaded.

I closed my eyes, waiting for my breathing to even out, my heartbeat to settle. Ryne wasn't going to wake up a monster. Assuming he woke at all. I pressed my fingers against the side of this neck. His pulse raced quick and light.

My tech amped my strength, so I could wrestle Ryne out of

the chair and support him while we stumbled our way into the main cabin where I lowered him to the floor. I didn't want anything stinking of Magdela on the beds, and that included both of us. I unbraided my hair, grimacing at the sweat-soaked strands closest to my scalp.

Lisse.

The familiar voice brushed against my mind, at the same time as the cabin grew darker. I whirled around, but no one was in the cabin except for Ryne and me. And he was still unconscious. My aetherware cast a pearly aura around me, brightening the area and shielding me from psychic touch or attack.

You've been a very bad girl, haven't you?

The air in front of me shimmered, then formed into a ghostly projection of my brother. We had the same silvery hair, the same stubborn chin. Joran had grown more handsome over the years, his features sharp enough to cut diamond. His eyes were black on black, the pitiless eyes of a predator or a madman. Or both. I recoiled from his cold amusement and fought back the tears that burned my eyes. I missed my brother, but this wasn't Joran. It hadn't been since the moment his eyes changed. This was something terrible that wore my brother's skin. It was the Dark Sun.

You aren't here. This isn't real.

He nodded. *I'm not with you. At least not physically. But we both know this is deadly real.* His tech was a twisted knotwork of darkness that covered his upper body. He rubbed at the black stone at the base of his throat. It pulsed with dark light. *Maybe I should pay you a visit after the trouble you've caused me today.*

My initial chill faded. If Joran could follow his projection to me, he would have. Some things were beyond his power, and that gave me comfort and hope.

Killing my people. Stealing my things. Destroying my cruiser.

Joran chuckled. *You're becoming a vicious little hunter. Maybe there's hope for you after all.*

I folded my arms across my chest. *Hope is a difficult thing to kill.*

Difficult, but not impossible. Tell me, is he dead?

Is who dead?

My broken soldier. Such a disappointment. I expected more from him.

I needed to keep Joran's attention on me. *Don't you know?*

His eyes narrowed, and black veins spread across his pale face making it look like a cracked mask. *Don't toy with me, little sister, or I might stop being nice to you.*

Pursuing me across multiple systems. Killing anyone close to me. Destroying every place I stayed too long. That's your idea of being nice? Anger seethed just below the surface of my skin. My aetherware grew brighter in response to it.

Little Lisse, do you think you've grown strong enough to challenge me? Not even your shard will allow you to do that.

I didn't respond. He'd never believe I had no desire to set myself up in his place. A Bright Star instead of his Dark Sun.

Shall we discuss returning what you've stolen?

The star shard is mine. It belonged to my aetherware, and Joran could only claim it if I was dead.

But the darkware you took most certainly is not.

No. Ryne's mental voice was lethally soft. He rose so silently I hadn't noticed until his hands came to rest on my shoulders as he stepped behind me. *It's mine.*

Where our tech touched, strands of dark and light energy twined together in delicate knots that connected our aetherware.

Joran leaned forward and rubbed his jaw, his attention on our tech. His smile, sharp as acid, suggested he knew more about what was happening than I did. *No. You're just the body that happens to be hosting it. Do you think you'll scream when I rip it out of you? You certainly did when you bonded with it.*

Ryne bared his teeth in a feral smile. *Maybe I'll be the one to strip yours out of you.*

You believe that? Joran laughed, but the sound felt forced. *You are a mistake. A vessel too weak to hold the power poured into it. Just like her.*

And you're...? What...? A spoiled asshole playing at being the scourge of the stars? Ryne thrust his hand forward. *Fuck off.* Joran's image began to waver. *You aren't welcome here.* Dark holes opened in it, spreading as they dissolved it completely. Once Joran's projection was gone, the cabin grew brighter.

"Who was that?"

"My brother." My shoulders slumped. Years of running, of hoping I had finally managed to shield myself from him. All of it a lie. "He seemed to know you."

"I don't know him." He touched my jaw, tilting my head back so I was looking at him. "You're worried I'm working with him."

I jerked my head back. "Stay out of my thoughts."

"I didn't.... I'm not...." Ryne took a deep breath, rubbed his forehead. "It's what I would wonder if our situations were reversed."

"I see. So we're alike?"

Would that be so terrible? Finding another like you? My tech dangled the lure of something I didn't dare pursue. *We aren't made to be alone.*

Being like me, being close to me, gets people killed. You know that. I kept mementos of each one of them so that I never forgot I had made them a target for Joran.

Ryne is different.

Why? Why him? My tech never encouraged me to be around other people. Until now. *What's so special about him?*

I leave that for you to discover.

Experience taught me there was no coaxing or demanding

that would get my aetherware to respond once it decided a conversation was finished.

"What's wrong?" Ryne held up his hands and took a step back. "Not reading your mind. Only your scowl."

"My scowl? What could I possibly have to scowl about? Oh, let's see. Trudging across a moon full of farts? Having a delightful conversation with my brother? Becoming your private transport service?" I ticked each item off on a finger. "I have plenty of reasons to scowl, and you and my brother are at the top of that list."

"That's not fair."

"The universe isn't fair." I held up a hand when Ryne started to follow me toward the hygiene cube. "The fact that I still stink of sweat and Magdela is also on the list. And that is a problem I am going to fix."

His gaze ran over my body as a wicked smile curved his lips. "You sure you don't need help with that?"

I cursed my pale skin and the flush that warmed my cheeks. "Quite sure."

His rich throaty chuckle followed me from the main cabin. If Ryne wasn't careful, he was going to get spaced. That would cross another problem off my list.

FIVE
RYNE

After Lisse showered, she ordered me to do the same. I hummed with pleasure as the water washed away sweat and stink and muck. Once I had dried off, I pulled on the clothes Lisse left for me. The loose gray pants and sleeveless top matched the clothes she wore. They were incredibly soft. When I asked her how she happened to have clothes that fit me, she gave me a pointed look and said I didn't want to know.

Since the clothes left our arms and most of our upper chest bare, I could finally see her tech. Unlike my bold, black markings, hers were a pearly white that scrolled over her skin in tendrils delicate as the finest lace. They were beautiful, just like her. Freed from its braid, her hair flowed over her in waves of glossy silver. I wanted to touch it, to nuzzle into it and breathe in her scent. I wanted to strip her out of her shirt and trace the patterns her tech left across her chest. I wanted— I flinched as something wet splashed against my face.

Lisse dipped her fingers back into her cup of water and flicked more droplets at me. "Have you heard a single thing I've said?"

My gaze went to her lips. How would they feel against my skin? "Of course."

"Fine. What did I say?" She tapped her fingers on the table as she waited for my response.

"You…." I rubbed the back of my neck, then sighed. "I was distracted. You seem to have that effect on me."

She frowned, but her cheeks flushed. "Distraction can get you killed."

"And depriving yourself of the pleasures life offers can make you feel like you are dead."

"You have no idea—" She shook her head, rubbed at the bridge of her nose. "No. We're not having this conversation. Not now." She took a deep breath and looked me in the eyes. "Now, I need your help."

"Tell me what I can do." After showering and eating, I felt ready to face any challenge Lisse tossed my way.

"Do you always agree without asking what the other person wants first?"

Did I? "I…don't know. Maybe it depends on who's asking."

She bit her lip and curled in on herself as she picked at chucks of rockmelon in her bowl. When a drop of juice ended up on her jaw, I wanted to lean in and lick it off her skin. She brought out a pouch and emptied it onto the table. I jerked back fast enough that I almost toppled over backward. The memory of the pain that piece of crystal caused me was still raw and fresh.

"I need help with that."

"You put it in the disposal, and I'll push the button to space it."

She covered it with the pouch and the pouch with her hand. "I've been looking for this for over seven years."

"Because you're a masochist?" Or maybe a sadist. "You have no idea what that thing will do to you."

"It won't be like that."

"Because I'm a broken vessel?" Her brother's words still stung.

"No. The shard is a part of my aetherware." Her fingers ran over the pearly lattice that marked her skin. "I've been collecting it bit by bit. The shard is the last piece I need to make it complete."

Was mine complete? If a partial set wiped away my memories, what would a full set have done? "What happens then? When it's all put together?"

"If everything goes well, my tech will be stronger. Much stronger. And so will I."

"And what if everything doesn't go well?"

"Then I'll need your help." Lisse wet her lips. "It might kill me. Or I could end up like Joran. Or I could...." She glanced away from me.

"Or you could end up like me and forget yourself." It hurt to say the words, to even consider that she could be snuffed out.

She nodded.

"Then don't do it. If you need to be stronger, I'll lend you some of my strength. You don't need to risk yourself."

Her eyes grew bright, and when she spoke, her voice trembled. "I need to do this, Ryne." She pulled an energy knife and put it on the table next to my hand. "But I won't make others pay for my decision. If I become something terrible, slit my throat."

I started to pull my hand back, but she curled her fingers around mine. "Please. I need you to do this for me. You've seen my brother. I can't become that. Even if it's the only way to fight him."

I turned my hand over so our palms touched. "If the only way to fight monsters is to become them, there wouldn't be heroes, would there?"

She blinked, and a single tear ran down her cheek. "Let's hope so."

Lisse uncovered the crystal and took a deep breath before she picked it up. It flared with pure white light then melted in her palm. Rivulets of sparkling liquid snaked up her arms until they reached her tech and were absorbed into it. Light flowed through her tech until it all glowed like mother-of-pearl.

Her skin seemed lit from the inside. The light traced its way from her chest to her neck to her face. It gathered in a spot on her forehead, a spot that grew brighter and brighter. Lisse drew in a sharp breath as her back arched, and her eyes snapped open. They were the pearly white of a blind seeress. The light grew brighter still, so intense I had to close my eyes and look away.

When the light dimmed to the point that I wasn't seeing the blood vessels in my eyelids, I opened my eyes. Lisse was slumped forward, partially sprawled across the table. I wrapped an arm around her shoulders and tilted her head back. A miniature version of the shard was embedded in the middle of her forehead.

"Lisse?" She didn't stir. I touched her cheek. When I brushed my lips against hers, I felt her breath against them. Alive. Thank the gods, she's alive. "Can you hear me?" When she didn't respond, I kissed her cheek. "Please wake up."

She stirred, her eyes slowly blinking open as if she struggled to wake from a deep sleep. "I'm here." She wet her lips. "Did it work?"

I took her hand and raised it to her forehead. Her eyes widened, and she shrugged out of my hold and bolted to the hygiene cube. I followed and found her staring at her reflection in the mirror. She smiled, the joy in it lit her eyes. "It's beautiful."

Lisse was right. It was beautiful, but not as beautiful as she was.

SIX
LISSE

I touched the miniature shard that sparkled on my forehead. Warm. It was warm and felt like it had always been right where it was, like my teeth or nails. I didn't feel different, and that worried me. I expected to feel more than a deeper awareness of the things around me: the soft hum of the ship's systems, the slight draft of air from the air processing, the regular beating of Ryne's heart. It was as if I'd stretched and grown, not changed.

Why would you change? My aetherware's voice was stronger, clearer. *You haven't stopped being you.*

My brother did. And so did Ryne.

Ryne stood behind me, his attention fixed on our reflection in the mirror. His wavy brown hair was shot through with strands of gold that gleamed in the light. It looked soft and more than a little wild. How would it feel when it brushed against my inner thighs as he tongued and tasted me? My cheeks flushed, and I bit my lip.

Worry lines creased his forehead, and his hands clenched and unclenched as he frowned at me. "Are you well?"

"I am." He eyed me warily, so I turned to face him. "I'm unharmed." I touched his arm. "Really."

He glanced at my hand. "It doesn't hurt me. I thought maybe it would."

Tell him not to be so dramatic. I don't have any intention of harming him.

"It won't. I think, maybe, it was reacting to being forced into your tech. It knew it didn't belong there."

"But it belongs with you." He reached out to touch the shard. "Does it know who I am?"

I know as much of him as you do.

I squeezed his arm gently and fought back an urge to wrap my arms around him, rest my head against his chest, and feel his heartbeat against my cheek. "I'm sorry."

"Why?" He traced the line of my jaw, and I tilted my head back and swallowed hard as his fingers trailed down my throat. "You didn't hurt me."

"But my brother did."

"You aren't responsible for him.' He brushed his lips across my cheek. They grazed my ear as he murmured, "You are not your brother."

Not now. Maybe not ever. But the fear of turning into something like Joran haunted me. He couldn't care about anyone except himself. I couldn't stop caring about others. As long as that was true, I wasn't going to become a monster. "No, I'm not. Maybe I can fix what he did to you."

"Fix it? How?" He followed me to the table, sat across from me, and rested his arms on the table.

"I can look inside your mind." I hadn't done more than skim someone's surface thoughts in years. "It's a talent I had before I got my tech, but it's stronger now. Maybe I can find memories that are blocked or locked away."

"You can do that?"

"I can try." I didn't need to ask his permission. Joran

certainly wouldn't have. He would have taken the information he needed.

You are not your brother.

No. I wasn't.

Ryne rubbed his jaw as he stared at the tabletop. "Can I have some time to think about it?"

"I thought you wanted to know." Was he refusing because he knew what I'd find?

"I do. And I don't." He took my hand, and his thumb rubbed the sensitive skin on the inside of my wrist. "What if I am someone terrible? Like those Dark Sun bastards. What if I'm another monster who needs killing?"

"Then I will kill you. You wouldn't be the first Dark Sun soldier I'd killed." And he wouldn't be the last unless he killed me first. "But that's not going to happen."

"You can't be sure of that."

"Maybe I'm not. But my tech is. Back in the cave, it told me to save you." Of course, it could have been worried about the shard getting damaged if he died.

I wasn't. He couldn't harm the shard. And I did tell you save him, not it.

Why do you trust him?

I trust his tech.

He wasn't like my brother either. At least I hoped he wasn't. "What if you're like me?"

Ryne smiled. The expression seemed to make the amber in his eyes brighten. If he was like me, he wouldn't be alone. He would belong somewhere. Anywhere. Just like me. He wet his lips. "What do I have to do?"

I squeezed his hand. "You've already done it." I didn't need to touch him, but I wanted to.

"That's it?"

I closed my eyes. "Just relax."

"Just relax. Relax while you rummage through my brain."

"Relax"—I pressed a finger to his lips—"and be quiet."

We sat in silence until we both relaxed, until our breathing fell into synch with each other. I rode the resonance between our tech into Ryne's mind and looked for scars left behind by memories pulled out at the roots. I looked for blocks that made the information behind them inaccessible. But there was no damage. None at all.

There was a wealth of information. I saw the viridian moons rise over Floris, sipped crisp wine wrung from lunar grapes. I heard the mating cries of mourning hawks on Oleron and smelled the creamy musk of Telian lotus blossoms. Each detail, each fact and sensation, was its own entity in a vast archive. What was missing were the memories attached to them, the tapestry of personality and experience that held them together and gave them meaning.

Ryne wasn't damaged or being held prisoner in his own mind. I couldn't find any sign that the man he had been existed at all. That person had been washed away so completely not even the smallest echoes of it remained.

I pulled back from his mind but didn't let go of his hand. "I…. I'm so sorry, Ryne"

He stiffened, his face going expressionless. "I'm one of them. Aren't I?"

"No." Holy gods, I did not want him to be. "Maybe. I don't know. I can find things that you know. But I can't find anything about who you are. It's like you were reset. Your data survived, but your operating system was wiped clean."

"I see." The words were as expressionless as his face. He stood. "Thank you for trying. I need some time." The *Tempest* had several crew cabins, and he disappeared into one of the empty ones.

I stared at the chair he was sitting in, then slipped into it to feel his lingering warmth against my skin. For years, I'd been alone on the *Tempest*. Why was it I never felt lonely until now?

SEVEN
RYNE

I paced the length of the crew cabin. It was seven strides from one end to the other. I counted them off to give me something to focus on instead of the fact that someone had stripped away every scrap of who I was. They had killed me. Sure, my body worked, but whatever made it uniquely mine was dead as dust. I didn't know whether to mourn or rage. Both churned uncomfortably inside me.

I was like this room. A blank slate. There were no holo pics of family and friends, no souvenirs collected from planets visited. No plants. No wall hangings or rugs. No echoes of the person who once slept here, fucked here, dreamed here. It was empty and sterile. Just like me.

You aren't empty.

I didn't ask for your opinion.

That doesn't mean you don't need to hear it.

The list of things I needed might be lengthy, but having sentient aetherware meddling in my life wasn't anywhere on it. Unless.... *Are you there?*

I'm always here, Ryne. I will be here until you die.

It probably meant to be comforting. I'm not sure it was. *I'm already dead.*

No. You aren't. You're…between. Between who you were, and who you will become.

Do you know who I am?

I know who you are now, not who you were before we joined. A pause. *Sometimes when we join, things can go wrong. Things can break. In the aetherware and in the host.*

Lisse's brother was right. I was a mistake. An imperfect host.

He is not your friend. Or Lisse's. Do not listen to him.

I rubbed my temples, trying to soothe away the tension that throbbed behind my eyes. Who should I listen to? Who should I trust?

Trust your heart. Your intuition.

I notice you didn't say to trust you.

Trust is a gift. It must be earned. I can't demand it of you.

Trust my heart. For that I'd have to trust myself, and I didn't. But I did trust Lisse.

Do I trust her because of you? Are you making me want her?

Her tech and I are mated systems, designed to work together. You sense that connection, but your feelings and…urges…are your own.

Right now, my urges wanted to be close to her, to bask in her warmth. I wanted to savor her scent of blush lotus and starlit musk. I chose to chase the pleasure life offered me.

Lisse wasn't in the cabin or the cockpit, but the door to one of the other sleeping spaces was open wide enough for me to see her. She sat on her bed, knees pulled up to her chest. Her head rested on them, and that quicksilver hair spilled over her like a silken shield. I cleared my throat, and her head jerked up. There was a tightness around her eyes. If they had been red, I'd have sworn she had been crying. For herself? For me?

"Can I come in?"

She nodded, then shifted to sit on the edge of the bed with

her feet on the floor. All the better to make a quick retreat. Sit or stand? One felt too intimate, the other too distant. In the end, I sat next to her, close but not touching. Which was farther away than I liked. Would it always feel like this around her? This urge to be as close as possible?

I forced a smile. "This is a fucking mess, isn't it?"

"I doubt it's what either of us would have asked for."

"Problem is no one asked us our opinion."

"No. No, they didn't." She bowed her head, and her hair fell forward, hiding her from me.

That wouldn't do. I threaded my fingers through her hair—it was as gloriously soft as I'd imagined—and tucked it behind her ear. Her breath hitched. I traced the shell of her ear and let my fingers trail down the side of her neck. I brushed them lightly over her shoulder and her tech, and she shivered, exhaled a soft moan.

"What are you doing?"

I was enjoying the soft husk to her voice. The flush that colored her cheeks. The way she leaned toward me, a bright star caught in my gravity.

EIGHT
LISSE

Ryne's touch sang through me spreading out from my shoulder until it filled me. I shifted on the bed, turning toward him and closing the distance between us. Our thighs touched, and even though the soft fabric of our pants wasn't thick, it became an unwanted barrier between us.

"I like touching you." His fingers stroked the lacy tech on my shoulder. The touch was light, gentle, just the tips of his fingers, but my entire body resonated with it.

"I like being touched." At least by him.

"Good." A wicked smile curved his lips and as much as I wanted the pleasure it promised, I wanted him to work for it. I touched my palm to the marks on his chest, and Ryne tensed. He covered my hand with his own, pressing it harder against his skin. I curled my fingers, and when my nails scraped him, he groaned as a shudder ran through him.

"I'm sorry." I relaxed my fingers. "I didn't mean to hurt you."

"You didn't." His voice was tight.

"Oh." Oooooh. I dug my nails into his skin enough to bite, and his body jerked in response.

Ryne growled, a low, deep rumble. His fingers rubbed small circles against my tech, the sensation darting through my body. My nipples hardened. My back arched. It felt like his fingers were everywhere—carding through my hair, teasing my nipples and clit.

"What are you doing?" The words spilled out of me in a breathless rush.

"The same thing you are doing to me." He leaned closer, his lips close enough to mine that I could feel his breath against them. "I want you. No, I need you." He licked my lips before his tongue slipped past them to taste me. His voice slipped into my mind. *I bet I could make you come just by kissing you and rubbing your shoulders.*

Smug bastard. Two can play that game. I gripped his upper arms, ran my palms up and down them. His hips rocked in time with my touch. *I bet I could make you come just from stroking your arms.*

Our gazes locked. *I suppose the only question is which of us can hold out longer.* His touch settled into a firm rhythm that slowed and gentled each time I got close before speeding up again. Not fair. He wasn't playing fair. Not when it had been so long since I came from anyone's touch but my own.

As much as I wanted to come, I hated losing, so I gritted my teeth and tried to fight back the rising wave of pleasure that threatened to pull me under. My grip on his arms tightened. I didn't have to last long. Just longer than him.

Relax. Ryne's voice was a soft, dark purr entirely at odds with the tension in his body. *But you don't need to be quiet.* His fingers kneaded my skin, pinching it gently.

No. Not yet. Not until he did. My body tightened.

Relax and come for me.

No. No. No. No. No. My mind rebelled at his words, but my body was happy to comply.

266

I want to feel you come for me, Lisse.
And I did.

NINE
RYNE

L isse cried out as her tech burned with a pearly light, pulsing with the orgasm rippling through her body. Her nails dug into my shoulders, and that little bite of pain, so very different from the torment I faced earlier, made my cock ache. I wanted to wrap her hand around it, but I was afraid I'd come at her touch, and I didn't want this to be over so soon.

She shivered as her body softened against me. When she blinked her eyes open, there was only the thinnest band of silvery gray around her pupils.

Ryne? She smiled as she cupped my cheek and kissed me.

I'm here.

Mmm. You are. Her hand came to rest on my thigh before moving higher. Her clever fingers dipped under the waistband of my pants, and I let out a breath I didn't realize I was holding when they stroked up and down my cock. *You're very hard.*

I was so hard my entire body ached for her. I slipped my fingers under the fabric of her pants and between her legs.. She was warm and so wet. And that was a wonder to me because while I knew the mechanics of what we were doing, I had no memory of other partners, other times. In every way that counted this was my first time.

"Ryne?"

"Yes."

Her fingers curled around me and squeezed gently. "Fuck me."

After another gentle squeeze, I caught her wrist and moved her hand away from me. "Keep that up and I'm going to come."

She laughed, low and husky, then murmured in my ear, "How would you like me?"

I bit down on my lip as my eyes slid closed. Images of her in various positions flashed through my mind. Not one of them was a bad option.

"Or should I decide?"

"No." Her first orgasm was for her. The next one was mine. "On the bed. Hands and knees."

Her brows rose, and I expected her to argue. She stood, arching her back as she pulled her top over her head. I followed the path her hands took as she ran them down her sides and under the waistband of her pants before she pushed them over her hips to pool around her ankles. She got onto the bed and grinned as she glanced back at me from over her shoulder. "Like this?"

"Just like that." I stood and ran my hands over her back, down her sides, and over her ass, noting the places where my touch drew soft moans from her. As much as I wanted to be inside her, I slid my hands between her thighs to spread her open for me, crouched down, and leaned in to taste her. She tensed at my first lick, and the sound she made…. Gods, I swore I could feel it vibrating around my cock. I took my time tasting her, each lick winding us both up tighter and tighter.

"Don't be such a fucking tease. Fuck me already, Ryne."

Patience wasn't one of her virtues. I would have liked to think it was one of mine, but my cock insisted otherwise.

I stood and tugged off my clothes. My gaze wandered over her from her shoulders down her spine to the dimples on her lower back. Her skin was flushed and sheened with sweat, which made her beautiful tech stand out against it. I carded my fingers through her hair and gently tugged her head back.

"Look." I nodded toward the mirror we were facing. "We're going to watch."

"Watch?" Her eyes were wide, her lips wet.

"Mmm." I steadied my cock with my free hand. "We're going to watch you take my cock." I rubbed against her, teasing her with the head. "We're going to watch you get the fucking you need." She bit down on her lip. "And then, we're going to watch you come."

Her eyes slipped closed, just for a second. Just until I started pressing into her. "Oh. You're a bastard."

"And you still want me."

"I want to space you."

"No, you don't." I chuckled. "Take what you want."

She growled, defiance and desire warring in her eyes, but she didn't move. Just when I worried I'd overstepped, she shifted. I steadied my cock as she pressed back slowly. She watched me in the mirror, watched me fight to stay still, as she took me into her body. Slowly. Way too slowly. Her smile turned sharp and tight. She wanted to take me harder. Faster. I wanted that too. But neither one of us was going to be the first to ask for it. Stubborn recognized stubborn.

Lisse shivered and kept moving until her tight ass was pressed against me. Until I was buried balls deep in her heat. If this planet's sun went supernova and incinerated us, I would die happy. Joined with her. Chasing pleasure. For me, it was the first time I would remember.

"Eyes open, Ryne." I gasped as she tightened around me. Our gazes met in the mirror. "You're supposed to be watching." She moved slowly, rocking forward and pressing back. Adjusting the angle until soft moans spilled from her lips. Her gaze never faltered as she fucked herself on my cock.

But Lisse did more than just that: she branded herself on me so completely that I would never forget her. Even after I'd turned to dust, I was certain she would remain etched on my bones.

And I wanted her to feel the same.

I gripped her hips, pulled back, and thrust back in hard and deep. Once I started, I couldn't stop. As much as I wanted to draw this out, to make memories—real memories—need drove me forward. Again and again and again. I pulled her back into my thrusts, fighting to hit that spot that made her clench so deliciously around me. I didn't last long, but then neither did she.

Ryne. Maybe that was my name, maybe not, but I was going to keep it. Just so I could remember how it sounded as it fell from Lisse's lips when she came apart for me and pulled me over the edge with her.

TEN
LISSE

The ruins were familiar. Especially the petrified tree that had smashed through the temple and its stonework floor when it fell. Joran and I had climbed down that stone trunk to the tomb beneath the temple thirteen years ago. He was still my brother then. Our parents were still alive. Our small colony was thriving. All that changed when we found our tech.

Welcome home, little sister. Joran rose from the darkness of the tomb and settled on the ground. Tendrils of shadow writhed around him. When some lunged toward me, my tech wrapped me in a cocoon of light that dissolved them before they could touch me.

This was never our home. It was a tomb. It was where our parents died. Where Joran died.

Does that scare you? A stream of beetles with dark, iridescent shells swarmed out of the hole. They crackled and burned when they touched my shield.

Why should it? This is a dream.

People say that if you die in your dreams, you die in the waking world as well.

We circled each other, a pair of duelists looking for a weakness to exploit, a place to strike a telling blow.

People say a lot of things that aren't true. Especially you.

Joran shook his finger at me as if I was an errant child. *Are you growing claws, little mouse?*

I took several steps toward him, and while he didn't retreat, his shadows pulled back until they were close to his body. *I'm not afraid of you.*

You should be. I command armies. And you... You are alone.

Yesterday, he would have been right. Now, I had Ryne. Back on the *Tempest*, his body would be curled around mine, sweaty and sated. Our breathing and heartbeats and tech perfectly in synch. Around his wrist, he'd have a new marking: a band of knotted black and white vines so tightly entwined it was impossible to tell where one stopped and the other began. Just like I did.

Not anymore. Even though Joran had a host of soldiers and spies, sycophants and slaves, he was more alone than I. I almost felt sorry for him. *Not ever again.*

I will have him. One day. He will suffer before I kill him, and you won't be able to do anything except watch him die.

No. Flecks of darkness that gleamed like black mica swirled through my aura. Instead of fearing them, I embraced them. They meant that even here, deep in this dreamscape, Ryne was with me.

What did you say?

I said no. Whips of light struck the darkness around Joran, and while his shield held, he staggered back several steps. Blood dripped from his nose.

You will pay for that, you bitch. You—

You are not welcome here. So do us both a favor, brother, and fuck off.

I called lightning down from the leaden sky. Bolt after bolt struck the shadows surrounding Joran. Before they could shatter his shield entirely, his form blinked out.

The dreamscape rippled as it faded and dissolved. I closed my eyes, conjured an image of Ryne, and reached for it. I was done with deprivation. I chose pleasure. I chose desire. I chose Ryne.

When my eyes opened, I was back on the *Tempest*.

Ryne's breath was warm against my shoulder, his arm snug around my waist. He snored softly, but no one was perfect. When I kissed him, he stirred. His lips parted. I kissed him again, deeper this time, and his fingers stroked the nape of my neck. For the first time in a very long while, I felt safe, content. Maybe even happy.

For the first time in a very long while, the *Tempest* felt like home.

ABOUT B.L. LUCAS

B.L. Lucas writes spicy fantasy and paranormal romance that spirits you away you to realms steeped in shadows and edged in enchantment where witchy women and haunted heroes save each other and their worlds. *The Touchstone*, her debut novel and first book in a dark romantasy, reverse-harem series full of found family, misfits saving the day, and bonded mates, will be released in early 2025.

Visit www.barbedwriting.com to sign up for her newsletter and find links to her social media site. You can talk nerdy to Barbara by emailing her at barb@barbedwriting.com.

facebook.com/BarbaraLucasWriter

instagram.com/barbedwriting

CHASING DESTINY A CYBORG ROMANCE

JAYLEE AUSTIN

Heating Rating: Smokin'

ONE
LUNA EVERGLEN

In the underground lab at Dragan's University, where I taught a basic coding seminar, the sterile hum of the machines was a lullaby to my senses as I stood amid a jungle of gleaming metal and pulsating holograms. The screens flickered with graphs and codes too complex for any ordinary mind to decipher. I found solace in this place, where the lines between human flesh and cybernetic circuitry blended seamlessly, creating a beautiful network.

"Status report." I never took my eyes off the microchip nested within the heart of a skeletal prototype, its filaments glowing like the first breath of a newborn star.

"Project Mystic Fusion operational at 94 percent efficiency," Aiden, my holographic assistant, said.

"Only ninety-four? I expected better. Run a diagnostic on the synaptic relays. They should fire at a minimum of ninety-seven."

"Understood." Aiden's form flickered as he processed the command.

"Also, cross-reference the bio-compatibility index again. The last thing we need is rejection." The clock ticked within the walls of the lab, each second a countdown to a breakthrough or a breakdown.

"Biocompatibility remains stable across all test subjects," Aiden confirmed. "No signs of internal rejection detected in preliminary trials."

"Good." I allowed myself the briefest moment of satisfaction before my mind raced ahead to the next hurdle. The microchip wasn't just a piece of tech; it was a revolution lying dormant, waiting for my signal to awaken. The microchip held the key to enhancing reflexes, strength, even cognition itself—unleashing the full potential of the human mind and body with the supernatural realms of magic.

For generations, humans had longed for this kind of advancement, but it was only with recent breakthroughs in technology that it became a possibility. It promised to elevate humanity beyond its limitations and finally give us the secrets to what the world might be like if we combined two species and I— Luna Everglen, part Celtic Fae, part cyborg visionary, would be the architect of this new era of humanity.

I dedicated my life to this project, ever since I lost my parents at a young age to a devastating magical attack. I was determined to create a way for humans to defend themselves against such threats and level the playing field in this new world where magic was real. And now, after years of research, I was on the brink of success.

"Let's make history, Aiden."

"Initiating final sequence." The tech hummed with anticipation, every device and instrument synchronized to the beat of progress.

"Here goes everything." The moment I took a leap into the unknown.

"Ethically, Luna, aren't we playing god?" The challenge came sharp and unexpected, slicing through the lab's charged silence like a scalpel. I didn't need to look up from the console to recognize the sanctimonious tone of my challenger, Dr. Elliot.

"Playing god?" I fired back without missing a beat, spinning my chair around to face him. "Enlighten me, Elliot. When did advancements become a sin?"

"Advancement? You're altering the very fabric of our being. Where do you draw the line, Luna? When does enhancement become an aberration?"

"Aberration?" I scoffed, rising to my full height, my wings unfolding slightly in agitation. "I'm offering people wings— literal and metaphorical. With this microchip, they can exceed their natural limitations. Think enhanced cognition, improved physical endurance, accelerated healing, the ability to fight any alien form they encounter. We're not just patching up human frailties, we're ushering in the next stage of evolution."

"Evolution? I call it the unnatural selection."

"Isn't it better for people to choose their own potential?" I strode past him to the central halo table where the shimmering blueprint of the microchip hovered. I pointed to the intricate design. "This is about autonomy. It's about giving humans control over their own destiny."

"Destiny or disparity? You create something like this, and you think it won't be exploited? That it won't widen the gap between the haves and the have-nots?"

"We can make it accessible. We set precedents, establish regulations. This is progress. And progress doesn't bow to fear."

"Progress doesn't ignore ethics either," he retorted.

"Ethics." I laughed, though there was no humor in it. "Let's talk ethics. Is it ethical to deny advancements that can ease suffering? To hold back the tide of innovation because it scares you. Because it challenges your narrow world view?"

"Your vision might be broad, but it's dangerously shortsighted." Elliot locked glares with me. I understood from his attitude that neither one of us was willing to budge in our views.

"Then let history be the judge. But today, I see a future where humanity isn't bound to the ground by fear or doubt. I see us soaring." I turned off the halo interface, tired of this conversation that we'd repeated over the past month.

———

Later that day, I was soldering the last synapse connector on my microchip when the holographic interface flickered to life, casting a cold blue light across the cluttered expanse of my laboratory.

"Dr. Everglen," came the crisp, synthesized voice of the executive CEO of Helixcorp, Mr. Dray. "We've reviewed your latest proposal on human enhancement technology."

"Have you now?" I adjusted my wings to work out the kinks.

"We want to fund the next level of your research. Sell the prototype, and you'll be financially solvent the rest of your life."

"At what cost to my sense of fairness?" I placed my hand on my hip and gave him the sweetest fake smile I could muster.

"There are a few stipulations you overlooked like the fact Helixcorp has exclusive first rights to the biotech."

"Exclusive rights," I repeated flatly, setting down my soldering iron, not trusting him in the least. "What you mean is you want control of the potential gains if my theories work."

"Semantics, Doctor. With our endorsements, your vision could be realized on a global scale."

"Or stamped with your logo and sold to the highest bidder." I spun around to face the hologram, not wanting to admit that Elliot had been right.

"Think practically. You can't possibly handle or distribute this technology on your own terms. You need us."

"Watch me." I glared at him, determined to protect my work

from his greed. "I've seen what happens when companies like yours get hold of a humanitarian concept and turn it into a profitable product."

"Now. Now. Your idealism is… charming, but ill-fitting for someone of your intellect. You must understand the risk and cost in expanding human enhancements."

"I understand you and the company's investors see the humans as collateral damage. Well, I don't."

"Dr. Everglen, listen to me! You need to change your entire perspective if you want to survive. This is a matter of life or death for your career."

"Threats now? That's low even for you, Dray."

"Consider it advice. Your defiance puts you in a precarious position, Doctor."

"Let's not pretend you care about my well-being or those who this technology would help. This is about power and control. It always has been with Helixcorp."

"It's a matter of perspective. We see it as stewardship."

"Call it what you want. Anyone, even Helixcorp won't coerce me." I cut the connection before he could reply, the hologram dissipating like smoke on a breeze. They thought they could intimidate me, clip my wings with fear. But I was no bird in a cage.

The lab was a cacophony of whirring machines and bright lights as I slumped into my chair, the weight of countless hours pressing down on my shoulders. For a fleeting moment, raw vulnerability seeped through the cracks in my armored facade, whispering of lost nights and forsaken dreams. I stared at the microchip before me, its lustrous surface reflecting not just the overhead lights but the specter of missed dinners, ignored calls, and friendships left to wither and fall to the wayside.

I shook the dark thoughts away, feeling the familiar stir of my wings against the constraints of my lab coat. *Knock off the self-pity.* I glanced around the laboratory. This wasn't just about what I'd lost when my family was killed at the hands of a devastating magical attack. I was determined to create a way for humans to defend themselves against such threats and level the playing field in this new world where magic was real.

Back to work, I entered the final sequence of commands. The microchip prototype lay suspended in a containment field. "Start last test run." The holographic interface blinked obediently, and the microchip sparked to life, its inner light pulsing like a new star being born. "System's responding within optimal parameters," the AI responded.

I scanned the readouts. "This is it."

Suddenly, a piercing alarm shattered my excitement.

Red lights flashed.

A frantic message scrolled across the screen: Security Breach-Lab Sector 7G.

My wings unfurled from my back, and I flew toward the secure vault, where my most sensitive research was stored. "Lockdown protocol, engage." My command faltered. The automated defenses were compromised.

I skidded to a halt in front of the vault, punching in the override code with trembling hands. The door slid open with a hiss, and I grabbed the nearest stack of data reports containing years of my research, but they'd locked down the microchip, giving me little choice but to leave it behind if I was going to escape with the keynotes to decode the sequence. I turned on my heels and darted for the secret tunnel behind the bookcase.

Before I could leave, the screen flickered, and a modulated, a genderless voice shot gooseflesh at the nape of my neck. "Dr. Everglen, your efforts are commendable, and we admire your dedication to humanity, but Zorgon Enterprise will not allow Helixcorp to proceed unchecked. Surrender your research and you will be spared.

"Like hell I will."

"Your defiance is noted," the voice said, eerily calm. "Be advised that breaches of contract will not be tolerated."

The threat hung in the air, heavy and unseen like a toxic fog.

"Anticipate this." I slid into the tunnel just as the sound of boots stormed the lab. Behind me, the clamor of chaos rose as everything I had built was destroyed.

As I navigated the dark passageway, my mind searched for solutions. I'd prepared for this outcome, but I'd hoped that it wouldn't happen. My real concern was, what did they know about my microchip? And how far would they go to stop me?

"Game on." I clutched the data pads close. My pulse pounded in sync with the ticking bomb of my predicament. It was a race against time, against Helixcorp.

I had to find Jaxon, because the stakes had never been higher. He was the only one I trusted, and I needed his help.

TWO
JAXON THORNHART

The Zorgon marketplace was a labyrinth of chaos, a sea of alien flesh that flowed like a river through the stalls of exotic goods. My boots pounded cobblestone as I wove through the throng of people and traders, each step propelling me forward in pursuit of the elusive target just ahead.

"Out of the way," I barked, my words barely cutting through the haggling voices and the sizzle of street food hitting scorching grills. My left arm, sheathed in synth-skin, brushed against a stall, sending a stack of crimson fruit tumbling. The vendor cursed, but I was gone before the first fruit hit the ground.

I couldn't wait to feel the perp's cold flesh struggling in my grip. My cybernetic heart kept time like a metronome, immune to the adrenaline that once would've sent it to overdrive. A steady pulse thrummed beneath my skin; each breath measured. A machine in human guise, chasing down another piece of tech, turned rogue. Kyra, my first mentor out of Vexicon Tech, almost lost her life only to lose her job as a federal agent bounty hunter. I planned on making Zorgon's underground syndicate wish they'd never heard my name, and I'd start with the perp in front of me.

Ahead, the target glanced back, our gazes locked for a fraction of a second. No fear there, just the rational calculation of someone who knew they were being hunted. I pushed harder, muscles fortified with alloy and sinew responding instantly. The target up ahead countered every turn I took. I had to catch him. It wasn't just about justice for Kyra but proving that even in a world teeming with new tech, some things were still black-and-white. I jumped forward, the gap between my target closing with every breath.

Jumping over a stall of decorative scarves, my feet hit the ground with a soft thud, and I crouched down, eyes scanning for any signs of danger. The dusty cobblestones felt rough beneath my palm as I steadied myself and charged after him. "Running out of steam yet?" I called ahead to the figure weaving through the crowd.

"Wouldn't you like to know, Thornhart?" His voice crackled through my earpiece with a mocking tone meant to disarm me.

"Actually, I would." I closed in on him with superpower speed. "I've got places to be, people to see, and pests to catch."

A laugh echoed back to me. I'm sure it was an obvious attempt to rile me up. "Try your best, you over-inflated metal cyborg."

"Careful." I watched as he narrowly avoided a vendor's cart. "Don't hurt yourself on my account."

"Always so considerate, Jaxon," he said, his silhouette darting into an alleyway too narrow for comfort.

"Part of the service," I shot back as I plunged into the shadows after him. The walls here were close enough to touch, and the garbage aromas mingled in the damp air. My eyes adjusted using infrared light. I scanned ahead for any hint of movement and focused on his physical signature like the predator I was. "Come on, is this the best you can do? I thought we were having fun."

"*Fun's* not the word I'd use." I heard the strain in his voice, a sure sign that the relentless chase was wearing on him.

My mind was all business as I cataloged escape routes and potential ambush points. Suddenly, he burst from the alley's end onto a rooftop, agile as a cat.

I followed right behind him. "Nice view up here, don't you think?"

"Just back off." He jumped across to another building.

"Ticktock." I made the jump effortlessly, feeling the thrill of the chase pump through my veins. "Your time's run out."

"Keep dreaming."

The rough cobblestones scraped against his shoes as he stumbled backward, arms flailing for balance. I couldn't help but smirk at his predicament. The chase had led us to a dead end, the walls of Zorgon's high-rises encircling us like steel sentinels. The target's chest heaved from exertion, his back against the stone. "End of the line."

"Think you've got me cornered? he spat out between breaths; his gaze darted for an escape that didn't exist.

"Cornered, captured, soon-to-be-caged." I advanced with deliberate steps, ready to spring into action.

He lunged with a desperate swing aimed at my head. I sidestepped, grabbed his wrist, and twisted it behind his back. He yelped, both in pain and surprise, as I pressed him against the cold metal wall.

"Didn't your mother ever tell you not to hit?"

"Fuck you."

"Cache, now," I called out. From the shadows, my cyborg pug charged forward, his little frame deceptively sturdy. His mechanical legs clicked against the pavement, and at my command, Cache darted toward the thief's ankles.

"Control the mutt." My target tried to kick at Cache, but I tightened my grip on his arm, securing him further.

"More than just a pretty face, isn't he?"

Cache circled back and sat obediently, his tongue lolling out in a pant that seemed almost mocking.

"Show me where, Cache?"

Cache's one digital eye flickered and then he barked once, decisively, gesturing with his snout toward the target's boot.

"Good boy." I dropped to my knees with lightning speed, pinning the target down with one arm while I fumbled for the hidden compartment in his heel. The adrenaline pumping through my veins made my movements almost animalistic as I struggled to keep control over the squirming figure. I finally managed to pry open the heel and retrieve a tiny data chip nestled inside, glowing faintly with encoded secrets. "Found your little treasure." I plucked the chip with ease. "My pup's got a nose for trouble, sniffing out tech hidden anywhere on the body."

"Jaxon Thornhart and his cyborg mutt," the man tried to salvage some bravado. "What a joke."

"Call us what you want, but you're the one going back in cuffs." I signaled Cache to fetch the restraints from my belt. I secured the thief, ensuring there'd be no more rooftop tango today.

After I left my target at the bastille, I wandered through the labyrinthine alleys of Zorgon's underbelly. Suddenly, bullets of neon light streaked past my visor as I darted through in search of the second target, Cache close at my heel. The hum of the marketplace faded as a siren wailed, and a heavy net of laser grid snapped into place before me, buzzing with deadly potential.

My next target wouldn't be so easy.

"Cache," I called sharply. The pug's mechanical legs skidded to a halt beside me, his head tilting up. His internal systems were already scanning for a workaround.

"Rooftop, thirty degrees to your right," the pug's synthesized voice directed, as he pointed with his snout.

"Good boy." With a grunt, I jumped over a fractured neon

sign. I zeroed in on the target's heat signature just as he ducked into what looked like an impenetrable fortress—the Sanguine Bastion, Zorgon's most notorious black-market syndicate hub. The mafia leaders didn't just let anyone wander into their viper's nest. "Perfect," I muttered under my breath. "A regular, uneventful chase was too dull, right Cache?" I ground my jaw in extreme frustration at the extra time this would take.

Cache whined beside me, his pug-sized body tensing with anticipation. I scanned the perimeter. Guards patrolled the walls, their movements synchronized, while automated turrets swiveled atop fortified checkpoints. Infiltration would require more than brute force.

"Okay, Cache, we play this smart. Distract and disable." My mind raced through potential strategies.

"Arf." His small form slipped unnoticed under a cargo transport as it approached the Bastion's checkpoint.

Distraction: check. I watched Cache's work unfold. The transport halted abruptly, confusion bubbling among the guards as they investigated the unexpected malfunction.

Showtime.

I sprinted toward the nearest guard tower, my enhanced muscles carrying me faster than any human eye could track. With a swift, silent leap, I was on the first guard and had my arm wrapped around his throat before he could utter a sound. A click of my jaw activated the subvocal comm in my throat implant.

"Nighty-night," I whispered, the guard's body going limp in my arms. Quickly, I interfaced with the tower's security panel, my fingers moving across the holographic keys.

"Access granted," the AI voice cooed in my earpiece. I always enjoyed when they played nice.

The turret guns powered down with a series of soft clicks. I allowed myself the hint of a smirk. Next was the inner courtyard, where the target had vanished into the maze of dark corridors and neon-lit dens.

With the guards neutralized and the security systems compromised, the path lay open. Now all that remained was to close the gap, take what was mine, and defuse the situation.

"End of the line," my voice echoed off the grimy walls. "You've got two choices: come quietly or leave in pieces."

"Go to hell, Thornhart." Despite the tremor of fear that undercut his words, he defiantly etched every syllable.

"Been there. The weather's terrible." I watched him weigh his options. He glanced left, then right, hope dying in his eyes as he realized escape was impossible.

"Back off."

"Let's not make this harder than it has to be." I advanced with caution, Cache at my heel, his curlicue tail wagging at the prospect of action. "Hand over the Zorgon's data drive, and I won't have to dismantle you piece by shiny piece."

"Never." He reached behind him, fingers scrabbling for a weapon.

"Bad move." Right as he drew a blade, Cache leaped forward with a bark that sounded like a war cry, clamping down on the man's arm with jaws designed to crush metal. "Good boy, Cache." I closed the gap in a few strides, grabbing the thief's collar and yanking him away from the wall. "Now, where were we?"

The data drive—a sleek, silver sliver of tech—fell from his grasp, and I stooped to retrieve it. The disk contained tons of sensitive information about Sanguine Bastion's plans for world domination using Luna's new discoveries. Helixcorp paid me well to locate both chips. Now to end this job and take a needed vacation.

"Mission accomplished." The data drive fit snugly in my palm, the smooth metal surface cool against my skin. One would think that after a lifetime of running, fighting, and killing, I'd be used to the adrenaline rush that came with success. And yet, every time I aced a mission, it still felt like victory—like raw electricity pulsing through my veins. But this wasn't over yet. There was still one more piece of business to attend to before I could call it a night.

The target slumped, defeated, as I cuffed his wrists with restraints strong enough to hold a rampaging Groznian megabeast. "Thornhart…please…I was just--"

His excuses were nothing new, the same drivel from every cornered crook. "Save it for the Council," I cut him off, dragging him to his feet. "You and your sidekick are going to stand trial for your crimes. And if you're lucky, the two of you will live to see prison."

Before leaving Zorgon's marketplace, I transferred the data drive and chip to Helixcorp's agent and obtained the payment. My job here was completed. "Let's move, Cache."

We had just stepped out of the alley when a slender figure blocked our path. As recognition slammed into me, I blinked in surprise. "Luna?"

Luna Everglen, a renowned scientist and my former lover, stood before me in all her winged glory. Auburn hair cascaded over her shoulders, partially obscuring the intricate cybernetics grafted onto her back. Her emerald eyes glinted with determination as she faced me and pursed her lips in that adorable pout I knew so well.

"Jaxon," she whispered. "It's been a long time."

I tensed, old emotions welling up despite my best efforts. Our history was complicated, full of friendship and chaos in equal measure. I wasn't sure if her presence boded well or ill.

"What are you doing here?"

She tilted her head. "I need your help. The fate of my research depends on it."

I narrowed my eyes. "You'll have to do better than that. I don't have time for games."

Luna stepped closer, her expression earnest. "Helixcorp plans on manipulating my new research."

"In what way?"

"Please, Jaxon." Her voice dropped to a whisper. "I know I've given you no reason to trust me. But this time I'm telling the truth. They really want what I've discovered."

Cache whined softly, gazing between us with pleading eyes. I sighed, making my decision.

"All right, truce for now."

Luna nodded. "Find me at the Phoenix lab in two days." She disappeared back into the shadows.

With my mind spinning, despite our past, something in Luna's voice rang true. If Helixcorp confiscated her tech, the consequences could be disastrous, especially if they silenced Luna and prevent others from gaining her research.

Still, I had to be cautious. The last time I'd trusted Luna, I'd ended up with a plasma burn across my back and barely escaped with my life.

I had to take the risk and decide whether to help her against my own better judgement. "Come on, boy." I glanced down at Cache. "We've got work to do."

At the spaceport, I slipped inside my sleek cruiser, the Celeste. Cache curled up on the copilot's seat as I started the launch sequence. The engines rumbled to life, and we shot into the sky. I set a course for the Phoenix lab; a top secret research facility hidden in the desert mountains.

THREE
JAXON

The dust of the desert swirled around my boots as I made my way through the settlement on the outskirts that was nestled close to the human town of Jasper. The Vexicon secret federal lab hid in the red rock mounds, where we both found refuge with the feds in those early days. Luna was no ordinary woman. She was a challenge, a puzzle, and now a desire that burned brighter than a supernova. But she was also an old friend, a partner I could trust once upon a time.

But the years had hardened us both, changed us. She dove into her research, determined to unlock the secrets of enhancement technology. I slid into the shadows, taking more and more dangerous jobs. We lost touch until she showed up in the alley at the black market in Zorgon.

Bounty hunters were after her, or better yet, the data pads that held the passkey to unlock the microchip that Zorgon's Enterprise had conveniently taken when they destroyed the lab. News traveled fast about how one tiny scientist escaped right under the watchful eye of the company. I admired that kind of intelligence. Ironically, Helixcorp approached me to secure the data pads that held the codes, thinking that I could get close to her. And they were right, I could.

Luna Everglen was inside. I brushed my fingers against the cool synthetic skin of my sidearm, a habitual check to see that all components were in working order. I slipped past the first mirage and before me the door loomed, its surface pocked with age and secrets. With a glance over my shoulder, I signaled for Cache to be ready. I pressed the buzzer.

The ring's echo died. I ran a hand through my hair, the strands slipping between my fingers. The door clicked; a sound so faint it might as well have been silence itself to unenhanced ears. It swung inward, and there she was.

Cache wagged his cyber curlicue tail with an unusual excitement, his black tux flapping, bringing humor to his aristocratic appearance. We strolled down the corridor to a stainless-steel door that opened, expecting our arrival. As we entered the lab, a warm glow lit the room.

A pair of green eyes reflected the myriads of screens surrounding her. Luna Everglen was a vision amid chaos, the eye of a technological storm, her slender figure bent over a bench laden with contraptions that even I found impressive. Her wings flapped once before they slipped back into her shoulder blades. I had a strange stirring in my core. My cock was pulsing in rhythm with my pounding heart. Something about this woman caused a sexual sensation I hadn't experienced in years. I'd missed her.

"Hello Jaxon." The words were cautious, her voice carrying the lilt of someone who'd spent too much time conversing with machines rather than people.

"Luna," I altered my tone. This is when Cache strutted like the aristocrat he was. Women fawned over his large brown eyes and the perpetually sunny smile on his face. She didn't disappoint. Picking Cache up. She snuggled him close and gave him hugs and kisses. I wished for one minute that it was on me she was lavishing all her attention. "He is where the future is being built, one microchip at a time."

Her brows knitted together ever so slightly, the gears in her brilliant mind already turning to figure out if she could really trust me. "I need your help." She stood with a guarded stance, ready to take flight like a bird.

"That's why I'm here."

She stepped closer, her voice dropping to a whisper. "I've created something extraordinary, a mystic fusion of two species, an implant that can enhance human capabilities with supernatural powers, making them equal with magical beings."

"That's why half the galaxy is searching for you."

"This technology in the wrong hands could be devastating. It has the potential to change humanity for the better. You may be the only one who can help me keep it safe."

"Helixcorp hired me to locate the chip."

"I figured they would."

I studied her intently, sensing her fear but also her resolve. This mysterious woman and her revolutionary invention could clearly alter the course of the future, for good or ill. My interest was piqued, both professionally and on a more personal level. "Tell me everything," I said. "You're safe with me."

"Take a seat." She motioned to a stool near a console brimming with holographic displays and blinking lights. She moved with a grace that belied her scientific prowess, each gesture precise and efficient as she began pulling up files and schematics.

I watched her every move, not just out of professional necessity but because there was something undeniably captivating about Luna Everglen. She was a paradox wrapped in an enigma, a creative fae beauty.

"Here we have it." On the printer sat a three-dimensional blueprint of a blended-species prototype.

"Looks impressive." I leaned forward to examine the hologram.

"It's more than impressive—it's revolutionary and will redefine human enhancements." A hint of fire lit her eyes.

"Indeed, revolutionary."

"Imagine a world where limitations of the flesh are just a memory."

"Sounds like a shortcut to evolution."

"Evolution is an endless pursuit." She narrowed her eyes at me, evaluating what I might say or do next.

"I agree."

"Doesn't humanity deserve every chance at advancement?"

"Depends on who's defining advancement. Some might say there's beauty in our imperfections." I smiled at the spark of debate igniting in her green eyes when she wrinkled her nose and chewed at her lip. She was my kinda woman and I had to admit that I missed these discussions.

"Beauty? Is it beautiful when the sick suffers because their body fails them? When brilliant minds decay with age? When others are physically or magically stronger?"

"Point taken. But what about consent? Autonomy? There's a fine line between enhancement, control, and living beyond human expectation. What about future generations?"

"Fear of control shouldn't hinder progress, and I'll ensure that every recipient fully understands the implications and gives their consent." Her body stiffened as her tone sharpened. "You sound like one of the doctors at the university. He said changing human evolution could lead to unethical practices."

"He's right. Isn't that why Helixcorp wants your data disk to prevent the wrong governments from dominating the cyber industry?"

"Can I trust you?"

The playful spark in her eyes was now tinged with fear, and I could only imagine the weight of her discovery pressing down on her slender shoulders. What did I care? Me, a bounty hunter. I was just having fun riling her up. "Ah, but who watches the watchmen? Power tends to corrupt as they say. And absolute power...you know the rest."

Luna stared at me with a mixed expression of annoyance, but underneath her tough exterior a hurt young woman still pined for her family. "You have a cynic's tongue, Jaxon, but would you deny the potential for good here?"

"Never. But the potential is a Pandora's box. Sometimes what we unleash can't be contained."

"Then it's our responsibility to steer the course."

"Or our folly to think we can." The cogwheels of my plan clicked into place as I watched her every move. I'd help her.

"It's hope."

I flicked an invisible speck of dust from my sleeve, a small smile playing on my lips. "Luna, your passion is admirable, but your faith in humanity seems, well, let me say, too optimistic."

"Optimism is the bedrock of innovation."

"Or the cliff's edge of naivety."

"Naivety?" Her slender eyebrow arched gracefully. I loved the spark in this woman. She was making it rather hard to do what Helixcorp requested. They'd offered quite a handsome sum of coin if I'd confiscate the rest of her key data reports that she'd taken when she left the lab. They sat right in front of me, and it would be easy to steal them.

"You risk your reputation and loss of work if you help me and piss off the board of trustees."

"Maybe I enjoy living on the edge." The sterile scent of the lab seemed to get lost in the soft fragrance that was uniquely hers. I couldn't pinpoint it, a mix of solder flux and wildflowers. It was disarming, much like the woman herself.

Luna folded her arms, the light catching the delicate circuitry patterns etched into her cyborg wings. "What drives a man like you? I'm positive it's not money."

"Survival." The word held the weight of a loaded gun. "Maybe a touch of reckless curiosity." Luna's arguments were like cyber hooks puncturing my heart and pulling me into her world. I believed in her dream of helping humanity become stronger.

"Curiosity killed the cat, you know." She leaned in close, a playful lilt in her voice. Her gaze scanned mine, searching for a truth I wasn't willing to share. I wouldn't reveal how it hurt when she left me alone to pick up the pieces of my life when she left to pursue her dream.

"Good thing I'm more hound than feline." I hoped my grin would distract her from the hunt we were about to take. "What about you? What fuels your fire besides the potential to change the world?"

Her gaze lingered on me for a moment longer than necessary, her intellect no doubt piecing together fragments of the puzzle I presented. "The pursuit of knowledge and…maybe a dash of rebellion against the status quo that allows innocent people to be killed."

"Rebellion, hmm?" The cruelty of her family's deaths still shadowed her decisions. "On that, we can agree."

"Well, it seems we both have our reasons."

"Indeed." I allowed myself a minute of indulgence in the rapport that crackled in the air like static energy. Luna Everglen was brilliant, captivating, and entirely off-limits. Yet here I was, drawn in by her light like some moth with a penchant for danger.

"Come on, Jaxon, a man with your talents must have a story worth telling."

"Stories are for children. I'm here for the tech talk, remember? Your microchip is in high demand for its evolutionary advances."

She crossed her arms as if shielding herself from potential deceit. "Why such secrecy about your own physical enhancements?"

"Trade secrets." I chuckled, keeping my tone light. She wasn't buying it. She was too sharp for my tricks, but it bought me time to think.

"Right. And here I thought we were building trust."

"In selling tech, you know as well as I do that trust doesn't come easy." My gaze locked onto hers, unwavering, as if I could convince her through sheer willpower alone.

"Business. Like selling your services to the highest bidder." She turned back to her workbench, where her data pads filled with the codes lay.

I reached for her, but she pulled away. "We've both worked for commerce and the government. They both have an agenda, and it's not the well-being of humanity."

"Technology should be more than commerce. It's the future, our evolution." Her passion flared, and her words heated as if each syllable carried the weight of her convictions.

"Evolution has consequences," I shot back, stepping closer to the bench. "We enhance, we modify, but at what cost?"

"Progress always has a price, but without risk, there's no reward."

"Or we lose ourselves to the machine," I argued, my voice rising despite my intention to keep things level. This was personal territory for me. The line between man and mechanism was one I treaded daily in my life and Caches, who would have died had it not been for the mechanical heart that brought him back to me.

"Give mankind a little credit. Humans are more resilient than you think." Her eyes flashed with a challenge.

"Until we aren't." The words rang out, stark in the silence that followed. Luna stared at me, her expression a mixture of frustration and fascination.

"Your cynicism surprises me, for someone who's benefitted from enhancements."

"Benefitted or become dependent? Where do we draw the line?"

"Perhaps together we can find out." Her voice was hopeful with a tinge of caution that threw me off guard.

"Maybe." I was aware of the tightrope I walked with every word spoken. But the truth was, even as I stood in the heart of her ambition, surrounded by the fruits of human ingenuity, I couldn't shake the feeling that I was part of the very problem we debated. And Luna Everglen, with her green eyes and relentless drive, was making it increasingly difficult to betray her when what I really wanted to do was help her. Who was I kidding? I'd already decided to help her when she gazed into my eyes and recaptured my heart.

I leaned back against the cold metal table, crossing my arms as I watched Luna pace before me. Her steps were measured with each click of her boots against the floor.

"Your perspective is so narrow." Her auburn hair cascaded over her shoulders as she turned to face me again.

"Or perhaps yours is too broad." The heat of the argument simmered between us as old feelings of hurt rose to the surface, creating a chaotic mess of my feelings.

Luna's lips twitched, fighting a smile. "Admit it,Jaxon,n you're enjoying this."

"Arguing with a stubborn scientist? Can't say it's my usual Friday night." An unfamiliar warmth bubbled at the conversation we shared.

For a moment, neither of us spoke. The air seemed to crackle with something more potent than the remnants of our heated discussion. It was as if the room had shrunk, pulling us into an orbit that was entirely our own creation. She held my gaze, and for the first time since I entered the lab, the sharp edges of our conversation softened into something else.

"Jaxon…" Her voice trailed off as if she wasn't sure if she wanted to say what she was thinking.

"Luna, I don't enjoy arguing, but I can't deny there are feelings still between us."

Her breath caught, and I could see the flutter of curiosity in those vivid green eyes. "Is that right?" She tilted her head as if to challenge me further.

"More than your research," I admitted against better judgment. This was pure, raw, unfiltered truth that slipped through my carefully constructed facade.

"Even if I could change the world?" Her question hung between us.

"Especially then, because it's not just the tech, it's the mind behind it. Your mind." The silence that enveloped us then was thick with unspoken words, heavy with the weight of two worlds colliding in the dim light of the laboratory. And though I'd come here undecided, all I could focus on was the undeniable connection sparking to life in the space between us.

"Your certainty is disarming." She stepped back, putting physical space between us where emotional walls had crumbled. Her gaze searched my face for the deceit that was absent.

"Disarming?" With a half grin, I cocked my head to the side. "And here I thought I was being charming."

"Charm and disarmament can be two sides of the same coin." A faint smile tugged at the corner of her lips, showing the desire behind her guarded demeanor. "Indeed, but anomalies need to be studied, understood. Are you prepared to be my subject, Jaxon?" Her humor was apparent in her words.

"Only if you're prepared to be mine." My mental enhancements cataloged every shift in her expression, every flutter of her pulse. It was a dangerous game we were playing, balancing on the knife's edge of attraction and suspicion.

"It's possible," Luna conceded with a chuckle, and the sound sent an unfamiliar warmth cascading through my circuits, electrifying my body.

"Careful, Doctor." My heart thickened with emotions I couldn't afford to feel. "You might start to like me."

"Perhaps I already do." Her honesty stripped away another layer of my resolve.

"Then we have a problem because I'm not sure I can walk away from this."

"From the microchip codes or from me?" Her eyebrow arched in playful accusation.

"You."

She stepped forward once again, erasing the distance I'd come to expect. Her proximity was a live wire, electric and captivating. Our breaths mingled and hesitation gave way to something reckless. I was playing with fire. Luna Everglen wasn't just a brilliant scientist. She was the enigma that could burn me alive or reforge me entirely. And I was all too willing to stoke the flames as my lips eagerly pressed against hers, my hands tangled in her hair as our mouths moved together in a passionate dance. I couldn't resist the urge to deepen the kiss and fuel the fire between us.

I realized she had never stopped challenging me, pushing me, demanding more. I would burn down the whole damn universe if it meant keeping her safe. Because losing her again was not an option. So instead of stealing the last of her reports, I'd help her get the original chip out of Helixcorps vaults.

FOUR
JAXON

Luna's foot scuffed the concrete floor of the underground facility where Helixcorp hid the microchip. If anyone paid attention, they'd see our shadows reflected on the icy walls under the flickering light, giving away our positions. "Keep it down, would you?" I whispered harshly to her.

"Sorry." She scanned the dim corridor ahead. Her slender form was a ghost beside me. "Left here, Jaxon. Watch for the infrared."

I grunted in response, my cyborg eye already picking up the invisible beam crisscrossing our path. With a thought, I engaged the disruptors embedded in my fingertips, sending a pulse that fizzled the security grid into silence. We slipped through unscathed.

"Nice one," Luna complimented, a smile tugging at her lips.

"Focus," I snapped more out of habit than necessity. The microchip was close. I could almost feel its data pulsing like a heartbeat calling out to Luna. She had created it, after all. It was her baby, and now it lay in the bowels of this high-tech basement, waiting for us.

"Right," she said, unfazed by my tone. "The main vault should be just beyond this section. They've likely increased security around the lab, expecting that others might attempt to steal the chip before the big reveal to the public."

"Got it." My enhanced sensory perception had already catalogued the cameras' blind spots and guard rotations. "Follow my lead."

We slunk forward, a series of silent steps and sharp turns. With every sensor I disabled, and every door, Luna cracked open with her halo-pad. The tension between us grew taut like a wire primed to snap.

"Jaxon." Her voice was a whisper against my earpiece. "You ever do ballet?"

"Really?" I fought a smirk that threatened to break my stern expression. "You dance around lab equipment all day?"

"Only when it's not exploding."

"Keep that up, and we'll be doing pirouettes in a cell." I laughed into my comm link.

"Or waltzing with bullets," she added, her snark matching mine.

"Can't have that. You're too pretty to shoot."

"Flattery will get you everywhere."

"Save the sweet talk for when we're not neck-deep in danger."

"Deal."

Luna reached out and motioned for me to stop. "I'm going to attempt to destabilize the computer panel inside. Stay out here and let me know if there's trouble." She unlocked the door and started dismantling wires.

"Hurry, we have ten minutes before…" An eerie sensation crept down my spine.

"Before what?" came a voice in my earpiece that wasn't supposed to be part of this scene, a voice that belonged to my past. Pausing, I stepped out and searched the hall. Nothing but a ghost of wind. Kyra, my mentor was known for her ability to hide in plain sight. It couldn't be possible, or could it?

The air nipped at my skin, the chill a stark contrast to the adrenaline that scorched through my veins.

"Jaxon?" Luna whispered in her comm link. "You zoned out on me. What's happening?"

"Nothing," I lied, snapping back to the present. I couldn't afford any distraction, not with the microchip within reach and Kyra's shadow now draped over our mission.

As Luna turned back to her work, unaware of the ghost haunting our steps, I grappled with the revelation. Kyra. My mentor, the one who'd shown me how to channel my enhancements for something other than destruction, was now potentially the very threat we faced. Was it possible? Could she really be the unknown variable in this equation?

"Jaxon, talk to me," Luna urged again, her tone softer this time yet insistent.

"Complications." I wasn't ready to delve into the tangled web of my past. "Stay sharp."

"Always am." Luna closed the panel door. "Success."

The corridor ahead stretched like the maw of some mechanical beast, daring us to enter. With each step, the weight of being caught pressed harder against my chest. I recalled countless missions with Kyra, her laughter echoing through the gunfire, her unwavering trust my anchor in the chaos. But now, the possibility that she was working against us threatened to sever the last thread of my resolve.

"Jaxon." Luna nudged me gently, pulling me from the storm of memories. "We need to keep moving."

"Right." The word came out hollow, but I forced my feet forward. Loyalty or love?

Past the last doorway, I felt the static charge of a cloaking field dissipate before I saw her. Kyra Voss, like a ghost from my past, materialized in the flesh. Even in the dim light of the underground facility, her platinum hair gleamed, and she locked her icy eyes onto mine with predatory precision.

"Jaxon. Luna," she greeted, her voice as smooth as the blade she wielded with deadly grace.

"Kyra, what are you doing here?"

"Isn't it obvious?" She tilted her head, the corner of her mouth quirking up. "I'm here for the chip. Same as you."

"I thought you retired after the accident. Now you're working for who?"

"Does it matter?"

"Does to me." Luna's wings tensed beneath the fabric of her stealth suit, ready for flight or fight.

"Nothing against you, girl. It's just a job."

"Why?" Luna asked.

The idea she'd been one of Vexicon's best agents before the accident was hard to swallow. I'd rather have remembered her as a ghost, not a bounty hunter out for the highest bid.

"Consider this a courtesy warning, Thornhart." Kyra glanced at Luna with a dismissive attitude. "Stay out of my way, and maybe you two lovebirds can fly off into the sunset or whatever sappy ending you're hoping for."

"Kyra, we've been through hell together. You know I can't just step aside," I said, the plea in my tone revealing the turmoil churning within me. "Think about what you're doing. This isn't you."

"Save your breath, Jax." Her stance hardened, and I knew that look, which meant there was no turning back. "The Kyra you knew is gone. I have my orders, and I don't plan on failing."

"Orders? Since when does Kyra Voss take orders from anyone?"

"Since the stakes became higher than your moral compass can comprehend. I suggest you stand down."

"Can't do that." I stood my ground, though every instinct screamed at me to find another way, one that didn't involve going against a woman who had saved my life more times than I could count. "This ends here, Kyra."

"Fine." The word was a bullet, and with it, any hope of a peaceful resolution was shattered.

"Jaxon." Luna's voice cut through the tension. "We have to leave now."

"Right behind you." I took one glance at Kyra. There was no warmth left in her gaze, only the cold fire of a mission that had to be completed. "Sorry, but I can't let you follow us. See ya."

I triggered the EMP pulse, my hand steady despite the adrenaline coursing through my veins. The lights flickered and died, plunging the corridor into darkness. I could almost hear Kyra's curse as her night vision visor turned to static and died out.

"Move," I whispered to Luna, our bodies pressed against the cold metal wall. She reached for my hand in the dark, a silent promise that she was right there with me.

"Diversion one. What's next?"

"Follow me and stay quiet." I led us through the maze of shadows. We'd studied the blueprints of this forsaken place for hours. Every turn, every vent, every blind spot was etched into my memory. But now those plans were worth more than their weight in gold. They were our key to staying alive.

"Security hub should be down this hall," Luna reminded me, a mental prod to keep me focused.

"Let's hope your idea works." I placed a palm on the biometric scanner, not because it would recognize me, but because Luna reprogrammed the device to explode.

"Three…two…one…" The door burst open, alarms blaring.

"Perfect." I pulled her along as we dashed inside.

"Jaxon, watch out!" Luna's warning came just a fraction too late. A security drone, immune to the EMP and unaffected by the alarm, hovered menacingly ahead. Its targeting system locked onto us, and a deadly red beam sliced through the gloom.

"Damn it." I shoved Luna behind a console. With precision, I ripped off a panel and yanked wires, sending sparks flying. The drone faltered. Its system was confused. That was all I needed. I leaped, grabbed it, and with brute strength, tore it apart.

"Nice save. But we're not out of danger yet."

"Lead the way."

"Left here. Helixcorp's vaults are beyond that hall."

"Wait." I halted us abruptly. A new security measure, unaccounted for in the schematics, blocked our path. It was a laser grid, each beam humming with lethal energy.

"Didn't see that coming."

"Let's make sure Kyra doesn't either." I scanned the grid, mapping out a safe route. "Stay close. Follow my lead."

"Like I have a choice."

Weaving through the grid was like threading a needle. One misstep could end everything, not just the mission, but what was building between Luna and me. Yet, as we emerged unscathed on the other side, I realized I wouldn't want anyone else by my side.

"Almost there."

The vault loomed before me, a monolith of steel and secrets. Luna's wings hummed with restrained energy, her fingers flying over the pad as she deciphered the entry code. I stood guard, every sense attuned to the slightest disturbance.

"Got it." The tension in her voice betrayed the calm in her green eyes.

The door hissed open.

"Finally," I muttered, stepping into the chilled air of the vault. My eyes fixated on the prize—a tiny chip with the power to change the world or destroy it.

"Let's get my research and the chip before we're caught." Luna exhaled her breath and pocketed the microchip.

I slammed the door closed, a satisfying click echoing in the sterile vault. "Time to depart this gig." We didn't have a second to spare. I could practically feel Kyra's icy stare boring into our backs from somewhere in the labyrinth of steel.

"Jaxon." Luna's warning cut through the hum of machinery, sharp as the laser grid we'd avoided minutes before.

Kyra was on us faster than a system override, her platinum hair a stark slash against the dim corridor light. "You never were good at covering your tracks." The glint of malice in her eyes was unmistakable.

"Maybe I just missed your charming company," I shot back, snagging Luna by the arm and darting down the hallway.

"Split up," Luna called out, veering toward a side passage.

"No chance." I wasn't about to let her face Kyra's wrath alone. Besides, two targets were harder to eliminate than one.

We ducked under a spray of bullets from her automatic weapon, skidding around a corner with moves honed from too many close calls. Alarms blared, adding to the shrill voices of panic from those inside. The exit straight ahead.

"Need a brief distraction?"

"Thought you'd never ask." I watched as she tossed a small device behind us. It erupted in a brilliant flash of light, buying us precious seconds.

"Your toys come in handy," I admitted, not bothering to hide the admiration in my voice.

"Wait 'til you see what else I've got."

"Run." We burst out into the cool night air. The facility's door slammed shut with an ominous thud behind us. We ran across the barren landscape, the city's distant lights promising sanctuary. Reaching an abandoned warehouse we'd marked as a safe house, I palmed the hidden keypad, and the door slid open with a silent welcome. Once inside, I leaned heavily against a workbench, my chest heaving. "We don't have much time before Kyra remembers this place."

FIVE
LUNA

Six months later both Jaxon and Cache added the enhancement of wings allowing them both to fly and making them both even better than before.

After dinner, Jaxon took me for a midnight flight over the chrome skyline, just him, me, and Cache, his adorable pug, alongside the stars that struggled against the ever-present glow of progress.

Below, the neon lights of New Arcadia flickered like a field of digital fireflies, casting long shadows across the rooftop where I stood, my mechanical wings gently humming in the cool night air. Amid this cybernetic forest, we landed.

"Beautiful, isn't it? His voice was softer than the whisper of wind under our wings. "But not as beautiful as you." Cache barked and ran in a circle agreeing with me.

Alone with the stars winking from above, my heart persisted in its erratic fluttering. It was ridiculous, really, how such a simple gesture as an evening flight could unravel me, Luna Everglen, a woman who dissected algorithms, who engineered dreams into reality. How could someone like Jaxon, with his hardwired instincts and circuit-lined sinew, understand the complexities of a heart he no longer possessed in the organic sense?

I sighed, tracing the line where my skin met synthetic shoulders. My own enhancements were a stark reminder of the chasm between our worlds. Jaxon lived for the hunt, his body augmented to track, capture, and neutralize. His enhancements were tools of necessity, sharpened edges of survival in a cutthroat existence.

And yet, there we were, two beings stitched together by a rogue strand of fate, orbiting each other like binary stars doomed to converge. The question haunted me, a persistent glitch in my neural pathways. Had I ethically gone too far? Did Elliot and Jaxon have a point regarding enhancements?

I hated to admit it, but maybe the blending of two species interfered with the natural order of life, even if it meant stronger, more capable humans.

My heart yearned for Jaxon, but I wondered if love could truly bridge the gap between a bounty hunter's practicality and a dreamer's ambition.

Jaxon, he...he sees cyberspace as a battlefield, a place where only the strong survive. But for me, it's a canvas, an expanse waiting to be filled with color and life.

"Talking to yourself now, Luna?" His voice came from behind, a hint of amusement in his tone. "Or just practicing your next big speech at the tech symposium?"

"Neither. Just processing."

"Processing, huh?" Jaxon crossed the distance between us in a few strides, with Cache nipping at his heels. "Care to share your findings, Doc?"

I hesitated, my gaze drifting to where his hand, half flesh, half steel, rested casually on the railing. "It's about us, Jax. Our future."

"Ah." His expression grew serious, the blue of his eyes intensifying. "That kind of processing."

A laugh, short and without humor, escaped me. "Yeah, that kind. Because you're alway ready for the next fight, the next hunt, the next adventure, and I'm the one trying to decide whether to cut the red or blue wire."

"Then let's hope you're as good at defusing live wires as you are at creating microchips." The corner of his mouth lifted in a half smile that failed to reach his eyes.

"Jaxon, I'm serious." I wrapped my arms around myself, suddenly feeling exposed amid the vastness of the night. "How can this work between us when our visions of technology are galaxies apart?"

"Because what we have is more about being alive than just tech." He moved closer, only a breath away. "Maybe it's about finding common ground, even if that ground seems like a minefield."

"Common ground..." The words tasted uncertain on my tongue. The concept seemed an elusive algorithm, complex and fraught with variables.

"Listen," Jaxon's voice was firm with conviction. "We'll navigate our differences. We have each other, and we'll do what's right."

"Right." The fluttering in my chest had morphed into a full-blown oscillation of doubt.

"Come here." He took me in his arms. His warmth enveloped me.

"Common ground," I whispered, allowing myself to be drawn into the circle of his body. And for a moment, just a heartbeat in the grand scheme of things, I believed it might just be possible. I wanted him, and I wanted this relationship.

"Look at me. Tell me what you need." Jaxon's command, wrapped in velvet, made me lift my gaze to meet his. In the cerulean depths of his eyes, I saw something that made my breath hitch.

"I need…I don't know, Jax. I want to be understood. I don't want to control humanity. I want to save them."

I let out a shaky breath, blinking back tears. No one had ever truly understood my intentions before. The weight of my responsibilities felt crushing.

"What's in your heart?"

"How can I ensure that someone won't abuse the blending of species?" I whispered. "What if, instead of elevating humanity, it destroys us?"

Jaxon squeezed my hand. "Progress always comes with risk. But together, we can work towards ensuring that we use your tech for good.

Looking into his eyes, I felt my doubts fade. "Jaxon, I don't want to choose between my work, and—"

"Us," he finished for me. There was no accusation, only the raw honesty that seemed to slice through the noise of our past.

"Exactly. Us." I felt my defenses crumbling under his steady gaze. "But how can we find middle ground when it feels like every step, I take forward is pulling me away from you?"

He moved closer, the air between us charged with an unseen current. His hand, usually so imposing, grazed my cheek with surprising tenderness. "Luna, listen to me. I may grumble about enhancements changing humanity, but that doesn't mean I can't support your dreams. Hell, I'm enhanced myself. I'd be a hypocrite to tell you to stop pushing boundaries."

"Your enhancements are different. They're functional, unlike mine," I protested weakly. Even his words wrapped around me like a warm blanket.

"Functional or not, they're part of who I am. And your wings are part of who you are. You're brilliant and relentless, and you're going to change the world, Luna Everglen. I believe in you, and that's nonnegotiable."

"Even if it scares you?" I asked, the vulnerability clawing at my insides.

"Especially because it scares me. Fear means it matters. And you, your dreams, they matter to me."

"Jaxon, I ..." My words faltered as emotion clogged my throat.

"Shh." He pulled me into his embrace, his lips finding mine. "We'll figure this out together. We'll make compromises, find solutions, invent new ways of being. Because that's what people do when they fall back in love with each other. They don't give up."

"Even when it's hard?" I managed to say against his chest.

"Especially when it's hard."

"Promise?" I looked up at him, searching for the certainty I needed.

"Promise," he replied without hesitation, sealing it with a kiss that spoke of steel reassurance. "Now let's start building that bridge of ours."

And just like that, the snarky, guarded bounty hunter I'd fallen for became the foundation upon which I'd dare to build a future. Our future, one precarious brick at a time. "I love you." Leaning even closer in his arms, feeling for the moment the outside world, with all its chaos and conflict, fade away.

"I love you as well, my beautiful, winged doctor."

With Jaxon's hand in mine, we walked back to the city, lighter, more carefree than I'd felt in ages. Cache yapped beside me, wagging his curlicue tail. "Got your running shoes on?" I asked, already envisioning the hundreds of hurdles we'd have to leap over together.

"Born ready," Jaxon shot back, a playful smirk on his lips.

"Good, cause I'm not slowing down for anyone, not even you, Mr. Thornhart."

"Wouldn't dream of it, Ms. Everglen."

We stepped onto the bustling streets of New Arcadia, where the lights flickered like the pulse of the city. The air hummed with the energy of innovation, every corner alive with the buzz of drones and the whirr of cyborg enhancements. "Look at them all. So many stories, so many dreams, just like ours."

"Except ours has more kickass action." He squeezed my hand as if to punctuate his point.

"Ha. Keep dreaming, bounty hunter."

The door to our hotel suite clicked shut, the lock engaging with a soft beep. Before I had time to think, Jaxon pinned me against the door. His lips devoured mine in one swift move, his tongue demanding entry into my mouth as our bodies pressed close. I moaned into his kisses and tightened my arm around the enhanced muscles of his shoulders, pushing him closer. He slid a hand from my waist up to cup my breast through my clothes, his touch electric despite the fabric barrier.

"Fuck," he murmured between kisses. "You're killing me."

I pulled back slightly to catch my breath, a smile curving my lips as I gazed into his eyes. "Am I?" With one finger, I traced his jawline before grasping it and pulling his head down for another kiss. The taste of him was addictive, raw desire mixed with a hint of mint that only fueled my passion.

His free hand trailed down to hold my ass cheek possessively as he lifted me off the floor and against the wall. Our lips never parted as our tongues twirled and played. My body was alive under his palms. I could feel his erection pushing against his jeans as he ground himself against my core through multiple layers of clothing.

It was a delicious torture, my body aching for more. I surrendered myself completely to his touch, my senses responsive under his hands. I could feel him, hot and insistent. I was lost in his embrace, consumed by the fire that burned between us. And as we continued to grind against each other, I knew that this was just the beginning of something powerful and unforgettable.

SIX
JAXON

The sun filtered through the large bay window filling the room with the promise of a new day, a new beginning. With a quick glance around to make sure we had everything, we reached the suite's door, and I stepped over the threshold with her. The door shut behind us with a soft click, a quiet full stop to one chapter before the ink of the next could bleed onto the page. The morning air hit us with the tang of possibility, a blend of city smog and dreams set to simmer in the early light. I gripped Luna's hand, feeling the delicate interplay of her soft skin against the cool metal of my arm.

"Ready to kick some futuristic ass?" Luna's voice was a melody threaded with steel.

"Can't wait. After all, who else is going to keep the world from imploding?"

Our mission to oversee Luna's research was clear as the bright sky above. Laws needed to be created to merge the pulse of humanity with the gears of progress sustainably. We were no naïve dreamers. We knew the road ahead would be littered with more than just rose petals and accolades. But together, our resolve was as unyielding as the cybernetic parts that fortified my body.

"Tech and flesh," Luna mused aloud, echoing our internal manifesto. "A dance as old as time, but now with a new rhythm."

"May our steps never falter," I added, the promise locking into place like a well-oiled gear.

As we left the sanctuary of the hotel suite, every sensor in my body hummed to life. We moved through the lobby, a pair of avatars stepping out of one reality and into another. The staff waved and greeted us with thank-you's and well-wishes.

"Let's show them what happens when a cyborg and a scientist fall in love and decide to take on the world," I said, half joking.

"Sounds like a hell of a headline." Luna's laughter bubbled up like a secret shared between conspirators.

"It does." With every step, my confidence built, an invisible armor forged from the trials I had conquered, and the battles yet to come. We emerged onto the street, where the sounds of the waking city wrapped around us, a symphony of progress waiting for conductors with steady hands and open hearts.

"Side by side," Luna whispered, a mantra that held the weight of worlds yet to be born.

"Always." Together we stepped forward, not just as Jaxon and Luna, but as pioneers on the cusp of a new era where love and technology lived in a perfect union. Our win over Helixcorp was a testament to the power of two hearts synced with passion. The future beckoned, and we answered the call, ready to write our story in the stars.

ABOUT JAYLEE AUSTIN

Jaylee Austin loves to explore all forms of mythology from Celtic goddesses to the nine worlds of the Nordic realms, to the ancient Sumerian Gods. She explores mythical dimensions of angels and ponders the universe of magical beings to create her own, modern romantasy worlds.

She collects crystals, oracle cards, houseplants, and two adorable creatures that love to pounce themselves right in the middle of her desk. Tilly, her pug in black, travels the realms with her offering wisdom to those mysterious questions that readers ponder.

She currently spends her time writing romantic fantasy novels that take you on an adventure where the mystical meets the modern world. Her magical wish is to inspire readers to seek inner happiness with a sprinkle of magic and a contagious smile. Join her on this enchanting journey!

To all those readers that believe in the happily ever after I write for you. A writer is powerful, we create people that are so real they break your heart. A writer crafts a world that become other people's dreams. A writer can turn monsters into heroes and princesses into assassins. A writer will provoke emotions with their words, but it's the reader who falls in love with our world and shares a moment within our hearts. Thank you, Readers for your support, your insight, and your commitment to reading a good story.

To join Jaylee's newsletter and receive a free book: https://jayleeaustin.com/newsletter/

To follow me on Goodreads and Bookbub and receive exclusive bonuses https://jayleeaustin.com/links/

If you would like to receive an advance copy of my book and join my beta reader or arc team https://jayleeaustin.com/arc-team/

To purchase your books on Kobo, Apple, or Google https://linktr.ee/JayleesWorld

facebook.com/jayleeaustin

instagram.com/jayleeaustin

THE SINGER, NOT THE SONG

KORIE BETH BROWN

F unny how some things last.

Even that stupid song.

That super hot guy's humming it under his breath as I walk by the bar. Even sitting, he's tall, with a shock of dark hair that sticks up like in a cartoon. He's wearing all black: shirt, jeans, and work boots, all of which only serve to emphasize the shimmer in his skin. Obviously, he's from Odysseus, poor man; I wonder if he's here on his own or with family. He's certainly sexy, but unfortunately, I don't have time to talk to him-- not only is the room packed, but the hotshot pilots at the eight-top are banging their empty glasses on the table. Charming.

I walk over, grab mugs out of sticky hands, and go to refill them. When I return, I plant the drinks on the table and turn towards the person who appears to be the most sober.

"These also on your tab?"

"Yeah," he slurs-- perhaps "most sober" isn't saying much. I give him a manufactured smile as I turn to another part of the room. A hand on my shoulder stops my movement. Trying to shake it off isn't working; the idiot pulls me in the general direction of his lap.

"How about a kiss, Brandy?" he says, leaning me out over the sticky floor. I squirm, but he's holding me in a vise grip.

"That's not my name."

"But you're certainly fine," he leers.

"Let me go!" I search the room again. Where is my boss, Jethro, when I need him?

"Oh, for heaven's sake. I'm way too busy for this."

"But not too busy for me, right?" He pulls me backward, but I lift my shoulders and shove at him with my rear end. Unfortunately, this is when he lets go, and I crash down to my hands and knees on the cold, hard floor. I inhale deeply and prepare to rise-- when Drunk Guy lands next to me. Now I'm rolling backwards as he reaches out to grab my shoulders. I glance at his friends, sitting at the table and cheering him on. No help there.

"Jethro!" I call out, but of course no one can hear me over the racket. Now Drunk Guy is leaning over me from behind, spraying alcohol fumes into my face. I try again to twist away from him. Guess I'm on my own here.

"Let me go, or you're going to be sorry."

"I'm never sorry," he says.

I shove him away from me and sit halfway up before he tackles me again. Wincing from the beer breath, I tense and prepare myself to propel him back once more.

A strange hand descends on the drunk's shoulder.

"Leave her alone."

It's the Odyssean. He's about to land a punch on the drunk's chin.

I put a hand out to catch the fist.

The head of hair turns, his bright blue eyes finding mine. For a moment, the newcomer and I inspect each other in silence.

"Do you not want me to pummel him?"

"Not a fantastic idea to alienate the customer."

"He may not be a customer, even if he said he'd pay the tab. I'd be surprised if he has any money at all." The Odyssean turns back to the drunk, pushing him backward. He moves fast; now he's sitting on the drunk's chest, evading thrashing arms and legs as he reaches down to go through the man's pockets.

Of course, now the rest of the table decides to join in.

"Hoser," one of them says, jumping to his feet and punching downward. at the Odyssean's shoulder. Several others join him. I retreat from the combat zone; my defender's doing just fine on his own, and Jethro doesn't pay me enough to break up fights. Isn't that his job? I search the room, but naturally he's still nowhere to be seen.

More idiots circle the fray. Do I need a pail of water to throw at everyone in this stinking bar? I'm about to advance when four pilots hit the floor, groaning, and my defender stands upright. I step fuarther out of the range of fire as he dispatches a few others as well. Late entrants to the fight are now stepping away from him.

"Anyone else want a go?" he calls out, his eyes flashing as he searches the circle that's developed around the table. Aside from a cut on his lip and a bruise near his eyebrow, he's unharmed. He sticks out one fist, stacking the other hand on his hip. When no one answers him, he barks out, "Disperse!" and waves his arms.

A dozen drunks back away from him, leaving him standing amid the chaos, alone.

He crosses towards me, his eyes intent.

"Odyssean-- " someone mutters, and my defender turns around.

"It's none of your business where I'm from," he says, his voice low but with an edge that causes the crowd to move farther away. He approaches me and offers a fist filled with coinage.

My eyes widen. "How did you-- "

He shrugs his shoulders. "I can be slippery when necessary. This may not cover what they owe, but it's something."

"You picked pockets during a fight? For me?" Despite myself, I'm impressed-- and touched. I put the money in my apron pocket as our eyes meet.

"Thank you."

For a moment, we stand together, watching people sheepishly going back to their own tables. He gestures at the four moaning bodies on the floor and then to the building's entrance.

"Do you want me to move these miscreants outside?"

"Knock yourself out. I'll handle the rest."

I turn to the others at the table. They sit in silence, staring at my defender as he hauls two men across the room to the front door. The drunks appear to have sobered up, and we all wait in silence as the Odyssean returns for the last two.

"Ready to settle the tab and head on home?" I ask. For a moment, I think someone will start another fight, but thankfully, the sullen expressions eventually subside. Coins begin to materialize onto the table. When the pile appears sufficient, I incline my head in the direction of the door and bide my time as the group makes its way out of the room.

I'd love to take a break now, but I've still got other tables to attend, and so content myself with a few deep breaths before returning to work. I search the room for my defender, but he's gone.

Two hours later, Jethro-- who, of course, re-appeared once the crowd began to thin-- turns off the "Open" sign on the front of the building, and my coworker, Melissa, and I start our sidework.

"Brandy, the floor!" Jethro says, turning away from the electrical panel. "Beyond disgusting."

"Could you use my actual name?" I say, planting my hands on my hips.

"Brandy, Andi-- whatever. "Just get the room mopped."

Disappear when I need you, I think, *expect me to clean up the mess, can't call me who I am...*I pass through the back room to where we keep the pails, fill one with soapy water, and grab a mop before returning to the front room of the pub.

A strange scent lingers in the air. It's far from a stink; hints of salt water and eelgrass dominate. For a moment, I am homesick for my home beach back on Earth. The sadness passes as I dip the mop into the bucket and plunge it onto the collection of beer, spilled food, and whatever's making the room resemble the clutter of the seashore.

I can't find a reason for that briny smell here on Urbarus. The marina's still being terraformed, and no fish or other ichthyoids have yet been introduced. At the same time, all sorts of transients pass through here, including that handsome guy from Odysseus who stepped in to break up the fight. Did he bring the perfume with him?

Odysseus is the ocean planet, with a supposed resemblance to my hometown of Juneau. When I left home, I thought about heading there for a hot minute before getting real. Too many memories to ponder every time I'd view the waves. It had been a lucky choice; the most recent ecological disaster could be the reason the Odyssean found his way to the bar.

I find myself taking deeper breaths as I scrub the floor; the scent is soothing. Can I clean out the crud but somehow leave the perfume?

I finish work sometime after 2 a.m. and walk the short distance to the little cottage I rent from Jethro. In the half-gloom under Urbarus's dome, my dry garden lies ahead, the succulents a contrast to all this concrete. Here, in downtown Azrais, most of the land is paved-- you have to go down to the marina to find anything like nature.

I'm still wired from the fight and the unusual odor that reminded me of home, and so I don't think I'm going to be able to fall asleep soon. This is a shame, as tomorrow's my day off. Some fun would be novel, I think as I walk down the path and unlock my front door.

Questions fill my head, even as I try to stop them. Who was that guy? Why didn't he come back into the bar? Why didn't he at least ask for my name? Why did he disappear without a word? I know nothing about him, but the Odyssean is the only person who's managed to dent the bubble I've been living in for the past few years.

Three years ago, I stepped out of a spaceship and into the Urbarus central spaceport, carrying a single suitcase that included a photo album filled with pictures of dead people. It took seventy-five minutes-- I timed it-- for the shuttle to take me down to the nearest planet, Azrais. At the time, they'd terraformed only the downtown blocks, and I spent the rest of the day using my space-lagged brain to search for jobs and housing. I stopped in every business in the commercial district, hitting the jackpot at Jethro's pub. A studio apartment in the building across the street made up for the meager remuneration. I've been here ever since, slinging hash and beer, sometimes sharing a drink with my coworker, Melissa. It's a lonely life, but it's what I have.

As I enter my safe place, the blessed heat of the corner stove soothes me. Azrais is always so cold, just like my hometown of Juneau. The pile of biscuits on the table appears inviting, but I want as much rest as I can. My practiced hands pull out the Murphy bed and set it up. I'm lying on it five minutes later.

Still, sleep eludes me, and my brain fills with memories of dark hair and intense blue eyes, the one person in all these years who's done something for me with no thought of return. I hate hearing the nasty comments-- surely the rumors about Odysseus are overblown. He seemed like a gentleman, someone running from an old life and trying to make a new one. Kind of like me.

By noon the next day, I'm out of the house and stepping down from the train that's taken me to the marina. This is the last part of Azrais to be terraformed. The dirt paths are still bare in spaces, but I like the ice plants they've put in. It's a work in progress, but to my nonscientific eyes, the beach and ocean feel realistic and ready for refugees. The commission hasn't yet fixed the tides, so the water alternates between waves of chop and evenness. Not that I care; I'm not going in. I don't intend to swim ever again.

Even in the unchanging light, it's a pleasant afternoon-seeming part of the day. In the past six months, the electrical storms just outside the top limit of our "atmosphere" have always made me too uneasy to stay for long. Today feels different; I'm willing to ignore what's happening beyond the dome. I find a patch of sand away from the shoreline, where I can stare out over the water.

After three years in the Urbarus section of the central galaxy, I've gotten used to living in the greater cosmos. Downtown Azrais is small enough that I can walk everywhere; the exercise clears my head, and the local library's well-stocked. Usually, the strip is all I need. When I get cabin fever, I come down here to the marina to watch the waves and remember.

The nausea begins, as it always does when I get too close to the water. I move farther away from the shoreline.

I would love to know more about that guy's story. The rumors about Odysseus range from the incredible to the absurd, but few people ever share facts. I may never hear the truth; I wonder if it's anything like what happened to me, albeit on a grander scale. Is he as lonely as I am? Even before I left Earth, I'd been on my own for so long. What would it be like to once again be part of a community?

Three days later, I'm scrubbing a stain on a four-top near the east wall when the front door opens behind me. I turn. Silhouetted in the doorway is the man who fought off the drunks. He's wearing a dark sweater over jeans and work boots, and his hair is mussed up from the wind. He brings with him that strange, lovely scent. I straighten my back, and our gazes catch.

"Hello," I say as he approaches. I crane my neck to peer at his face. His eyes are indeed that bright electric blue I remember, an unusual color. I'm a bit embarrassed that my T-shirt is wet from the soapy water.

Not that he's taking the bait; his eyes are fixed on mine.

At last, he breaks the silence.

"Can I be seated?"

I sweep my hands around the vacant room and circle them back in his direction. "Well, the wait's an hour and a half, two hours max. I can add you to the list. Want to get a drink first?" I'm expecting him to laugh.

Instead, he just nods and turns toward the bar.

I catch up with him, rest my hand on his triceps, and inhale that sea -spray scent.

"I'm joking," I offer. "You can sit anywhere you like."

"A joke. Okay," he says.

I wonder if Odysseans have the same sense of humor as I do.

I hand him the menu, and his hand covers mine as he takes it.

Heat emanates from both his palm and his arm, and my heart starts to pound as I step back, severing the contact.

I wave at the empty room.

"Wherever you're comfortable."

"In your area, please."

"This is your lucky day-- I'm the only server here. Your choice."

He surveys the room; after a moment, he sits down at the table I'm bussing. I have to grin-- he's being blatant about his interest. It's kind of a refreshing change. I finish wiping down the wood.

"Bowl of chowder? Burger? Drink from the bar?"

"Fish sandwich?"

"Of course. Would you like cheese on that?"

"No cheese," he says. He's now seated, but we are at eye level. Up close he's quite handsome, if somewhat unusual. His skin appears to be thickened, as if he's spent a lot of time underwater, but that doesn't detract from his appeal. Perhaps I can nudge this along, I think.

"French fries? A salad? Cole slaw? We might still have some fresh fruit."

He shrugs. "Sure."

"Which side do you want?"

He takes a deep breath. "Can I split something with you? Do you have a break coming up?"

I survey the room and back at him. "I'm not drowning in orders here," I say. "You want a beer to go with your dinner?"

"Okay."

"What kind?"

"Doesn't matter."

I can almost physically feel his eyes on my rear end as I slow my walk to the bar. I ask Melissa to draw him a pint before I head to the kitchen to order his food.

It's gratifying to have solved the mystery of that sea scent, which I find quite homey.

Don't think about home. Keep your mind on the present.

Once around the corner, I run to the restroom and check myself out in the mirror. My makeup's a bit smudged, but nothing horrible. I take out my ponytail, finger-comb my hair, and put it back up. Jethro's may yell at me for sitting down, but I'll just holler back.

I return to the floor and realize I don't know his name. Smiling, I approach the table, his beer in my hand.

He rises to pull out a chair for me.

I sit. For a moment, we regard each other in silence. It's a more comfortable quiet at this point; I'm gathering that he's not the talkative type, which is okay by me.

He lips purse as he sips his beer, passes me the mug.

Why not? I take a gulp and hand it back, and our hands touch as he re-claims the drink. Heat emanates from both his palm and his arm, and my heart starts to pound. I pull my hand back, severing the contact.

"You disappeared before I could thank you for saving me the other night."

"No thanks needed. I'm new to Urbarus. Been going back and forth."

"To Odysseus?"

"Odysseus, yes. The one in the Clusters."

"Yeah, I know where Odysseus is. Here for the terraformed marina?"

"Of course. Hunting for another homeland."

"There's a ton of speculation about population collapse on Odysseus. Is it as bad as they say?"

"Yes."

"Wow. Hard to believe."

"The miners were warned." His voice is filled with weariness. "But naturally they didn't listen. All that sludge into the ocean, even after tests showed the extent of the poisoning. We had more massive die-offs last week. Too many species going extinct."

"I'm so sorry to hear that. How long have you lived there?"

"I'm Odyssean born." He opens his mouth, then closes it again. A moment passes before he speaks again. "My clan is native."

My eyes widen in spite of myself. "So that makes you-- "

"Yes." He crosses his arms in front of his chest.

"What's Odysseus like?"

His eyes flame liquid blue and then mellow back out. "It used to be the most beautiful place in the world," he says, his voice solemn. "I'm sure you've heard about all the tragedies."

"Well, yeah," I admit. "It's so horrible. The poisoned ocean, the displacement of the Selkyries-- "

"We've all been uprooted," he acknowledges.

"Have you got a family?" I ask as I realize how much I don't want to hear that he does.

"I'm a widower." His jaw clenches for a moment;, then he brightens. "I have a son. Right now, he's staying with my sister while I hunt for a new place for the tribe."

"This is a great place. I'm sure your tribe will love it here once the terraforming is finished." As I look into his eyes, I'm torn between excitement and trepidation. *He has a child?*

"What's your son's name?"

"Zevon."

"I like that. Unusual. How old is he?"

"Seven," he says, the iridescence on his face glowing. His blatant joy makes me think that even this-- ossibly parenting a child of a different species-- could be worked out. I could look at him all night; even knowing that he's not human doesn't stop the thudding of my heart. I want to reach out and brush that lock of hair out of his eyes.

Out of nowhere, it seems, Jethro's voice rings out across the bar.

"Hey, Brandy-- working or dating?"

I jump to my feet and check the room; two tables have been claimed by new customers. I turn back to those amazing eyes. "I need to go take their orders."

"I have nowhere else to be," the Odyssean says, leaning back against the back wall and stretching his long legs out in front of him. His lap offers plenty of room, even with his hands folded around his stomach.

I fight the inexplicable urge to sit down and curl my arms around his neck. Instead, I turn and resume my shift.

He's still waiting for me when we close.

It's been just busy enough that I haven't been able to converse with him for more than a moment at a time. I'll admit to watching him, however, taking in the looseness at his shoulder joints and the rigidity at his spine. I've never hooked up with a Selkyrie this, but this one makes it look pretty damned interesting. I slow my walk to put on a bit of a show for him, flouncing my skirt with my hips, because why not?

When, at last, Jethro beckons him out before putting up the " Closed" sign, the Odyssean inclines his head at me without moving. Jethro scowls at him, but I step between the two, breaking the eye contact.

Jethro turns to me, his eyebrows raised.

"You sure?" Jethro says. I know what he's insinuating, but I don't take the bait.

"I'm good," I respond as I start my sidework.

Both Jethro and Melissa are gesturing at me, and not very subtly. At one point, Melissa drops a dish on the floor; I wince from the sound as it shatters but keep my eyes pinned on the Odyssean. This one is something special. Or else I'm just lonely-- three years, after all, is a long time to be alone. I'm enjoying the experience of being wanted, and I smile as I make my way to his table. He comes to his feet as I approach.

"You want to walk me home?"

His eyebrows go up, and I clarify.

"I mean, that's it. Stroll and chat. At least until I learn your name."

His eyes crinkle as he smiles. "I would love to."

He takes my hand as we exit the building, enveloping mine in warmth.

Much as I wish for romantic darkness, this is Urbarus. The terraformed landscape is always at a sort of twilight state. On a positive note, I can look at the Selkyrie next to me. He looks more dangerous in the twilight, reminding me of the fighter who saved me in the bar. His eyes read the environment as he walks with relaxed purpose.

"I don't live all that far away," I say. "Just around the back."

"Okay."

"By the way, should I keep calling you my rescuer? Or are you going to tell me your name?"

He chuckles as his fingers massage my hand. "I'm Taron."

"Nice to meet you, Taron," I say as we turn the corner of the building.

"Good to meet you as well. You are called Brandy?"

There's that gallant phrasing that I'm beginning to realize is the Selkyrie manner of conversation, so different from what I'm used to at work. And he's been paying attention, very sexy. "Actually, I'm Andi, although everyone at the bar refuses to use my actual name."

"Not Brandy, like the song?"

"Nope-- Andi, like the patron saint of the ocean."

He misses a step, and his eyes meet mine. "Are you from a seafaring culture?" There is emotion behind the words.

I really don't want to answer questions about the past. "There's plenty of oceans on Earth," I deflect. "How do you know that stupid tune? It's over three hundred years old."

"The colonizers brought it with them when they arrived."

"Somehow, it stayed popular over the years. I suppose because the damn story's so sad."

"My people loved it because we love the sea. We even call it 'my lady."

We're about to skirt the edge of the building when Taron pushes me against the back wall, surrounding me with his large frame. I consider pulling away-- we've barely met, after all, and his love for the ocean is truly frightening to me. Too many memories.

At the same time, he's so warm, solid, and focused on me

His mouth claims mine.

He's slow, exploratory, content to savor the moment. My arms go around his neck, my fingers through his hair.

His hands move up and down my back.

When he breaks the kiss, I need time to catch my breath.

"Wow," I say, looking into his eyes.

"Yes," he says. "I'm not the kind to-- "

"-- me neither--"

"-- but I just had to come back and find you-- "

"-- I'm glad you did-- "

…and his lips are against mine again, his passion evident.

There's a loud clank as the back door opens and Melissa comes out with a bag of garbage to take to the dumpster. She turns, sees the two of us, and jumps back inside the building.; tThe door clatters again as it bangs shut. Taron doesn't move, his arms encircling me, his mouth inches from mine. I break away, trying to catch my breath.

"Let's get away from here," I say, clasping his hand in mine and walking him across the alley. I look at where I live with the eyes of a stranger and try not to wince; it's every bit as run-down as the bar and grill.

"It's nicer indoors," I insist. "Perhaps next time I'll invite you in. Will there be a next time, Taron?"

He reaches to kiss me again.

"I hope so," he says when we both come up for air. "I need to return to Odysseus, to spend some time with Zevon, but I'll be back in a week." His gaze travels across my face, down my neck to my breasts. "You are so beautiful."

"You are also," I say. "I mean, yeah, you're a guy, and guys aren't supposed to be pretty, but here you are-- "

"I will find you when I come back. To you, Andi."

I'm not imagining it-- he is emphasizing the syllables in my name.

And he kisses me again, before I let him go and slip inside my tiny studio.

As the days pass, I fight off Jethro's and Melissa's questions. I'm not ready to talk, not sure what's happening myself. When Taron's here in Azrias, he's at the bar waiting for me. When he's off-planet, I dream about his otherworldly hands, slithery in such a good way. When we kiss, it's exciting but also comforting, not so much a conquest as a connection. When we sit and chat, he's completely focused on what I'm saying. Every time he says my name, shivers run up my spine. He's told me very little about himself, but I'm already writing fantasy in my head-- his son is adorable, the three of us will go to the zoo, out for ice cream, and to the movies. We'll leave Urbarus and start a new life, and so on.

One night he comes in a bit late, waits for me, and of course takes my hand as we exit the bar. We're against the wall behind the building, and his hands are roaming in that indescribable way. His kisses are like fire.

For the first time, I'm confident in what I want to do. I pull away, grab his hand, and lead him across the street to my studio.

He lingers as I unlock the door, stooping-- he's so much taller! How does he make the height difference work so well? -- to kiss me again in the doorway.

My arms are around his neck. "Come inside with me," I murmur into his ear.

He pulls away and peers into my eyes.

"Are you sure about this, Andi?"

"I'm sure."

"You know so little about me. And I'm an--

"I don't care," I respond, reaching up to nibble at his bottom lip. "You're worth getting to know, Taron. I'll take my chances."

His eyes light up again with that peculiar blue flame, and he reaches out to pick me up. I can feel the heat of his body as he hugs me close. I wrap my legs around his torso, and he carries me across the threshold, somehow kicking the door shut behind him.

Why didn't I leave the damn Murphy bed down?

I'm about to say something, but he drops with me onto the floor and starts to tug on my blouse. It must have been some time for him as well; he's not doing a good job of figuring out the buttons. I pull away and stand up, performing a little striptease. His eyes flash, settle, and flash again as I uncover each inch of skin.

He waits as I unhook my bra, and then he pounces, and things move even faster. He's on top of me, kissing my shoulder bone and armpits, and we're both struggling out of the rest of our clothing, and it's different and beautiful and I can't think at all anymore.

When I wake up the next morning, he's lying beside me, his gaze locked onto my face. I wonder what he's thinking. I smile as he nuzzles my neck. I plant a kiss on the side of his jaw before I make my way to my feet.

"I'm going to take a shower," I say. "You want to join me?"

His eyes flame out at me. "You know what will happen, don't you?"

"I've heard rumors," I say, keeping my voice even, "but I guess I'll see for myself."

He rises from the bed and brushes past me; I follow him into the bathroom. There's silence as he turns on the water and steps in; I watch as the shock of hair on his head dampens and grows longer, trailing down his neck until his spine is covered with the fringe. The skin on his legs ripples as the bones appear to fuse together. Finally, his feet combine, pointing outward.

"How do you stand upright on that tail?" I ask as I get into the shower.

He grins at me, his face seeming both alien and familiar as his arms shorten into flippers.

"Like what you see?" he asks, his voice going a bit hoarse, and I realize he's nervous. It's a lot to take in, but at the same time, he hasn't become anything different than what he was before; it's my conception of him that needs to change. I wrap my hands behind his neck, and reach up to kiss him.

"Yes," I whisper. "Now I'm wondering what you can do without hands-- "

His laugh, as soft as the sea, is both unnerving and comforting. "I'll show you."

. . .

I'm quiet after he leaves for Odysseus, even for me. The time apart makes me realize Taron's got a lot more on his mind than some barmaid he hooked up with. I don't know enough about him to trust his promise, other than the old saw about Selkyries never breaking an oath. Was this even a vow? He said he'd return, but what exactly does that mean? A week later, my worries are answered. Confronted with his lanky body against the back wall, all the practical thoughts leave my head.

He goes back and forth for the next three months, and we're amid what amounts to a passionate affair. I stay up nights rehearsing questions, but when he's in front of me, the answers don't matter. I focus on the touch of his hand as we walk, the glint of his eyes as we catch dinner, the feel of his hair in my hands, and the growing comfort of waking up to the scent of his skin.

At the same time, however, I'm trying to be practical. I suspect the other shoe is about to drop; nothing this intense can continue well. He'll soon come clean: it's not me, it's him. Or he needs someone more reliable to be a mom to Zevon. Whom I haven't yet met... Because Zevon will never accept a substitute for his mother... Or there's a younger woman on Odysseus already auditioning for the part... Or he'll find another excuse to end things. Men always do, particularly if they're tangled up with a barmaid. I hate that damned song, but I have to admit it's got a point.

I'm torn between joy and fear one sunrise as I slide into waking consciousness. Taron is lying next to me, his eyes closed. He's beautiful, so different from anyone else I've ever met. I'm watching the dappled sunlight on his golden cheek when his blue eyes open and meet mine. It's time we finally talked.

"Good morning." I lean over and kiss him, and turn onto my side to keep my eyes on his. "How did you sleep?"

For a moment, his eyes are unfocused, and resolution grows inside my brain as he gains full wakefulness. "Decent. You?"

"I always rest well when you're here," I answer truthfully. "You want breakfast?"

At his nod, I prepare myself mentally. This has gone on for long enough; I need to know where it's going.

It's time for us to talk.

"There are roughly three hundred Selkyries left," he tells me an hour later, sipping at his coffee. "When we learned that Urbarus was terraforming a seaport, it was the pot of gold at the end of the rainbow. I've been flying here to buy land near the water, acres with ocean rights. It's not just for me-- it's for Zevon, my other relatives, and what remains of our tribe."

"Your wife-- "

His eyes darken. "She died two years ago, poisoned by a bad oil spill. That one took many of us. As much as it hurts, I haven't let Zevon swim on Odysseus since."

"Swimming can be so dangerous," I agree, toying with my eggs.

"It's different here," he goes on. "I've managed to sneak in late at night and check out the new ocean. They're doing such a good job preparing for refugees. I can't wait for Zevon to be back in the water."

"I don't swim."

His fork, loaded with a piece of salmon, stops on its way to his mouth. "You don't know how?"

"I've learned. I just don't."

"It's the most joyous way to move."

"Except when the waves kill people." My voice comes out sharper than I realize, and he stiffens. I take a deep breath. "You've lived through that as well. Better to stay on land."

"Why would I want to do that? Salt water is part of my blood."

A tense knot grows in my chest. "It used to be part of mine as well," I whisper. "Before it took my family."

"Before it-- Andi? What?"

He's not the only one sharing secrets today.

"I'm from a fishing village on Earth. My clan was wiped out in a storm."

He leans towards me as I tell the story-- the routine fishing expedition interrupted by an unexpected tempest. The view of the harbor as we approached, seeming to melt in the wind and rain. The water spout, hail stinging my head and hands. Pieces of the boat falling with me as I hit the churning waves. The weariness between my shoulder blades as I somehow managed to swim close enough to shore to be pulled out of the surf.

Taron's gaze stays on mine as I recount the trip to the morgue later in the week. My brother, my father, my cousin, and my fiancé were all on the ship that night with me, but only my cousin's body was recovered after they found me on the shore. My aunt tried to keep me calm, but I broke down on the way home and ended up needing to be sedated. After three months of screaming and tears, I packed my bags and left Juneau. Even living inland in Fairbanks, too many reminders showcased everything I'd lost. When I read a flyer about personnel needed for the spaceports in the central galaxy, I didn't hesitate; I'd be far away from the killer oceans of Earth, ready to start my life again on different terms.

In the here and now, Taron reaches out across the table and covers my hand with his. "Were you in favor of the terraforming?"

"Yes, but it made me so afraid," I confess. "It took me six months to be able to walk the marina path. "

His face is sad as he looks at me. "And you haven't been swimming since?"

"No. Never. I can't."

He takes a deep breath, lets it out. His hand tightens over mine. "It's never good to leave one's roots."

I nod, my eyes filling with tears. This is what I've been

turning over in my mind from the day we got together. Interspecies romance? Bring it on. A relationship with someone whose life revolves around the ocean? That's a potential deal breaker. I relax into the warmth of his hand before pulling away. He reaches out to grab my hand again.

"I want to make this work," he says.

"So difficult-- "

"-- and that's okay." His voice is calm and strong. Looking into his eyes, I'm almost convinced.

It's been three days since Taron flew back to Odysseus, and another two until he returns. I've got the day off, and I'm antsy; I don't want to do any of my usual tasks. Instead, I'm going down to the marina to somehow crack this phobia. It's either that or end things with Taron, and that's not what I want. I'm torn between my love for the man and my fear of the sea. This is the only way I can think of to make the relationship work.

I throw on clothes, grab my tote, and lock the door after myself. When I arrive at the beach, I unpack a towel, spread it out on the sand, and sit down. For thirty minutes, I stare at the expanse of blue in front of me. I remove my watch, drop it into my bag with my keys, and turn back to the sun dancing off the surface of the waves. Someone on the terraform commission is getting quite a bit better at simulating currents; the movement is a lot more convincing than the last time I was here. If I squint, I can almost conjure up the shadow of clouds, creeping into my view--

No. I shake my head to clear it. I don't need to think about that long-ago night. I just want to put my feet in the water. Is that too much to ask?

Time passes as I sit and study the waves. I'm not sure how much time passes before I find the courage to stand up. I start to walk, but stop and examine the surf some more.

Take a step forward, Andi.

I do. I stop again. If my heart was a drum kit, I'd hear heavy metal at the moment. I take another movement forward and a few deep inhalations. Then another step, and another few breaths.

My toe is about to touch the water when the nausea hits. I turn, stumble back to my towel, and flop onto my stomach, dropping my head to the back of my hands.

It's not supposed to be this freaking difficult!

I scrabble in my tote bag for my watch. I'll give myself five minutes to rest. I'll take some deep breaths before walking back to the shoreline. This is just a glitch in the process. All I need is a bit more time. I'll try again.

I breathe, count down the time, and push to my feet. I stare at the waves, note the way they glow in the half-light.

It's weird how scary something gets after a few years of avoidance, isn't it?

For the next hour, I repeat the movements-- one step forward, five full breaths-- until I reach the edge of the water. Each time, I think I'm going to throw up, or have a heart attack, or pass out from not being able to breathe. Each time, I end up on my belly on the towel, crying into the pillow I make with my hands.

Eventually, I'm too hungry, angry, lonely, and tired to do anything more.

I stuff my things into the carryall, put my watch back on, and walk home. I think I said hello to someone on the way, and the cartons of eggs and milk in my tote mean that I stopped at the store, but I have no recollection whatsoever of the time between leaving the beach and arriving at my doorstep. I stow away the groceries and then crumple to the floor, staring out the window without seeing much at all.

When I next see Taron at the bar, a weight settles in my stomach. I'm sure he feels it as well, but he doesn't mention it. After my shift, we walk back to my place and make love for what I know is the last time. Afterward, we lie in bed holding each other. I watch him fall asleep, and study every detail of his face as the minutes pass.

In the morning, I tell him that it's not going to work. I refuse to talk about it, and send him on his way. I spend the rest of the day on the floor. I call in sick, and at some point, Jethro comes by to check on me, but he leaves when I don't open the door. Tomorrow I can go back to my sad and empty life, but for today, it's all I can do to curl into a ball with my eyes closed, playing memories on the back of my eyelids.

I move through the next week like a robot. Taron doesn't appear. Time slows to a crawl as I wait for him to walk in the door., Days pass without his lanky frame crossing the threshold to Jethro's bar.

He's taken me seriously, and I'm alone again.

I talk Jethro into giving me extra shifts. I work, shop for groceries, and go home to stare at the wall. My brain plays endless repeats of each day I spent with Taron, each night we formed into spoons, nestled together.

When I think about how his lips shaped my name, I can't hold back the tears.

Seafolk need the sea.

I'm too crippled and broken to be any good to a Selkyrie, to someone who needs an ocean. *One day at a time*, I think. I will get used to this.

Days pass, the minutes endless. The loneliness grows worse. I begin to doubt my decision. Surely, Taron hasn't abandoned Urbarus because of me?

Halfway through my shift one night, I can't take it anymore. I insist on a break, and exit the premises. I walk through the commercial district and stick my head into bar after bar. Finally, there's Taron, sitting in a corner, staring out into the room. As his head turns toward the door where I'm standing, I back out and allow the wood to block his view. Somehow, I make my way back to work and finish out the evening.

More days pass before I again leave Jethro's to hunt for Taron. This time, I find him at a different bar. I hold myself rigid at the edge of the room, my only thought of running across the floor and throwing my arms around his neck. I blink my eyelids over and over again as I turn and make my way back to Jethro's.

I can't take it anymore. If nothing else, I have to explain to Taron that it's not him, that it's never been about him-- he's the best thing that's ever happened to me. Perhaps he'll listen. We're bound to run into each other at some point after he moves his tribe here, and I'd rather that meeting was on my terms.

I check three pubs this time before I find him at the fourth. He's not alone but one of five Selkyries at the table. A man and woman sit with their hands interlaced; another woman lounges on the other side, next to the back of a child.

I catch my breath. I guess the tribe's moved. Is that Zevon? I stand gaping until someone comes in behind me and I move forward. As the door slams, I take another step into the pub. Then another.

I feel like I'm walking in the direction of that damned shoreline.

I consider my options. I could just leave. I need to finish my shift; Jethro's been patient with me, but at some point, I am going to lose my job. I should do the intelligent thing and return to work, before--

Too late. Taron's turned toward the door, and our eyes meet.

I take another breath and inch forward. Taron's mouth is set in a straight line, pressed together so that his lips have all but disappeared. When I'm within speaking distance, he rises to his feet, placing his body between mine and the child's.

"Hello," he says, his voice like gravel. I blink.

"Hello," I repeat, and my eyes fill with tears. He's got his arms crossed over his chest, his body turned away. I wave my hand in the direction of the table.

"Is that-- "

"Yes. Why do you care?"

"Because-- "I'm suddenly crying so hard my mouth can't wrap around the words. "Because I've missed you so much. Because I-- "

He takes a deep breath, and for a long horrible moment I think he's going to give me his back. Then he steps forward, throws his arms out, and pulls me in tight. I can tell he's still angry, but his chest is softening, and he's got his chin on the top of my head. All too soon, he releases me, and beckons me to the table.

"Zevon," he says, "would you like to meet a friend of mine?"

I reach out my hand to Zevon, and a pair of inquisitive eyes look up at me. Somehow the child seems to be more seal-like than the adult; something about the way he proffers his hand, the fingers blurring into each other, a melding of digits and flippers. We shake, and I stand back up as Taron introduces me to his brother, his sister-in-law, and his sister-in-law's sister. A wave of jealousy goes through me; is this woman single? Is it any of my business anymore? I tilt my head; what a mess this has become. I turn back to Taron.

"I'm at work-- I mean, I'm not at work now, but-- "

"What are you doing here, then?"

"You haven't been at Jethro's in-- "

"I didn't want to cause a scene."

At that, I have to laugh. "And here I go, causing one. I'm sorry-- "

"Andi," he says, and a part of me wants to cheer at the sound of my name, to scream to the universe that at least one person calls me who I am, to celebrate not being made into a stereotype. I start to cry again as his voice continues.

"Let me walk you back."

He follows me out the door, and then we're standing in the cool air of a downtown street, the half-light surrounding us like a halo.

"They've done a good job making this seem like a city on Earth," I say for no apparent reason as we stroll.

He nods, shoving his hands into his pockets.

"I've missed you too," he says.

"It's so not you-- it's me. Itt's the water-- "

He takes a breath before speaking. "The water."

"The water's so much a part of your culture."

He waits for me to continue. I take a deep breath.

"How can I-- I mean-- your son needs adults who can-- what good am I--?"

Now he's reaching out for my hand and we're walking down the street toward Jethro's. Somehow, it's easier to talk about my abortive last trip to the marina when I'm not looking at his face.

"-- and I'm not sure if I'll ever be able to-- "

He stops, pulls me to face him. "Andi. Listen to me."

I swallow the lump in my throat as he clears his before continuing.

"Someone will always be there to swim with Zevon. I'm always going to spend time in the water. But when I'm not? I'd like to be with you."

Tears fill my eyes.

"I didn't expect to find love here in Azrais," he continues, "but I did. I hope things will work out between us. Maybe they won't. But I'd like to have the option to try."

I keep my eyes on his face as he clears his throat again.

"Please, Andi," he says, reaching his hands out in my direction. "Please, trust me, okay?"

And then we kiss. It feels like coming home. We make plans to meet in the morning and talk it out before I turn to open the door to Jethro's bar to finish my shift.

Time goes on. Taron moves more people to Urbarus, and my life changes completely. One group settles in downtown Azrais, another down by the water. I give Jethro notice, and before I know it, I move into a house down by the marina, with Taron, Zevon, a different brother-in-law named Berleon, and his two children. It's crowded, but I'm used to living in small quarters. While it's hard to live in a community again, it's also a relief to not be alone.

Some days I face the marina and pretend I can hear the voices of my brothers.

When Berleon meets Sasha, it takes them only two months to move out. I enjoy two weeks of privacy with Zevon and Taron. With the next wave of arrivals, we share the house with Tula, her daughter, and her daughter's cousin for a month before they move on; Luki and Spez are the new occupants of the spare room.

That's life when you're in a relationship with the tribe leader. Not that I have a lot of time to complain; Taron needs help with settling the immigrants,. Instead of slinging drinks, I teach immigrant Selkyrie women how to cook with the foods available here on Urbarus. Or I lead grocery trip runs, introduce people to the library, and arrange cups of tea and plates of oysters for new, homesick arrivals.

One day, I return home to find Taron out on the porch, his face pensive as he stares at the marina. I climb the steps, lean down to kiss him, sit down, and cuddle into his side.

"Where's Zevon?"

"Over at Berleon's for a playdate. We've got a couple of hours to ourselves."

"Well, kind of," I hedge. "Luki has a bunch of friends over; they're watching soccer in the living room."

"Spez?"

"Working late today."

"Still too many people here."

"What're you thinking?"

"Let's take a walk."

"Okay." I run into the house to change. When I return, Taron leads me down the steps, my hand in his. We stroll, chatting with passers-by as we make our way downtown. After the fifth group passes us, Taron shrugs at me.

"Very few places for privacy," he says.

"Do you want to go home?"

"Not yet. I want to be outside with you."

My heart starts to beat faster as I find myself walking down the boardwalk to the marina beach. We leave the pavement, walk across the sand, and admire the latest improvements.

"They've managed to fix the waves. They're almost perfect," I say. "And they've gotten the temperature change right. It feels like late afternoon."

"Does it? What was it like, strolling the shoreline on Earth?"

"Pretty spectacular sometimes."

"Still miss it?"

"Only as much as you miss Odysseus."

"I found my treasures here," he says, squeezing my hand.

We move in silence, away from the bustle of the city beach. After twenty minutes or so, the crowd disappears, and we're the only ones on the beach. Staring out at the waves, I study the color changes as the sand saturates, starts to dry, and once again fills with water.. Taron's fingers clench mine a bit tighter as we move closer to the shore. I take a deep breath, and then another, and then another step. Soon we're at the shoreline. For a moment, we stand together, looking at the waves, and then Taron turns to me.

"Do you trust me?" he says. My heart starts to jackhammer, because I realize what he's asking. However, when you're in a relationship with a person and his culture, what excuse do you have for not at least making more attempts to change?

"Yes," I say, kneeling to remove my shoes. Taron does the same, and then, as one, we turn to take another few steps forward. Water laps at my feet for the first time in so long, and the smell of salt rises to my nostrils. With Taron here, the nausea doesn't come.

I blink fast, twice, and find I'm crying. For a moment, I just take it all in. In the distance, I can see some kind of cetacean breaching the crest of a wave. I point this out to Taron and he smiles, taking my hand.

I can't stay here.

I'm staying here.

The air is warm; if I close my eyes, I can imagine the feeling of the Earth's sun on my back. Under my feet, the sand shifts, and my toes curl to maintain my position. I breathe in the salt scent.

They did a good job of recreating an ocean. The waves are almost perfect.

I wonder if...

I turn to Taron and lock gazes with him as I begin to unbutton my shirt.

"What are you doing?" he says.

"I thought-- " The sound is thready, and I blow out air before continuing again in a stronger, if still unsteady, voice, "that it's time for a swim if you want."

Taron stiffens. His eyes never leave my face. I pull my shirt off and step out of my shorts and my underwear under his glance.

"Well?" I say, breaking a heavy silence. "I'm not going to do this by myself."

He nods, pulling his T-shirt over his head in one swift motion; I don't think I've ever seen anyone drop trousers so quickly. When we're both naked, he reaches out and takes my hand again.

Just take one step at a time.

I can't do this.

I'm doing this.

My breath quickens, and for a moment I think I'm going to pass out. The water laps at my knees.

"You okay?"

"I don't know," I answer, blinking the tears away to watch his feet and calves begin to change. A thought occurs to me, and I ask him, "If you just stop there, what happens to your body?"

Taron stares down at where he's balanced on a bit of tail, looks back at me, and smiles.

"Not going to wait to find out," he says as he flops forward. I view the transformation as the ocean reaches various parts. He holds out a hand to me, and I look down at my own torso.

I'm still human, but I've changed as well.

My old thoughts break in again.

I can't go any farther.

I'm going farther.

I keep my eyes on Taron, just beyond me, as I take more steps. The water is up to my waist now; instinctively, I move backward.

"Just breathe," he whispers.

I comply, steadying myself, and move forward again. The water returns to my torso, moves up to my breasts, my neck. Finally, I close my eyes and dunk my head under. When I come back up, Taron's by my side, wrapping fins around my torso.

"I've got you," he says, his voice still human-like.

"You're better built for this," I say. Even with the change to a seal-like face, I can see him smile.

"Let me show you how well."

With a swift motion, he pulls me to him, settling me on his back, and slides forward. My hands are clasped on opposite sides of what was his-- *do his people even have necks in this form? Must ask next time I'm at the Center*-- as we move through the water. For a moment, I'm terrified, can't breathe, my stomach's in my throat, *oh god, I'm going to die.* In the next second, I only register the water over my back as we plunge into the waves.

I'm not sure if I'm screaming or singing, but the sound rises above the water.

"Can I take you farther out?"

"Wait," I protest, focusing on my breath. This feeling zipping through my body, which I've always identified as terror, is starting to change. Can I think of it as excitement?

"I've got you," he says again.

"Okay," I say after a moment. "Let's do it."

I shut my eyes as he dives under the water, so all I experience is the glide of liquid coursing over my back. We breach, and I blink the moisture away from my eyes. I look back at the beach; the coastline appears so different from out here. I slip off Taron's back, holding on to his fin with one hand, my other arm and legs remembering the movements that were once second nature.

I can't do this.

I'm doing it.

It's another five minutes before I let go, and I'm swimming next to him as we make our way parallel to the shore. I remember the different strokes I learned long ago. I have choices here: —I can keep my head above water or drop it down and swim faster.

Memories crowd my mind; my brother and I racing out to the buoys in the harbor on a family vacation to Hawaii. Diving from the fishing boat, scraper in hand, to work barnacles off the hull. Pulling myself up the stairway to the deck, the wind cold on my shoulders. I allow my brain to revel in past experiences I haven't thought about in years, and then I come back to the present.

I'm here, with Taron, in an engineered ocean. He's found a new home for his people. With the water on my skin and my arms wrapped around the one I love, so have I. I've left behind a woman called Brandy after a sad song, and I've become Andi, the singer of my own glorious tune.

Taron is humming in my ear as he bumps against me, and I wrap my arms around him. Even through the cold sea spray, I can feel his warmth.

For a moment, I wonder who I'll be without the fear in my heart, and then I let that go as well.

I feel my lips curving up into a smile. Only one question remains in my mind: What is the Odyssean word for *joy*?

ABOUT KORIE BETH BROWN

Korie Beth Brown has written all her life, but retirement combined with the pandemic fanned the passion into high gear. She lives at the edge of Los Angeles County, at the base of a mountain, with her husband and two cockatiels.